THE HALLOW CURSE

A LEGEND OF SLEEPY HOLLOW RETELLING

THE HALLOW CURSE

A LEGEND OF SLEEPY HOLLOW RETELLING

KAYLA MCGRATH

CONTENT WARNINGS

This book includes content that may be disturbing to some readers, discretion is advised. Content includes graphic violence (blood, gore, decapitation, murder, death, exsanguination), sexually explicit scenes sexual blood drinking, binge drinking, drugging, cult-like environment (non-religious), stalking, dreams-stalking, madness/insanity, gladiator-style fights (slavery), abuse from an ex-partner, firearms, depictions of demons/demonic influence, mentions of Hell and Heaven.

For those who have always been the second choice.

...and the Astarion girlies.

PROLOGUE

OCTOBER 3, 1820

Horace Ross had murdered his young wife only twelve days past, and tonight he was whistling in the woods. Without remorse, he had done the deed just to pave the way for new paramours to take her place. He had defended his actions; she was no looker and a man of his station must have a beauty on his arm. Devoted, she may be, passionate she was not.

Drunk his mind, sloppy his step, he traversed the woods with the moon filtering through the skeletal fingers of the branches high above. Leaves crunched beneath his well-oiled boots when he heard a whisper on the wind.

Horace paused his whistling with a slow, depressive note as he turned to look over his shoulder. All that spanned behind him was darkness and the way back to the tavern through the trees. He resumed his melody with a skip in his step, dreams of the sweet Catalina he'd met that evening on his mind. Damn, did he want to taste that spitfire.

"*...Horace...*"

This time, Horace whirled, his joviality muted immediately.

"*Wretched man...*" the voice continued, a sharp feminine cackle following.

"Reveal yourself!" he called out into the night, feeling like a fool. But panic was making him ridiculous, poisoning his blood to force him to act like a simpering woman.

A swift breeze kicked up, stirring the leaves to swell around his feet. The gust heaved and tossed his tricorn hat from his head, disturbing his loose brown curls around his shoulders. Carried on the wind, his hat tumbled into darkness.

Horace quickly twisted his fingers and orange light bloomed between them as he created a sigil of protection. It took shape and hovered behind him, flickering. Then gone.

He was not a powerful warlock, but he more than made up for it in status.

Nothing answered him.

Not his voice

Not his magic.

Not his command.

Horace huffed and then turned back around and set off for his home, intent on two fingers of whiskey and his hand around his cock as he pictured the blonde from the other night with her mouth around it.

Suddenly, he heard a crack from behind him and the scent of brimstone flooded the air. He knew that scent. He'd never forget it. He'd performed the Staying thirty years ago, but one did not forget their trip to Hell so hastily.

Behind him, an infernal rune burned in the air, like a dreamcatcher from a babe's mobile. All sharp slashes, and severe lines. It grew and grew, until it was more than two men tall and twice that across. The hellfire black shape split in half, and like a gate, it opened and from it appeared a horse and rider.

Horace gave such a violent start that his bladder threatened to let go.

The hellhorse's hooves thundered across the earth, nostrils chuffing pure flame, the rider's long dark hair a war banner behind them. They ate the distance between them faster than Horace could react, his clumsy fingers trying to work his feeble magic before they were upon them.

The steed raced to him and not ten feet from him, the rider dismounted, leaping from the saddle. She landed without stumbling and kept walking. Beneath the moonlight, she shook out her long black hair and tilted her chin up. Just as she passed beneath a beam of light, Horace recognized her and all the blood drained from his face as his bladder truly did let go.

"You waited not a fortnight before my body was cold beneath the ground to replace me," his dead wife said. "Not just once, but twice. Days after I was gone you found a new lover. But she wasn't enough. Was she? It was your ego that allowed you to pursue another and create the Rival." Victoria Ross laughed—a too bright and violent sound.

"How are you here?" Horace asked, attempting to cast another sigil.

Victoria curled her fingers—faster than he knew she could—and her golden magic erupted in her palm as a deflection sigil launched into his hand, dissolving his paltry trick.

"You have filled the requirements of a curse. I am enacting it."

"Which curse?"

"The Hallow Curse."

"You lie."

"I do not. I expected to have to wait longer to pursue my revenge, husband. But you never were one for considerations or gifts. No jewels or baubles—just a necklace, once."

Her fingers went to her throat and the dark purple imprints on her cream white flesh.

Perfect impressions of his fingers from when he strangled her to death and had it covered up with his political and law enforcement related connections.

The hellhorse cantered in circles around them, an anxiety-inducing rhythm that felt like it was pressing against Horace's heart. Squeezing it.

Victoria looked down and smiled a soft, sad little thing. "I intend to pay you in kind." She lifted her gaze to his and her once brown eyes lit with hellfire and that sweet smile turned absolutely wicked.

She crossed to him, a devious look covering her face.

Horace realized with horror that in death his wife had become a deadly beauty. Ebony locks, moon-white skin, blood-red lips. In life he hadn't noticed how striking she was—why did he not realize?

Regret suffused him.

"I'm so sorry. I wish I could take back what I did," he groveled. "I love you, Vicky."

Victoria inclined her head as if slapped. "You love me?" she spat acidly.

"I do," he said, tears streaming down his face at the harbinger of death that stood before him. He sank to his knees. "Please. Come back to me."

"Beg."

"Wh—what?"

"I said beg."

Horace swallowed. Fear and desire, and shame and regret boiling in his blood. He prayed she didn't notice the dark stain on his trousers.

Victoria leaned down and bared her unnaturally white teeth. "*Beg.*"

"Please, Victoria. I beg you. Come back to me. Save me from this torment. I regret all that I did. I am sorry that my fit of rage ended so tragically. I need you back. You are the love of my life, the light of my life. You are the sweetest thing I've ever known. Please."

The hellhorse paused its threatening circles and stood behind Victoria, smoke curling from its lathered coat.

Victoria placed a hand against the horse, stroking its neck. Its eyes were the same hellfire red as hers. She looked to the beast thoughtfully.

"No."

Horace froze. Blinked.

"I beg your pardon?"

"I said no."

"B—But you said to beg!"

"I did," she confirmed, reaching for something hanging on the saddle. "I didn't say it would do anything. I just wanted to hear your pathetic attempts before I end you in turn."

Fury rocketed Horace to his feet.

"You deceitful bitch."

"Oh, I'm a deceitful bitch, now? How quaint. I thought I was the light of your life."

"You were a boorish wife and I am glad you are gone."

Victoria tsked. "Such a shame."

Horace, with his drunken fingers drew lines of magic in the air, but Victoria, his suppressed wife was more talented—faster—than he, and her golden sigil took form and she speared pure power at it. It passed directly through his chest—nicking his heart.

Blood spread rapidly against Horace's chest and pain erupted—an exquisite bolt of agony. Victoria's golden magic tore through him and Horace collapsed to the forest floor.

A shaft of moonlight cut across his face as Victoria approached him, rope in hand. Her visage obscured the light and she instead was haloed by it.

A demonic dream.

"It's time you come to Hell, husband."

And then, Victoria tied his hands and looped a noose around his neck.

Anger lanced through him.

He wanted that whiskey.

He wanted that blonde.

He wanted that Catalina.

But instead, the universe was intent on punishing him for his desires and the actions he took to secure them.

Horace, hardly alive, watched as Victoria, satisfied by her handiwork, tied the rope to the hellhorse's saddle and mounted her steed while her husband bled to death behind them.

Victoria commanded the horse and they took off like a shot, dragging Horace behind them as they charged forward.

The scent of brimstone suffocated him as the screams of the damned swallowed him whole while they passed through that still open portal to Hell.

INTERLUDE

What neither Horace nor Victoria noticed was the midwife gathering herbs a mere seven yards from the confrontation, silent and still. Hidden in the trees.

But with their departure to Hell, she ran for home, basket forgotten. Come the dawn, the midwife recounted the tale to all that would hear it, and those that questioned her sought proof.

Only to find Horace Ross's empty dwelling and hoofprints seared into the forest floor, the scent of brimstone lingering in the breeze.

It was then that all truly feared what they had all learned.

Some curses the dead could cast.

VALE
WOOD

10

The Hallow Curse

OCTOBER 1, 1867

The nude model bore a terrible likeness to her ex-lover.

Sabine Van Arsdel ducked her head, flushing, discomfort in every stroke of her brush as she swept over the canvas. Her cheeks flamed as the model tilted his head and new softness entered his features, banishing the sharp lines and shadows of her past.

But not all of it.

The model was still fair of hair, so light it was white. Not the white of an aging man—no, this man, like her former lover, appeared not even thirty. His waves were that of the unusual sort of beauty. Lashes lifted over eyes of heather gray and Sabine clenched her teeth, knuckles whitening on her brush.

Her inner wrath added an air to her study, turning the slender form of the model into one of wasting. Shadows. Hollows. Darkness. It all seeped through her portrait. And the silk that covered space between his legs was wrought in ebony, though the fabric was pearl in actuality.

Sunlight filtered down from the glass ceiling, dust motes danced in the air, while around Sabine the susurrus of brushes slicked with paint glided across canvases. She was one in a circle of twelve, the dozen students studying art just as she was.

Only they were not running from the events of the past winter and trying to escape feelings of betrayal and inadequacy.

Probably.

Sabine quashed the thoughts of what had happened back in Vonor. She was in Vale Wood now; pursing artistic liberties and techniques free from the repute of the scandal of the century.

Luckily, such scandal was quieted by the exponential growth of the magically paralleled world. Once, it was mere pockets of cities filled with warlocks and threatened by demons, hemmed in by borders of shadowy nothingness and accessed only by portals. Now, entire countries were beginning to develop as a match to the mortal world. Velleth now existed just as Mortal England did. No longer was it just Vonor to London. Now it was Wendallan and Birmingham, Reathon and Brighton. The country had widened its magical borders to encompass all of the Mortal United Kingdom.

And it was growing every day.

Over the oceans channels were growing, and now one could take a ship to Vonor all the way to Syxon—which in the mortal world was Cairo—and then another to Vale Wood.

Which was to mortals, New York.

The new world.

And the new world within the new world was exactly what Sabine was searching for.

Sabine wanted to reinvent herself. She wanted to be the mysterious artists who almost exclusively wore pants and didn't talk about her past. She didn't want to be known as always second-best.

At least for a while.

A small bell tinkled, and with that clear chime, the nude model wrapped himself in the blanket of silk at his groin and descended from the dais. He smiled and gave a flirty little wave, then disappeared into a room at the back.

There was a brief reprieve where the students and artists replaced or applied finishing touches to their canvases. Sabine carefully tucked hers away and out of sight—she needed not be reminded of the similarities she'd rendered and tried to alter out.

Leaning back, Sabine stretched her legs in the cotton leggings she wore, the flex of the muscles beneath her curves evident in the form-fitting garb. Her arms extended above her head, the hem of her black peasant blouse rising to reveal a line of golden midriff. Everything about her would be an utter scandal in the mortal world.

"There are eyes on you," Winifred said in her Midith accent from next to her, pinching her corset-clad ribs.

Winnie still held a bit of Vonorian influence in her cadence—perhaps from parents or grandparents—but it was very different than Sabine's full accent from the mother tongue. That had been one of the largest culture shocks coming across the water—the dialect.

"Ah yes," Sabine demurred, flexing her stiff fingers. "I sense them. Under the guise of artistic study, they dream of me unclothed on that dais so they have an excuse to stare. I am not a fool. I am the shiny new bauble they want their hands on."

Winnie cocked a strawberry-blonde brow. "You seem to not enjoy the attentions. I would kill to have men look at me as they do you."

Sabine internally cringed, but kept the aloof air. "Dear, it's not as glamorous as you may imagine. It comes with much heartbreak, and I, for one, am sick of it."

"*You*?" Winnie asked, incredulously.

"Indeed."

Winifred stared uncomprehendingly, as if she couldn't fathom anyone having ever passed up or quit on Sabine.

Sabine knew she had beauty, but beauty was fuck all when the person you were with wanted someone else and they'd do whatever it took to get them.

Just then, Sabine picked up on concerned mumbles and noticed the instructor wringing his hands and gazing at the clock. He poked his head in the model's quarters, but they were presumably empty—Sabine had distantly noticed the first model's departure.

A few more breaths passed before the instructor took out a pocket watch and sighed.

"It seems our next model has neglected to arrive so unless we wish to practice still life…" he said and cleared his throat. "I'll need a volunteer."

There was a tense silence. Sabine sucked in a breath. She'd not painted herself, nor allowed anyone to paint her image in nearly a year. Not since—no. No, she would not let her mind wander.

A hand across the room rose.

The instructor's gaze locked on it gratefully.

"Oh, Mister Emmons. Thank you for your willingness to help."

"It is my deepest pleasure," a purring voice returned and Sabine became alive with the sound.

His accent was Vonorian. Like hers. Like home.

Sabine's eyes landed on the dark-haired warlock who'd spoken and her heart gave an involuntary flutter as he set aside his supplies. Her gaze was trained on him, so she took in all his movements.

Mister Emmons got to his feet—he wasn't a particularly tall warlock; a man of average height, but he carried himself with the utmost confidence and grace. Slender and lean, he crossed to the center and pulled the laces on his billowy white blouse.

Sabine instantly locked on his fingers—and oh how she wanted to capture them! Long and tapered without being unusually so, fingertips stained with ink and paint, and both hands were beringed with silver.

Without her having realized it, Sabine had begun to draw all she was taking in with her fingers on a fresh canvas.

As he tugged the shirt free from his person, all his delicately pale complexion was on display with even more silver around his neck. Emmons took the recently vacated pedestal, and lounged sensuously, tilting his chin ever so.

Sabine bit her lip as she resettled herself on her stool, straightening her shoulders as she assessed her canvas and the shadows she'd begun to depict. Glancing up, she caught Emmons's gray eyes and jolted.

They were otherworldly silver in the sunlight, fortuitously different from the storm gray ones she'd been trying to forget. Framed by thick black lashes and smudged kohl applied with a light hand.

He was breathtaking.

Entranced, Sabine started painting but couldn't take her eyes off him. Emmons, seeming to sense her potent attention, slowly brought his gaze to hers. They locked, and a pretty little devious smile spread across his lips.

Breath caught in her throat and heat burned in her cheeks, but she did not stop.

She did not stop painting.

And she did not stop looking at Mister Emmons.

Nor did he stop taking her in.

In the fingers of sunlight that still tried to hang on after the summer, Sabine and Winnie stood outside their art class arm-in-arm. Winnie was chittering animatedly, but Sabine's mind was otherwise preoccupied.

"Do you happen to know much about Mister Emmons?" Sabine asked, summoning the courage without balking. "He's quite striking."

"Oh, I noticed you were quite taken with his looks," Winnie said teasingly, giggling. "I've never seen you so flustered."

"I was not flustered, darling. I was aroused—or at least my creativity was."

"You have no troubles speaking your mind, do you? Even if it's considered uncouth?"

"Attraction exists. I see no reason to deny it. I do not shy away from topics of sex or sex-adjacent."

"Is that the norm in Vonor?"

"Not exactly. Though, it also isn't prohibited and won't have me shamed out of high society. But you're neglecting to answer."

The two girls began walking down the street to their favorite modiste. Winifred had ordered a new dress and Sabine had a custom corset designed. Their heels were clicking on the cobbles, crisp leaves crunching underfoot, the scent of autumn thick in the air. The slight decay of foliage, the hints of smoke from chimneys, the barely cold bite to the wind.

"No, to answer your question. Mister Emmons is evidently newer to Vale Wood—even more so than you. But it is a big city."

"You are quite right. Perhaps we should make a warm welcome to the fresh blood in the New World." Sabine leaned in conspiratorially. "Make the mystery a familiarity."

"Coquette," Winnie called her as they stepped through the threshold of Spider Silk.

The modiste was all heavy, orange-toned wood, walls papered in black damask, sconces of amber, and chandeliers that dangled crystals and topaz. The tufted chaises and ottomans were deep, chocolatey brown, fine floral patterns upon them, with tasseled pillows of rust and gold. All the darks of the shop brought out the bold jewel tones of the dresses, or the soft pastels of morning gowns.

Sabine winked over her shoulder. "I take that as the utmost compliment. If I didn't know any better, I would accuse you of wanting to court me, darling."

"Hush. Take those flirtations out on the men tonight. There will be plenty of available warlocks at the Harvest Party." Winnie whirled from the cinnamon-colored dress she was admiring. "You're still coming, right? Perhaps in a new confection by this brilliant dressmaker?"

"Of course," Sabine said as the modiste retrieved her corset. "But you won't catch me dead in a dress."

The Harvest Party was full of the merry drinkers and filthy dancers. The party in question was hosted by the Kilgore family at their ancestral manor—ancestral only in the way it had been passed down a single generation— the exterior of which was sandstone and ivy, and the interior was gothic elegance.

Sabine danced with Winnie; glasses of mead clutched between their fingers. Sabine twirled in her heels, utterly free to move in the black leather pants stuck to her like a second skin.

She was the only female present not in a dress, but she'd had one too many dresses catch afire for her likes.

Sabine sipped her drink and shook out her long auburn waves as she swallowed. Winnie's fingers trailed across her throat, as she followed the steps of the dance to slide behind Sabine. Sabine in turn, grazed her fingertips against Winnie's forearm as they came together and then apart.

The music was a deep heartbeat, low drums and horns, eerie strings, and throaty voices that were growling, moaning, and singing in an old language Sabine didn't recognize.

It was heady.

Intoxicating.

Sabine finished her mead, and with speed that was envied by every warlock she knew, she twisted her fingers and casted a sigil to safely deposit the glass away as she continued dancing. Winnie copied the action as Sabine stroked her fingers down Winifred's jaw, throat, and down her arms as she slid behind her. All the dancers around them were doing the same, but unlike all the other's Sabine had attracted a particular male's attention.

Emmons watched her on the sidelines, half his profile in shadow as he brought a glass of wine to his lips. Just as they had locked in on each other during the class, they watched now.

Sabine's and Winnie's hands were all over each other as the dance rose in its sultry movements—hands on hips, arms around waists, palms to cheeks—but her eyes were for him.

He licked a drop of wine from his lip.

Sabine blushed, sweat making strands stick to her skin. She was hot, and alive, and new, and mysterious.

The dance began winding down to its conclusion, which involved the partners drawing close. The movements were synchronized as chests bowed and bent forward and back, hips guided by hands, until hands rose up and cut between hearts—cleaving them—and effectively ending the song.

The two of them smiled at each other and Winnie kissed both of Sabine's cheeks—she smelled of incense, lavender, and the lingering hint of mead.

"I think I drank too much," Winifred giggled. "I'll be right back." And then she scampered away to the toilets.

Sabine heaved a breath and made her way to one of the serving tables to parch her sudden thirst.

"The Faust Curse, that's a twisted curse, for certain," a woman was telling a man by the barrel of mead. "Or the Lovers Curse."

"Forget the Lovers Curse, the Vengeance Curse is the wickedest I've ever heard," he returned.

"Bloody Hell, I know someone who survived the Vengeance Curse!" an eavesdropping man nearly shouted, belligerent with drink. He joined the mead-drinking couple.

"Bullshit!" the man responded, blond hair the color of hay brushed back from his brow. "Barely anyone has ever casted that curse."

"But it's true! And I know another who was doomed to the Cupid Curse—he did not survive it, I am afraid to report—but that one is an annual curse."

"Just as the Nightmare Curse is. Say, did you hear that no one was cursed this most recent winter?"

Sabine tuned out at that point, she knew the truth even if no one else did.

The room was overheated with bodies and dancing and the pressure of reputation. It was all heavy tones of gold decadence and garlands of dried flowers festooned from the ceilings, which were painted with murals of angels and demons in varying degrees of pleasure and agony.

Though a misconception to many, demons were not figments of imagination or threats from a book. They were very real, and they took the human—or very near human form—of their prey. But they were not senseless. In fact, demons were alarmingly intelligent and loved to play trickster games like how mortals had depicted capricious gods.

Gods, however, did not exist. There was no celestial deity, just as there was no paragon of evil below. Angels and demons roamed their realms freely without any sort of omnipresent overlord.

Sabine sighed and poured herself some water and stepped towards the open doors that led to a terrace. She leaned against the frame, luxuriating in the brisk night air, cooling the perspiration that beaded.

"…what about the Lover and Rival?" the belligerent

drunk was continuing his intercepted conversation.

Sabine rolled her eyes and stepped out onto the stone and to the railing.

Anti-demon sigils hung in the air, marks of protection and defense surrounding the grounds of the manor. Sabine could see the work of at least three different warlocks judging from the shades of green, yellow, and orange that made up the sigils.

Every warlock's magic manifested as a color unique to them. You could certainly find other green casters if you yourself were one, but you'd never find the exact same shade—evergreen to hunter, or viridian to emerald—even if it was indistinguishable to the eye.

Sabine's magic was crimson, which carried somewhat of a stigma. The bigotry was mostly banished, but some still lingered. Especially when infernal runes were once believed to be red—they were black with tinges of other colors—and could only be cast by demons of the seventh circle of Hell, and even rarer, some warlocks. Though that ability was often kept secret because corruption was rampant in the magic world and those who could cast runes would become weapons.

"Is that you out here, Miss Van Arsdel?" a deliberately softened voice called from the threshold.

Sabine recognized the voice and a slight smile crept across her lips. She turned and leaned her lower back against the rail, glass of water dangling from her fingertips.

"Hello, Idris," she greeted warmly. "I didn't think you were much for parties."

Idris stepped out onto the terrace with her and shrugged sheepishly—which was a feat considering the man was built like an ox. He was tall; six feet and several inches, with muscles cording his arms as if he were a laborer, but

Sabine knew he was not, because she knew he was a librarian.

Sabine knew Idris from her studies. She'd come to him on more than one occasion searching for an anatomy textbook or histories of famous and infamous artists to better learn her craft.

"I'm not," he said carefully, his flatter accent curving over the words strangely to her. "But I was convinced by a friend that I needed to experience life and not just let it pass me by."

She laughed as he sidled up to her. "Has this friend performed the Staying?"

"Yes, actually," he chortled gently. "More than seventy years ago if I remember correctly. Have you?"

"Two years ago," she confirmed.

Forever she would appear six-and-twenty, even though the spinning of the Earth revealed her to be twenty-eight. It would be so, even when she was an old woman, yet still retained her youthful form.

The Staying was a ritual most warlocks performed at their choice of age that granted them immortality after finding pieces of their soul. It was unheard of and near unethical to commit to it before the age of twenty-five; before one's brain had reached full development. Each afterlife—Heaven and Hell—kept a piece of a warlock's soul so that each had a claim upon them when they died.

The Staying upset that balance.

The ritual involved a descent into Hell where one searched through the circle of their most prominent sin—lust, in her case—to find a shard of their soul, absorb it, and then ascend to Heaven where the warlock split the other shard in half and cast the pieces to each afterlife to lock them in an eternal battle over one shard. Doing so immediately halted the aging process.

It, of course came with drawbacks—such as the Staying was sometimes fatal, and the risk of contracting immortal diseases—but eternal life and all the perks of healing, stamina, and power was much too alluring.

"I performed it five years ago," Idris told her. She wasn't sure if she'd asked him as well, but she was not upset by him telling her. "I couldn't decide for the longest time when the best age was as each of them seem to have drawbacks to some degree."

Sabine eyed him, trying to gauge what age he'd chosen.

His aquamarine eyes were bright and intelligent, filled with a certain kind of naivete that came from not having encountered true violence and conflict, yet he had the slightest beginnings of aging around the eyes—nothing off-putting, but rather distinguished and mature. His nose was strong and straight with a slight hook, with sharp cheekbones, and a squared jaw. Dark brown curls were pushed into some fashion of submission, styled to be slightly swept away. It was alluring, certain to say. She imagined painting him sun-kissed and by the ocean—which, she assumed from his olive complexion that his lineage followed the sea to Syva.

After her assessment, she settled somewhere between thirty-three and thirty-five.

"It's a predicament to even decide; what with the risks and all," Sabine said off-handedly, staring back in at the party. "Though most of the concerns to the diseases are less than they were in years past."

"Ah, yes," Idris began, excitement in his tone. He visibly brightened. "I meant to ask. You are friendly with the professors that have worked on the cures for immortal diseases, correct?"

Sabine squashed a sigh. She knew she shouldn't have

mentioned anything about the fucking diseases.

"Yes, that is true."

"I don't mean to be presumptuous, but would you be opposed to me calling on you this week to perhaps discuss it further?"

"Oh, I am not the intellects they are, but if I do not have the answers, I'd be happy to put you in contact with them."

"My, you have a kind heart—one of gold—and I'd certainly appreciate your generosity. I'd also like to say, I'd be remiss if I did not tell you I was charmed by you from the beginning."

"You flatter me," Sabine said politely.

What no one but those closest to her would know was that she'd retreated into herself. The talk was wandering too close to bad memories.

"Idris Swan!"

Idris turned, and there was a man Sabine vaguely recognized from the café she frequented. He was cheery and his face was rosy with drink as he lumbered over. He approached and produced from his pocket a silver case and opened it. A cigarillo appeared between his fingers and he summoned a sigil for fire and quickly sparked the end.

Sabine hated smoking.

"I shall leave you to your date," Sabine said, sauntering away. "Looks like there are sparks."

As she made her way inside a new song started up and she was inexplicably drawn to it. She felt the vocals pull on her heartstrings as surely as she was pupeteered. Sabine's lashes fluttered with the surge of emotion.

"You feel it too, don't you?"

Sabine whirled at the voice and found herself face to face with Emmons, his seductive eyes heated on her. There was something mysterious and challenging about him. Something ever so…quietly *wicked*, that called to her as surely as a siren's song.

"The tension?" she queried, shoving down the slight surprise that betrayed her. She added a devilish lilt as she cocked her head. "So thick you could cut it with a knife?"

Emmons smirked and his eyes slid down her frame, resting on her breasts before continuing his lazy perusal. "Oh, that too, little artist. But I was alluding to the musicians subtly weaving suggestion sigils into the notes."

Sabine's eyes widened as she glanced at the band, and sure enough there were discreet sigils fluttering in the air. They were minimized by a warlock whom possessed the ability to shrink the appearance of magic, just as she was blessed with rapid speed in her casting.

"What reason would they have to bespell the guests?"

Emmons gave her a droll look. "Nefarious reasons ranging from gaining political affluence to persuading more amorous attentions."

Sabine wanted to scrunch her nose in distaste, but refrained. "And would you have nefarious reasons for approaching me this night?"

"If you call asking you to dance one of them, then I am guilty as charged, love."

"I don't dance with strangers," she said coyly, her voice full of flirtation as she trailed a finger down his arm. He caught it and entwined their fingers.

"Then allow me to introduce myself. I am the tortured artistic soul who couldn't keep his eyes off you because you were undressing me with those mysterious dark bedroom eyes."

"Not much undressing was to be had as you did much of it yourself."

"So, you admit you wanted me naked?" His tone matched hers as he tugged her towards the dance floor.

"Whether I want or wanted you or not isn't of relevance; you were either way as fortune had it."

Emmons leaned toward Sabine in such a sultry way her heart leapt unevenly. She tried to quell it, but he pulled her closer. Emmons stirred something visceral and lusty in her.

"I like hearing that," he whispered. Pausing. "'*I want you*' sounds so divine from those lips."

They were fully on the dance floor now, the music something primal and heartrending. Sabine could feel the rhythm pounding in her chest, aching for the warlock who held her in his arms—aching to touch the heart that was beating against hers through flesh and blood and the layers of their clothing.

"I can think of something better."

"Oh? Color me intrigued, darling."

Sabine brought her face to his ear as they spun together. He smelled of crushed leaves and smoke, and the sweetest hint of apple. "Hypothetically speaking, wouldn't '*I need you*' be the greater conveyance of desire?"

Emmons dipped her. "A man would beg on his knees to have the pleasure of tasting those words on your tongue." He tilted his face to her throat, nose skimming her jugular.

Her pulse hammered.

"Silver-tongue rogue," she rasped teasingly.

He pulled her back up for the next steps of the dance, his hand at the nape of her neck, the back of his hand tracing down her face. Sabine's palm was on his throat, the other sliding down his ribs.

"Temptress."

"Charmer."

"Siren."

"You've given me many names during this dance."

"Only because I do not yet know your given name, little artist."

"Sabine," she told him.

"Sabine," he repeated. "Sabine, suits you."

"Charming me, are you?"

"As long as you like it."

Sabine's emotions were in her throat. She hadn't let herself feel a pull to anyone since *him*. She'd had physical encounters, but she hadn't allowed anything to interfere with her heart while she was healing. But all this seemed to be undone because Emmons was under her skin; such attraction damning her.

"I like it very much."

The last steps of the dance were upon them. Hands were intwined above their heads, chests pressed together. He was only a few inches taller than her so when his eyes flickered down her face it was only a short distance more to her breasts. They fell there, taking in the swells that were pushed up generously from the custom corset that was stitched with bats and brambles.

Their breaths mingled as those silver eyes of his rose to her midnight ones. Their fingers disentwined and then they were palm to palm as they slid down their bodies and between their chests, parting them.

The song ended.

"But you won't find out how much tonight," she whispered as she broke from him and strode for Winnie.

Winifred was balking by the door and Sabine knew she had Emmons on a leash behind her. She grinned to Winnie but did not turn. She enjoyed the tension.

"*Sabine*," Winnie whispered in a scandalized fashion. "That man is panting for you."

"He's going to ruin me, Win." Sabine's voice was low and despairing. "I just don't know if it's the best way or the worst way."

"Are you going to find out?"

"Oh, for certain. I've never felt such attraction and I'll damn myself to all the demons in Hell if I don't pursue it."

Winnie's brows rose. "More than—?"

"More," Sabine interrupted. "But I must keep my head about myself. There are suggestion sigils woven into the music."

"*Is there?*"

"Mmhmm. Subtle, but there."

"Devious."

"Indeed."

Winnie shook her head. "Bloody hell. Well with that said, I should leave before I make any poorly influenced decisions."

"I shall as well."

Winnie glanced over Sabine's shoulder. "I wouldn't be so sure." Winnie winked. "I'll see you tomorrow."

Winifred left and as she stepped through the door a throat cleared behind Sabine.

Sabine turned and was surprised to find Idris standing behind her, a glass of water and a glass of mead in hand. He extended both to her.

"Care for refreshment?"

Sabine smiled, banishing the slight surge of disappointment at the identity before her. "Water, if you please."

Idris smiled and extended the clear glass to her.

Sabine took it gratefully and drank deeply and glanced over to the place she'd vacated. Her heart launched into her throat as she saw Emmons propositioned by a beautiful brunette dancer. Her eyes met his as he accepted.

Her throat tightened and she drank again, returning her attention to Idris.

"Thank you for this. I seem to be more parched than I thought."

"Your dancing was quite…hypnotic." Idris cleared his throat. "Not that I was—rather that I wasn't, I—"

Sabine laughed, betraying eyes catching glimpses of Emmons dancing with the brunette just as he had her. Jealousy bit her. "It's quite all right. Whatever it was you were trying to say."

Idris heaved a sigh of relief. "Good. Good. That is good news. I…are you planning on staying much longer?"

"Ah, no. I'm actually planning to leave right now."

"May I walk you home?"

"Do you live near the docks?"

Idris grimaced. "No, I ah, I actually live next door. Upstairs."

Sabine smiled softly and patted his shoulder. "Oh Idris, you are kind but I cannot allow you to do that. I am much too far out of your way and I am used to a city with much more demon activity. I will see you tomorrow at the café."

"The same time as always?"

"Same time as always."

"May I walk you out at least?"

"You may," she said as she finished her water and deposited the glass on a nearby table.

"Do you have a cloak?" Idris asked.

"No, just my jacket," she said as she pulled the fitted red piece from the rack and onto her body. It was hourglass-shaped and hugged all her curves. "I try to refrain from having too many loose layers."

"Does that include dresses?"

"You noticed?" she asked, fitting the gold buttons through their holes as they stepped out the door and left the manor behind them.

"I did. Is there a reason?"

"There is. But it is a very long, very tragic story not fitting for Harvest Party nights like this."

They had begun to walk down the street during their conversation and already they were at Idris's apartment.

"Well," he said. "Perhaps another time."

"Perhaps."

They stayed locked in an air of uncertainty until Sabine broke it, nodding and striding away backwards, a wave on her fingers.

"Until tomorrow, Mister Swan."

Sabine followed the line of the streets, casting red sigils about her person. Protection. Strength. Power. Carefully crafting an arsenal should she need it. Vale Wood had far less demonic attacks than Vonor, and last year she'd had more than her fair share. In fact, she'd had far more than the average warlock typically experienced in their lifetime. All courtesy of a curse she'd gotten tied up in.

Even so, the constabulary dedicated to policing demons were out in their black regalia and casting sigils just as she was. They patrolled the streets in pairs, hyperaware.

While warlocks could only travel from the magic world and mortal world through the portals formed between bridges, demons did not have such constraints. Even with wards some managed to breach through and into the cities.

With a veritable halo of crimson sigils orbiting her, Sabine crossed the street where the spaces between shops and homes became larger and quieter. It was dark, nearing midnight, the nearly full moon hung bright and white in the sky.

Kilgore Manor was in the city center and Sabine's apartments were on the edge of the docks, nearly an hour's walk from the party. But more importantly, much of that travel was through dense woods, the trees of which were sacred and said to house the spirits of those passed.

Sabine wasn't sure if she believed in that, or even spirits of that sort. She'd encountered demons who'd taken on the nicknamed mantle of ghost when chained to a curse, but never had she met a mortal or once immortal spirit.

Sabine passed the last inn before the forest began, the sounds of the bawdry tavern below it fading as the trees swallowed her.

Moonlight filtered through the skeletal branches above; all the leaves having been stripped bare of it to now carpet the forest floor. The leaves crunched beneath her boots as she navigated the roots and foliage of the well-traveled path. Birds chirped intermittently and nighttime critters rustled in the undergrowth. Lanterns were sparse but present through the woods, even so, Sabine twisted her fingers and summoned a bright ball of crimson light.

She'd heard rumors of ruffians hiding inbetween the trunks in the dark, but Sabine had sigils prepared for untoward individuals. Regardless of that, she kept aware the longer she went into the woods.

After twenty minutes, the forest quieted.

It was eerie how everything silenced.

Sabine halted, turning on her heel and peering through the fingers of trees and moonlight, using the dim lanterns to the best of her ability. Everything hung suspended, as if holding its breath as she searched.

Nothing spoke to her.

Suddenly, the scent of brimstone suffused the air.

Pure, unadulterated fear skittered down Sabine's spine at the scent of Hell. It struck her senses and froze her into doe-like panic.

Then, from where she'd been traveling, an infernal rune appeared in the air, burning hellish dark, sparking as it grew. The rune stretched and lashed with flame as it became taller than herself and more than that wide.

And then, like a gate, it opened.

And out leapt a hellhorse, whinnying. The beast let out a bellow that chuffed with smoke as the rider yelled and spurred it onward.

Ice plunged through her blood as she heard that voice.

No.

No, it couldn't be.

But it was.

Nicholas was astride the horse, almost exactly as she'd remembered him. Appearing no older than thirty, young and handsome with skin as pale as cream, hair so fair it was platinum, still lithe and tall. But what was different were the eyes, now burning scarlet with hellfire, and the new addition of the angry red scar that ran down the center of his face, throat, and disappeared beneath the neckline of his shirt.

But she knew how far it went.

"Oh, *fuck!*" she cursed.

And then she ran.

OCTOBER 2, 1867

Sabine bolted on swift feet, unhindered by the various skirts she once used to sport. The dirt and leaves flew up around her in her haste and she rapidly twisted sigils between her fingers and threw them back at Nicholas.

Power, speed, cutting.

She cast it all at him in crimson blasts but he battled it with violet violence. Nicholas gained on her astride his infernal steed, shields of purple blooming against the gothic dark.

Sabine knew her one advantage over him was speed in her magic. She'd always possessed the inherent ability of a quicker cast than other warlocks—though she wanted nothing more in that moment than to have the capabilities of manifesting infernal runes, rare as it was.

Nicholas's horse was far faster than she could ever attempt to be, even after impressing upon herself speed spells.

Abruptly, an unwanted sigil flashed in front of her and Sabine banished it with a yell. She recognized the shape and saw it for Nicholas's proficiency.

Seems dying had not killed his penchant for illusions.

"*Sabine*," Nicholas taunted. "You cannot run from me."

"The fuck I can't," she muttered as she pumped her legs harder as the horse's hooves clopped dangerously loud.

He was close.

Too close.

Sabine cursed and threw a handful of defensive sigils over her shoulder. She didn't consciously decide which she attacked with—they just twisted and formed in her hands, her magic moving faster than her mind.

A sigil must have struck true because Nicholas bellowed behind her and his horse faltered. She allowed herself a small smile as she made for the bridge up ahead.

There was a thump behind her and just when she chanced a look over her shoulder, she was met with the sight of Nicholas dismounting with a façade of fury. His longer legs eating up the distance, egging on an inevitable confrontation. He was all silver-white against the night-dark, the only color the terrifying burn of his newly acquired eyes—villain-red.

Nicholas was upon her, fisting a hand in her hair. He grabbed her long auburn hair and forced her to the forest floor. Sabine fell, earning a mouthful of dirt and decomposing leaves as she hit the ground. She spluttered, tasting blood and earth as Nicholas turned her over by her shoulders.

"Look at my face, Sabine," Nicholas commanded through his teeth.

Sabine stared up at Nicholas hatefully, his hands manacles to her wrists, his knees digging into her thighs. His eyes returned to their once gray and her heart tore.

"Look what you did to me, my dear."

She yelled and tried to claw at him, thrashing like a wild cat dangled over water. Sabine kicked and bucked, fighting him off—all to no avail.

"I am nothing to you, you bastard!"

"You are everything." His voice lowered to a caress and Sabine's stomach roiled. His mouth was near her ear. "My lover, my murderess."

Her killing him was true, but she wouldn't give him that satisfaction. She wouldn't allow him to have her admit any guilt—for she did not feel any.

"You're not real."

"I'm all too real. Don't I feel familiar? Don't you remember how I felt on top of you?"

Nicholas's nose grazed her throat and she screeched like a banshee. Unwelcome thoughts languished in her mind. Old memories of previous encounters turned sour. Intimate moments spoiled like milk left out for days.

She remembered how he'd been so soft that first time. How he'd carefully lifted her long skirts up her thigh, trailing deft fingers across her skin. How those fingers slipped between her legs and ratcheted her up before his length replaced them. How he took her on that lounge, and then later against a wall.

Forcibly, she pushed the memories away, locking them deep in the prison of her mind.

"How I felt inside you?" he continued predatorially.

Sabine summoned all her rage and spat at him, blood and dirt and saliva all in his eyes.

Nicholas reared back in disgust and when he loosened his hold on her, Sabine broke his grip, clawed the ground and cast a handful of dirt into his face.

He hollered, blindly reaching for her as she kicked him with both feet planted against his chest. She felt the give in his chest as she pushed, the splitting of his very center that she'd gifted him nearly a year ago, the line following the angry red mark that climbed his face. He rushed backwards, tumbling through the undergrowth and Sabine rolled aside, leaping to her feet, running once again.

"You stupid bitch!"

Sabine charged for the bridge, internally praying for safety, hoping to find one of the constabularies—fuck, even one of the Scarlet Brotherhood would do.

Behind her Nicholas reinstalled himself upon the hellhorse's saddle and kicked off. She could hear the volatile clop on the earth as she sent crimson sigil after crimson sigil behind. Her breaths sawing in and out of her chest, perspiration beading on her brow. She was too hot and adrenaline was turning her sick. A poisoned heartbeat hammered in her ears, the very sound of her blood thrumming through her brain, a matching rhythm to the currents of the river.

Sabine sprinted onto the bridge just as Nicholas gained on her. But steps before the arching stone path, the horse reared up with a distressed whinny, nearly unseating Nicholas. She was shocked to see the malevolent glare that he cast her way. To see the sudden lack of chase.

But then it clicked.

She looked down slowly, down at the wide, gray stone

bridge. And as if she could see further, she saw the gray waters of the river rushing below.

Evil spirits could not cross running water.

And Nicholas was nearly as evil as they got.

Sabine froze in the middle of the bridge, catching her breath, red magic pulsing around her. She stared at Nicholas as he stared back at her, loathing a veritable living thing between them.

Sudden frantic footsteps met her ears from the opposite side of the bridge and Sabine raised her hand with an incendiary spell caught between her fingers. She was prepared to take on whatever nefarious cronies Nicholas had acquired—or die trying. Out from the foliage came Emmons, light eyes blazing with protective anger and silver sigils hovering at his brow.

He gave a pause when he saw Sabine on the bridge and Nicholas and his hellish beast on the bank. Emmons swiveled his gaze between them, shock upon his face.

"Sabine!" Emmons called. "The unhallowed cannot cross here. Quickly!" He hurried her with his arm and she dropped her sigil in response.

As she skittered to the edge of the bridge Emmons caught her up and Sabine threw a glare at Nicholas.

"Fuck you!" she shouted at him.

"Oh, in your dreams, I shall, my dear." He sneered, lip curling in disgust. Those red eyes flickered to Emmons—intrigued. "I'll be back."

And then Nicholas took off into the woods, following the line of the river.

Sabine began hyperventilating. Her breaths sawed in and out of her chest, panic winding her tight until her gorge rose in her throat. She pressed a hand to her chest and the other to her belly, trying to calm the noxious tension souring her body.

"You're cursed," Emmons said baldly.

"No, I cannot be," Sabine rasped.

"You killed your lover, so I assure you that you are."

"How dare you accuse me of such a thing."

"Did you?" He lifted a brow.

Sabine inclined her chin. "I did. But I assure *you* that it was necessary."

"Necessary or not, the fact remains."

Fuck.

Sabine threaded a hand through her loose waves; bits of dirt and debris stuck to her fingers.

"And which curse do you speak of?" she queried, panic still fluttering in her chest.

"The Hallow Curse."

"I've never heard of it," she retorted.

"It's rare and mostly unheard of, and I only know two other things about it."

"Are you deliberately pausing for dramatics?" Sabine snapped, her fears turning her temper sharp.

"The cursed must have killed their lover, and you must be dead to cast it."

OCTOBER 2, 1867

He shouldn't have been attracted to a verified murderess, but here he was.

Sabine stood before him; face flushed with heat even against the chill of the night. Bastien could see the fear still written across her frame despite how well she tried to hide it—and she did try. Her generous chest heaved with breaths that she attempted to tame and it took all of Bastien's moderate—rapidly becoming subpar—self-control not to gaze at.

"Will he come back?"

Bastien blinked and refocused on her. Her full lips were parted and those night-dark eyes were ferociously vivid. Dirt speckled her chin and mouth, streaks like fingers carved down her face.

"Almost certainly."

She visibly blanched and Bastien's heart gave a tug.

"Can I kill him? Again?"

"I'm not sure. But I fear what is dead cannot die."

"Fucking great," Sabine huffed, tugging the roots of her hair and taking a few stomping steps away to pace—and presumably to think. "Any other crumbs of wisdom?"

"You shouldn't be alone right now?"

"I can take care of myself."

She was fiery, he'd give her that—and he'd be lying if he said he didn't like it.

Murderess or not.

Still, the fact she'd killed her lover had his curiosity wildly piqued. Was it self defense? An argument gone rogue? Infidelity? A betrayal? Or more nefarious…was it just because she was sick? She'd mentioned it was necessary, but how necessary was necessary? Necessitation was subjective— wasn't it?

Regardless, she was the perfect mark.

A thrum of worry threaded itself through him, wondering what secrets she harbored, and with that, his fear response which kicked up his hunger. An ache began in his gums. In his teeth.

"Yes, evidently," he finally responded, addressing the death without the direct words.

Sabine sighed and began walking away.

"Where are you going?" he asked, catching up to her.

"Home."

"Unless you live on the ocean or over running water,

he can get you."

"Well, I certainly shouldn't linger here," she replied easily. "There's a point where the river goes still and he'll cross there. It'll take some time but I'm not going to be sitting here in a tea party dress waiting for him, darling."

"You're not wearing a dress."

"How very cognizant of you," she quipped.

Just as he caught up to her, she stilled and reeled at him. He was taken aback by her intensity and it made his blood turn hot.

Perhaps perfect mark was not the right descriptor. Adequate could be sufficient.

"You said he was unhallowed? As in damned?"

"Yes, I believe so."

"So, like a demon he cannot step foot on holy ground."

"That is the working theory."

"Sublime," she replied, then continued on her way. "I'll pay a visit to Winnie then and pray she is not entertaining guests—she is wont to fornicate upon the altar." Seeming to sense his befuddled silence, she threw a devilish look over her shoulder. "She lives in an abandoned church."

"You could come with me instead," he suggested, falling into step with her once again.

He startled himself with this proposition. He hardly knew her and yet he was inexorably drawn to her as a moth was to the flame. Perhaps it was her fiery spirit, her vixen-like air. Or the fact she could be his tithe without guilt. Or perhaps it was all that coined with the promise of her blood and the way it crooned to him as the sigil-laced music had.

"Do you also live in an abandoned church?" Sabine asked, broaching the end of the forest, the tree line giving way to the sliver of moonlight and the breadth of the town spreading beyond it.

"No, but I do have very powerful wards—it's my specialty."

"Ah, well then, I must refuse. Besides, I told you I don't dance with strangers, and I certainly do not go home with them."

"Bastien," he told her.

"Bastien," she repeated. Almost like a purr.

He loved the sound of his name falling off her lips. The sweet cadence of her words like the most decadent of desserts. He wanted to devour it.

"You bent your rules once," he teased. "Care to do it again?"

"Ah, such lapses in judgment will become an anomaly, I'm afraid—especially in light of Nicholas's return."

They crossed the forest's boundary, leaving the trees and the horseman ordeal behind them. Sabine seemed brighter out of the trees—both in the physical and emotional sense. She seemed more present. Sabine turned her face up to the night sky and exhaled a long breath before a smile crested the dawn of her desolation.

"Are you sure you're well?" he asked, transfixed and confused by her behaviors.

This positively stunning warlock had just discovered she was cursed and her former lover was hunting her down and she was…smiling?

She was a puzzle he wanted to study.

"It's not my first encounter with a curse. I'll be fine."

She took a left onto the first diverging lane and Bastien saw an old church at the very end of it. Moss and lichen climbed the stone walls, ivy followed every line of the leaded glass windows, stuck to the trenches of the sill like water weaving a maze. The belfry was cracked and the spire leaned precariously. In the churchyard was a thriving pumpkin patch, the orange dimmed in the night's faint light.

Churches were not for worshipping a god, for one did not exist. They were sanctuaries away from demon-kind, where priests and priestesses could allocate resources and offer aid. The power in such people came from the energies of angels and demons.

"Are you certain the building will not collapse?" he asked with dubious confidence.

"Winnie is proficient in protection and preservation spells. I have the utmost faith in her." Sabine's hand landed on his forearm, and despite the filth of her nails, and the corduroy of his jacket, her touch scalded him in the best of ways. And beneath the soil scent he picked up the sweet note of vanilla and the faint spice of cinnamon. "The place will hold, Mister Emmons."

"Bastien," he corrected, desperate for her perfect lips to form the shape of his name again.

And as those perfect lips curved up in a warm smile, she did.

"I'll see you tomorrow, Bastien."

"Goodnight, Sabine."

She parted from him and strutted on confident legs.

"Goodnight, Bastien."

Oh, she knew. She absolutely knew.

He grinned at her departing frame, memorizing her curves.

In a fit of fancy, he called out his address to her.

"In case you change your mind!"

She cast a coltish smile over her shoulder. Because she knew—she knew—he was watching. He met that smile with a continued one of his own.

Goodnight, she mouthed.

He was done for.

Playfully, he rolled his eyes as she disappeared inside the church. Once the doors closed behind her, he stuck his hands in his pockets, rocked back on his heels—fucking smitten as all hell—and then turned to make his way to his flat.

Tithe or no, she was his—one way or another.

Bastien slowed as one of his wards pinged. He recognized the signature of the warlock and sighed as he caught sight of the glowing ember of a cigarillo beneath a shattered lamppost. Pinching the bridge of his nose, he met up with the shadowy figure on the corner of Hessian and Dullahan.

"I thought you were going to leave me alone while I was here," Bastien said conversationally, leaning against the wall.

The other warlock said nothing at first, simply passing Bastien his cigarillo in silence. Bastien took a drag from it and then slowly exhaled a coil of smoke. He wasn't much one for smoking, but in times of stress he caved.

He gave it back.

"Our time here is running out," Salem said regretfully. He side-eyed Bastien and took another puff. "She wants us back."

Bastien stiffened. "I said I was done after this last one."

"But you haven't left."

"You know perfectly well that I can't. I need more time."

"We don't have it." Salem held the cigarillo to his lips. "I've stalled as much as I can."

"When?"

Salem's dark eyes flickered. "First ship is tomorrow night."

Fuck.

"And the last?"

"Six nights after."

Bastien sighed.

He needed more time to attain Sabine's trust—but perhaps her being cursed was the perfect solution.

"You should know…" Salem began haltingly. "She got someone past your wards."

Fury lit Bastien up from the inside. His wards were unparalleled and there was only one person alive he knew of that could nullify them. Someone he thought was in his corner—not hers.

"Elvira?"

"Yes."

"Dammit," Bastien cursed.

"I hate to be the bearer of bad news, but I thought you should know."

"Thanks," Bastien said distantly as he returned to his flat.

The letter was on the chest of drawers. It was nearly two o'clock after scrubbing the night's events from his skin, but he finally gathered the courage to pick it up.

Upon seeing the black wax seal his heart hollowed

out. He swallowed. Stress made his teeth ache and it only highlighted the fact that he hadn't fed last night—or that night.

Bastien's battle with Midnight Malady was his secret to bear alone. He'd told no one in Vale Wood of his affliction, and the only people who knew about it were the same people who'd sent the letter—including Salem.

Bastien swallowed, reminding him of a growing burn in his throat. He could only live three days without drinking blood; without succumbing to insanity where death would quickly follow. He'd meant to find someone at the Harvest Party—just someone to take from, and he'd give in whatever mutual manner they'd request—but then Sabine was there and all those plans turned to ash.

Memories of the previous feed were upon him. A buxom woman with light eyes and smelled of lilies. She was all too willing in exchange for coin so she could flee her husband and his gambling debts. She'd confided in him the amount owed to the Scarlet Brotherhood and Bastien had let out a low and concerned whistle.

Even with discretion, he made sure to use a disguise, and even though the blood drinking aspect was highly erotic to the receiver and the giver, it was still taboo and only talked about or allowed in certain circles. Circles which Bastien had taken pains to discover and cultivate.

Scrubbing a hand over his jaw, Bastien banished the recounted events and leaned his shoulder on the doorframe, breaking the seal on the letter. The paper was pressed and textured, the ink bleeding in spiky lines. His eyes scanned the words and his hopes sunk deeper than the depths of the ocean.

"Fuck," he whispered to himself.

He was being summoned.

And they wanted the tithe brought to the island.

Directly there, not just deposited at a rendezvous point.

As he read on, his dread grew. They wanted him back immediately or else they'd hunt him. He thought he had more time. He thought he'd earned more leniency. He thought he'd deceived them into trust. But evidently, they hadn't bought his ruse and now he and others would suffer for it.

Not just one last one.

More.

Because she wasn't letting him go.

Bastien backed up with the letter in hand and kept going until the back of his knees hit the edge of the bed. He sank down and hung his head. The thin sliver of moonlight trickling in the room drew a line on the floor and it felt poetic. As if it were demarcating what was and what was going to be. The distance felt like a crevasse had been ripped into the floor and he was staring past the abyss of it.

What the fuck was he going to do?

OCTOBER 2, 1867

Some curses the dead can cast…

Those words haunted Sabine as she sat in the makeshift sitting room of Winnie's church home, nursing a cup of coffee spiced with cinnamon. She hadn't slept well. Every tap of branches upon the windowpane was Nicholas's fingertips. Every creak of the structure shifting against the wind was his footsteps. Every night creature's noise was a warning of his approach.

Sabine shook her head, tangled waves about her

shoulders, as she sipped from the mug.

"I assume you still don't want to talk about what drove you here around the witching hour?" Winifred asked as she puttered around the kitchen, wooden spoon in hand. When Sabine looked up, Winnie was cross-armed before the counter, stained apron over her day dress.

She'd used the key Winnie had told her was hidden on the eave and whisper-called to her friend. She'd found her by candlelight, sketching with charcoals. When she'd looked up her hazel eyes looked hollow and haunted, coils of soft ginger framing her face.

Eyes glassy with drink, she'd taken in Sabine.

"Unsettled?"

"Worse," Sabine had managed. And then her knees gave out and she sank to the floor, bowing her head.

She'd let all the pain Nicholas had put her through tear about her chest. All the betrayal. How he'd used her. How she was second-best. Always second-fucking-best. She couldn't even be the cigarillo pressed to the lips of a gentleman—she was the second-hand smoke that slipped through fingers and lingered only as long the stick burned. All her passion, intangible, paled next to the substance of what called to the heart.

Twisted and wicked as those affections were.

Sabine didn't cry. Nicholas didn't deserve her tears. She'd cried enough over him. Instead, she let those poisoned thoughts bleed out of her soul through every ragged breath. She let those noxious feelings turn into resolve.

Then, just as suddenly as she dropped, she stood. Regained her sense of self, lifted her chin and set her jaw. Beneath the candlelight, she couldn't see much, but Winnie seemed to jolt from the abrupt change in her demeanor.

"My past is coming for me, Winnie," Sabine had

whispered.

"Should you be afraid?"

"Oh, yes. Very."

"Should I?"

"Absolutely."

Sabine shuddered out of the previous night's memories and returned her gaze to Winnie. Her brow was cocked expectantly, lips thinned.

"So?" Winifred prodded.

Sabine shivered out an exhale then took a steadying second sip of her coffee. Setting it down, she then straightened her back and stood.

"My former lover is hunting me down and intends to drag me to Hell."

Winnie's eyes widened dramatically and her spoon tipped in her grip.

"Oh." She cleared her throat. "That's not what I imagined you would say."

"Yes, it's quite inconvenient."

"*Inconvenient*?" she echoed, voice high. The repeated word sounded flatter in her mostly Midith accent. "Inconvenient is when there's a long line at the shop and you're in a rush. This is terrifying, Sabine!"

Sabine nodded. She'd been trying to downplay it, but there really wasn't any way to downplay the situation—even with as minimal of information she'd given. She hadn't even disclosed Nicholas had returned from the dead and she'd been the one to kill him.

"You're right," Sabine agreed.

"Are you going to call any law enforcement? Tell them he plans to kill you?"

"I can't."

"Why not?"

"It's extremely complicated."

"And you've dragged me into it?"

Sabine blanched. "He—"

It was on the tip of her tongue to say he wouldn't do anything, but she knew that wasn't true. Not anymore. His greed and avarice had completely rotted whatever image she once had of him. She had no idea who he was anymore.

But she wasn't the same girl he'd broken the heart of.

Not really.

Something broke in her that night—turned her jaded to the idea of love ever again.

"I'm so sorry. I should leave. I can't believe I was so selfish to risk you like this," Sabine said, putting on her jacket—she'd used mending sigils to fix the tears and cleaning spells to dispel the dirt and whatever else had clung to her from the forest tumble.

"Wait," Winnie said, reaching as Sabine went for the door. She turned and Winnie continued. "Did you have anywhere else to go?"

Sabine smiled sadly. "Nowhere that would have been safe."

A knowing light appeared in Winifred's eyes. "Because it's hallowed."

Anxiety ratcheted up Sabine's throat but she nodded once.

"I see."

Sabine wasn't entirely certain Winnie did see. She was sure the other girl thought her old flame was a demon, not a warlock back from the dead.

Demonic paramours weren't unheard of but it was highly irregular and scandalous. Most demons were creatures of mayhem, destruction, and discord, but some had appetites that did not lean to anarchy. Some preferred the pleasures of the flesh—and rarer, pursued the heart. But warlock and demon couples were the ultimate of taboo and such true bonds would have both parties ostracized from their respective peers. She'd never met anyone who'd had a dalliance with a demon and all of her experiences with them had been positively abominable.

Sabine wasn't about to correct her, though.

"I should go," Sabine pronounced. "Thank you so much for your hospitality, darling. I'll see you in class this afternoon?"

"Of course," Winnie replied. "I'll be there. And Sabine?"

Sabine paused by the doors and turned. "Yes?"

"You're always welcome here—risk and all."

Warmth grew in her heart and she had to fight off the cresting emotion. It burned in her eyes and throat but she quashed it.

"Thank you, Win."

And with that Sabine strode out the door and past the pumpkin patch to the lane.

Her walk to the café was short and silent. She cast glances at the woods where Nicholas had hunted her, revulsion rolling through her. When she looked at the ground, there were no hoof prints which meant that either Nicholas hadn't found her on this side of the bridge, or the beast's presence was more a ghostly apparition—at least to tangibility on the earth.

When she arrived at her regular café the bell tinkled overhead. Tables were cluttered with people and papers. It was a popular spot for the early morning creatives. Poets and writers congregated near the back, sequestered in the atmospheric moodiness of the dark of October's dawn. Artists and painters took advantage of the light blue gloom against the large pane windows. The bench along the largest window was taken up by sketchbooks and flowers—gypsophila, carnations, and anemones—all in varying shades of white.

Sabine weaved her way past the teak wood tables and chairs and made her way to order where her regular mild-mannered barista tapped on a black and gold register.

"No sketchbook today?" he queried.

"No," she responded. "I'm trying something new."

"And you're early."

Sabine managed a tight smile. "Like I said—something new."

"Do you want to try a new coffee, then? Or stick with your regular?"

This time her smile was genuine. "My regular."

The transaction was completed and the barista handled the drink for her. It was moments of movement and swirling sigils of balance and speed before she had her steaming cup. Coils lifted from the surface as she took her coffee to a seat by the window, staring vacantly.

Normally she took this time to sketch, but today she didn't. Her thoughts were consumed with the conundrum of the Hallow Curse—if that's truly what she'd been doomed with. Even though her fingers itched to sketch and draw—sharp lines and slashes of bold red and burning crimson eyes, black of ebony steeds and shadows, all abstract and messy to convey the nebulous complexity of both her relationship to her curser and the entire situation.

Sabine shook her head free of the thoughts and sipped her coffee. She had plenty of time before her art class, but she had an inkling that her next stop would eat up all of that time.

She watched the clock and when the time struck, she finished her coffee and took her leave. As she traveled the streets, she saw more and more people milling about and starting their days. She passed a bakery and the scent of fresh bread was thick in the air, mixing with the crisp leaves and hint of smoke from the chimneys around. It was less than fifteen minutes before she found herself in front of the library.

The library was a white stone structure with tall, fluted pillars and statues of notable minds on plinths. Lilith Carrion stood with her arms upraised, forever frozen with an apple in one hand and a pomegranate in the other, immortalizing the perceived notion of illusion and misremembering while highlighting the abilities warlocks possessed—human religion dictated one was the forbidden fruit, but which one? On the opposite side Thanatos Ravyn had a book open on his palm, fire burning in the other, with a shield strapped to his back, portraying his advancements on combining like spells together in lieu of a physical defense. Ten statues lined the façade of the building on the highest level of the thirty stairs, broken only by a single landing.

Sabine ascended and when she got to the door, she twisted her fingers to create an unlocking sigil. The door, unwarded against such spells—only demonic presence—swung open. It wasn't an oversight; it was a welcome. After dawn had broken in full warlocks were welcome to enter and peruse the stacks. Always there was a librarian or scribe inside the building to protect all the knowledge it contained—as was the norm for every library in the magical world.

Inside, it was warm—the kind of bone-deep warmth that assuaged the soul—and saturated with the scent of ink and parchment. Heavy wood cases took up all the walls with only sparse windows breaking up the furthest walls. Shelves created a labyrinthine shape within the space, spanning more than two times Sabine's modest height. Amber lights dotted the interior, heavy rugs taking up much of the floor space, long tables set with chairs and lamps spread out across the surface.

Sabine bypassed the tables entirely and went straight for the stacks, cataloguing the organization system and pinpointing the curse section. As she turned the corner deep in the maze of the curses section, she stopped short.

"Are you stalking me?"

Bastien lifted his head at Sabine's accusing tone. She'd stutter-stepped upon discovering him standing there, shoulder leaned against a shelf, book splayed in his palm, an ankle crossed over the other. Her heart had stuttered just as surely as her feet had, but luckily her mouth was quicker.

"It appears that would be my line considering I was here first," he countered playfully.

Sabine huffed and Bastien smirked. She crossed the distance between them and reached for the book he was holding. She propped her back against the shelf, mere inches from where he was still leaning—he didn't move. Bastien hovered over her shoulder as she flipped to the title.

"*A Compendium of Curses: 1844 Edition*," she read aloud, then flipped to the open page and exactly right there was what she was looking for. "The Hallow Curse. Did you kill your former lover, too?"

"Afraid not. I wanted to share my findings with you this afternoon."

"I haven't scared you off?"

"You said you had your reasons. And on the contrary, it piqued my curiosity."

Sabine allowed a small smile to twist the corners of her lips.

Feeling the heat of his body envelop her like a corona, she tilted her head and read on.

The Hallow Curse is derived from the demon, Crom Dubh, with the first known case dated 1620. Characterized by a deceased lover returning on a brimstone steed to drag to Hell the one who'd slain them. Prerequisites for the summoning of the curse entail two new beaus to the cursed and the cursed having committed the unforgivable act upon their love.

"The Coquette?" Sabine asked dubiously, having read ahead.

"Oddly gendered, if you ask me," Bastien said, then leaned over her. She warmed further. "But look—" he pointed, "the Coquette may also be deemed the Rake."

Characters and roles include the cursed, known as the Coquette, the two new pursuant loves titled the Rival and the Lover (titles dependent on who the Coquette* is inclined to accept), and the Unhallowed*.*

NOTE: The Coquette may also be referred to as the Rake and the Unhallowed may be coined the Horseman. Regarding early texts the original cursed one was deemed the antithesis of the Unhallowed, titling the cursed as the Hallow, but that term has dropped in favor of the other cursed titles due to the often nature of the cursed one being adulterous. Even so, the name of the curse has remained unchanged.

Sabine tipped her head back and swallowed.

She was cursed. She fit the prerequisites. She knew the exact moment Nicholas could attack and it was last night. He was lying in wait. Biding his time until he could have his revenge. And she'd had no idea.

"I wonder which one I am to you."

She cocked a brow at him. "Your implication is noted."

Bastien shrugged with a smirk. "I'd just like to help you and knowing your key players could be useful in that endeavor."

Sabine nudged his shoulder and returned to the book.

The First Account.

She swallowed.

Katrina Van Tassel, the Coquette, had raced her betrothed in a field of wheat and during an unfortunate accident she inadvertently sent him to his demise in a fall where a stray farming scythe severed his head from his body. Years later, the Coquette was pursed by schoolteacher, Ichabod Crane, and local golden boy, Abraham Von Brunt— the former became the Rival while the latter the Lover. Upon both courtships, the Unhallowed returned for Katrina's hand and was dismayed to discover her evident betrayal. It was on his hellhorse that he sought to drag her to Hell with him.

Given a time of thirty nights—

"Thirty nights?" Sabine gasped. "He can hunt me for thirty nights?"

Thirty nights.

That gave him until All Hallow's Eve.

Oh, how toxically poetic.

She had to survive him for a month and she had no idea if he could die. All she knew is that she didn't want to go to Hell—again.

Thirty nights, from dusk until dawn, beginning midnight the first and ending upon midnight the final night.

"Breathe, Sabine," Bastien coaxed.

She hadn't realized she wasn't until he'd drawn attention to it—and he was correct. Her chest was tight and she could feel the distinct restriction of her corset.

She wanted to claw it off.

Her throat felt dry, her eyes felt wild. She glanced

around, fearing of demons in the library or Nicholas attacking in the daylight.

Suddenly, Bastien plucked the book from her and placed it on a shelf behind them, stepping in close to her. With one hand, he slowly reached for her lower back, the other cupping the back of her head. As he urged her backwards to the shelves where each edge pressed against her back, her lungs were consumed by the scent of Bastien—of crushed leaves, smoke, and the sweetness of apple.

"What are you doing?" she rasped.

"Making sure you know you are secure. You are safe."

"You hardly know me."

Her dark eyes searched his, finding only earnestness in his light gaze. He held her so steady with just a look some of the discomfort in her chest eased.

"Not in the sense of time, but I feel drawn to you, Sabine," he practically purred her name. "And I'd like to see you through this curse. I want to help you."

"Why?" she whispered. "I've done nothing to show you I am worthy of such thoughts."

His fingers tightened on her. She could feel the touch in her hair, slowly lacing through her dark red locks, the opposite one splaying at her back—his palm pressing firmly. Heated. Sabine's blood positively burned—she was scorched by him in the best of ways. She felt herself spiral downward with attraction. How he built her up and ratcheted high, simply by the barest of touch but the most devoted of words.

The words that conveyed she might not be the second choice she'd always been.

"That alone—that selflessness—shows me all I need to know."

His breath ghosted across her lips and she inhaled sharply. Bastien's eyes flickered to her mouth and she was completely transfixed by him.

Suddenly, the squealing of hinges broke their connection as someone entered the library. Bastien practically leaped back and grabbed for a random book on the shelf. Sabine quickly picked up the curses book once again.

For a few moments—cheeks burning—Sabine stared at the same page yet taking in nothing. Bastien was seemingly similarly flustered but neither of them said anything. Minutes passed before footsteps approached them and Idris rounded the corner.

Idris stopped short and his eyes widened. "Sabine!" His eyes flickered to Bastien. "Mister Emmons."

Bastien nodded. "Good morning, Mister Swan."

Idris returned his attention to Sabine. "You're here awfully early, I missed you at the café."

The realization struck her. Idris was the Rival. The one who'd helped kickstart this curse. He was the one who'd expressed enough interest in her—attraction or courtship, whatever it may have been, despite being unrequited. He was handsome and kind to be sure, but that was all—to her.

Sabine smiled lightly. "Yes, I was possessed by the urge to research curses this morning as everyone was regaling tales of them last night."

"Ah." Idris inclined his chin in acknowledgment. "May I see which one you are reading at current?"

"Certainly." Sabine tilted the book in his direction and Idris sidled up close—perhaps too close.

Bastien made a sound of displeasure and Sabine simply cocked a brow at him. Idris had no response.

"Oh, the Hallow Curse! A less known curse, but one of my favorites."

"You have a favorite curse?" Sabine asked, surprised.

"Doesn't everyone?" Idris asked, slight insecurity in

his voice.

Sabine looked at him unsure.

Bastien was looking down at his book, but cocked a brow.

"Not really, no," she said finally.

Color bloomed high on Idris's cheeks in embarrassment and it was a bold offset to his aqua eyes and royal blue jacket. Idris loosened his cravat, knocking his silver pin askew.

"I just find it poetic. You murder your partner and just when you move on to new paramours and think you've left it all behind, tragedy strikes serving unholy justice. It's karmic, really. Such a curse invoked and the only one to blame is the inciter of it."

Sabine felt shame flush through her. Bastien, sensing the change in her, straightened and moved slightly closer.

"What if it's a case of self-defense?" she suggested. "Or their spouse beat them and finally they had enough and now their villain returns?"

"I suppose I never looked at it that way." Idris shifted in awkwardness. "I saw too clearly in the black and white that doesn't exist. And that I never met anyone who'd survived the curse to tell their side—no one has survived longer than a fortnight."

"But the curse lasts a month," Sabine returned.

"It does. But it's either waiting out the month or whenever the horseman drags their cursed to Hell—whichever comes first."

Sabine let out a colorful curse that she barely understood.

Idris looked alarmed by her response. "Is everything all right?"

"All is well, thank you for your concern."

Idris hesitated and lingered, eyeing her uncertainly. "I should get back to work."

Sabine nodded and Idris left her and Bastien. Once he was out of side she deflated and Bastien was right there behind her. She sank to the floor and tipped her head back against the shelf.

"No good deed goes unpunished," she murmured to herself. She shook her head and held out a hand. "We have two more hours until class, hand me another text?"

And so Bastien did as he sank down beside her, the outside of his thigh pressing against hers solidly reminding her he was there.

When the two hours had passed Sabine was surprised that Bastien stuck by her, not wholly unlike a wax seal to a letter—and she tried very hard not to think about how, also like an unopened letter, she wanted to know what delightful secrets he kept inside. Anyone else this sort of closeness would be like a leech, but he was very decidedly not parasitic—a fact which startled her.

Did she…fancy Bastien Emmons?

Natural attraction aside—because it was ridiculous to deny—but beyond the physical, was she forming an emotional attachment?

As they walked into their art class Sabine was stunned when Bastien elected to take up the easel next to her, rather than the one across the room. She took her seat and just as he took his she leaned over.

"Not the center today?"

Bastien smiled a crooked little thing. "I'll give the stage to someone else today. But should you want any private modelling…" His eyes raked down her form in a promising fashion. "I'm available."

Sabine positively heated and she felt a surge of arousal between her legs.

They didn't speak again while the rest of the class filtered in, Winifred meeting her eyes and zeroing in on Bastien with an amused look of surprise. She took the seat he normally would have had and gave Sabine a little hip shimmy. The sound of chatter surrounded them, but nothing was louder than the silence of tension between her and Bastien.

Bastien rolled up his sleeves, showing off the smooth expanse of pale skin and the tracery of veins that stood out prominently. He rolled to three quarters and she was completely taken by the deft motions of his fingers, the way they curled and tucked.

Fuck, she wanted to draw his hands.

It continued like that for the rest of the class. Sabine utterly distracted by his presence. The way the paint smeared across his hands and tiny spots of red flecked his wrists. She had the wild and intrusive thought about paint streaking the two of them—

Bastien glanced at her, a knowing smirk on his lips.

She internally cursed herself.

In the absence of moonlight, the churchyard was haunting in its atmosphere and ominous in its presence. The light was hidden behind smoky clouds and it sent shivers down

Sabine's spine.

She was staying with Winnie once again, only this time there was a threat of tension that pulled taut like a piano wire. One she had visions of losing her head upon and her stomach roiled.

Outside, the gate whined in the breeze and the sound made all the hairs on the back on her neck stand up. Sigils of protection hovered around her, but even so she was on edge— even with being inside.

Even after casting countless strength sigils on every easement and entry. There should be no veritable access. Her signature magic hovered with Winnie's pear green spells, hers softer and less bold than Sabine's.

She'd retrieved some items from her flat to take to Winnie's earlier in the day while she stayed temporarily. Sabine had left art class somewhat reluctantly, leaving Bastien behind. She'd then immediately left for the abandoned cathedral and had slept much of the day due to the poor night's rest previously.

The heat from the fireplace warmed her, but she still felt ill at ease, so much so that her teacup trembled on its platter. She forced herself to set it all down as she stared out the window.

Sabine felt like a specter, amorphous and haunted. Once the night set upon the fence's brow, she'd rooted herself to place before the window, awaiting the horseman's return. Despairing about Nicholas's parting words.

"What are you doing?" Winnie asked from behind.

Sabine didn't turn around when she answered. "Keeping watch."

"You think he's coming back?"

"I know he is."

There was an audible hesitation from Winifred.

"Would you like me to stay up and accompany you?"

"No, you go to bed, darling. I'll be fine."

Winnie rested a hand on Sabine's shoulder. "Goodnight."

Sabine covered the hand with her own and tilted her head against it. "Goodnight."

As she listened to the sounds of Winnie retiring for bed, she didn't move. She just stared at that gate that rattled in the wind, knowing that flimsy bit of metal demarcated one of the only things to keep him at bay. Even if it couldn't keep the pumpkins within its enclosure, the vines snaking through the iron, cannonball gourds creeping towards the road.

Between her fingers, Sabine twisted a cutting sigil—the very same one she'd used to kill Nicholas nearly ten months ago. She could still remember it so clearly—the fury, the betrayal. Even thinking of it now burned her blood.

A sound cracked through the night.

Sabine's gaze zeroed.

There.

Through the dense fog rolling in was a horse's screech.

Her hearing piqued.

Hoofbeats.

Chuffing.

He was close.

She readied herself, threw the window open, and stood her ground.

Suddenly, the haze parted and red eyes broke through first. Two sets burned like braziers in a dungeon; all darkness save for their light. Too soon, the brimstone and charcoal horse appeared and there, its pale and vile rider, leering with sick pleasure.

Sabine's face was hard. She couldn't believe she'd

once loved him. How he'd cast such a mask of earnestness upon the depraved shell of his skeleton-soul with not even his dearest of friends knowing?

It seemed his penchant for illusion weaving extended to his presentation of self as well.

"Sabine," Nicholas said, breaking the tension from across the courtyard. "You wait for me, dearest? You shouldn't have."

"I wait for you only to tell you to leave. I will not be stepping foot outside these grounds after dusk until the month is up."

Nicholas canted his head. "You've done your research, I see."

"I have," she responded flatly. "So, you can fuck right off back to Hell because you can't touch me here."

"Oh, but that's where you're wrong, my sweet." He grinned a sinuous, creeping smile and raised his hand. It was wreathed in violet. His magic.

A rotten pumpkin rose as he directed the levitation sigil and it floated toward him. She watched in horror as he surrounded the pumpkin with a breaking sigil and it pulsed around it like a malevolent orb. Without flinching, he pushed it with a power spell and it shot across the grounds.

Past the wards.

Sabine, due to luck and her speed proficiency, managed to cast a locking sigil and threw it at the window as she dropped to the floor. The spell took before the rotten mess of orange and violet could crash through, and the whole thing slammed against the magically-reinforced pane with a violent bang.

Sludge slid down the window, greenish and pale seeds and slime stinking of decay.

Anger threaded through Sabine, and it finally made

her leave her post. She stomped to the front door and flung it open. When she did, the night air assaulted her senses, violated with the hellish visage presented past the gate.

Nicholas had another rotten pumpkin hovering close by.

Sabine held up her hand that still held the cutting sigil.

"You remember this, you fucking reptile?"

He flinched. His pumpkin wavered.

"It's the very sigil I used to kill you. Care to see if it can finish the job once again?"

I am your ruin.

Those were the last words she'd spoken to him and they hung heavy in the air, unspoken and tenebrous.

"It may hurt, but it will not stop me."

"I may decide to try."

And then she did.

The cut flew across the courtyard, across the wards, and him. It sliced through Nicholas's midsection. He hissed in pain. But as quickly as it crossed, it reformed, leaving not even severed fabric in its wake.

Fuck.

"Tart," he snarled, taking in the once-was damage.

"Oh, we're sinking to sexual-themed insults now?" she said, deflecting her fear. "Fucking delightful, Nicholas. It's pathetic you linger so."

"I won't linger if you come out, my dear."

"Fuck that," she hissed.

"Well, your options are exceedingly limited. Either you surrender yourself to me now and I take you to Hell. Or…" he tilted his head toward the pumpkin still levitating. "The next thing I send through that door will kill your little artist friend in there. Do you wish for her to die unnecessarily?"

Sabine froze.

Nicholas had already displayed quite clearly that despite his inability to cross, physical objects secured within a breaking spell had no such limitations. She was not safe here, but more importantly, Winnie wasn't either. Winnie, who'd opened her home to her without having to. Winnie, who remained friends with her despite believing she'd engaged in a taboo affair. Winnie, who simply cared about her.

She couldn't drag her into this—it was cruel. She had to leave. But how could she do so without Nicholas snatching her?

"If I leave, you will not touch her?" she queried.

"Not unless she wants it," he retorted.

Her lips twisted in a grimace. "She will not."

Nicholas shrugged. "Come to me and you shall not worry."

Sabine chanced a look behind her, half turning her body, and found Winnie standing silently on the stairs behind her. She was in her long white nightgown, an ivory bow at the bust, and her mouth was rounded into a small O. Faint moonlight traced her features and what she could see there was shock and fear and concern.

Guilt rampaged through Sabine as she twisted her fingers. Thoughts accompanied it all with a mantra of worthlessness and deserved loathing. It was every dark thought that had her questioning her morality and continued altered mortality.

"I'm so sorry," Sabine whispered to her. "I'll leave."

"You shouldn't have to," Winnie returned, silver lining her eyes with the glassines of tears.

"He's left me with no other choice."

"Please take care of yourself," she managed thickly.

"Do not stay here," Sabine whispered. "I do not trust

him. Find somewhere safe until the month is over."

Winnie inclined her head in understanding. "Anywhere specific?"

"Somewhere hallowed and over running water."

Winnie nodded and ascended the staircase.

As Winnie vanished, Sabine turned, hand raised with another cutting sigil, but as she did, quicker than was calculable, she threw a second sigil she'd been crafting secretively at Nicholas. He didn't even respond to it, blinded to distraction by the cut.

She walked out and his eyes tracked her.

Or rather, they would have if she'd continued walking.

Nicholas's gaze watched the illusion of herself she'd crafted and thrown at him. He watched a false Sabine descend the steps while the true one was sprinting for her life, casting silencing spells in her wake.

Ensuring Nicholas saw her slow surrender, still holding the cut, she raced past him and through the fog. She had one safe destination in mind and she intended to reach it.

31 Dullahan.

Bastien was her only safe haven. He was proficient in wards and that was her only sanctuary in the absence of available holy grounds. Vale Wood was spare with hallowed spaces simply because their demon attacks were minimal in comparison to the bigger cities—less prey. Even so, she was always readily armed with holy water and salt. It wasn't the first time she'd outrun a demonic creature and it certainly wouldn't be the last.

Sabine knew her illusion was still slowly walking. She couldn't hear it, but she knew Nicholas was leaving parting and farewell taunts, and she'd ensured her vision would respond similarly in curtness and coyness, as well as brusqueness and boldness—just as how the real her would.

She didn't stop running. Not even when Nicholas yelled when the foil was revealed and hooves crashed against the cobbles.

She just ran faster.

OCTOBER 3, 1867

The banging on his front door roused him from mild sleep just after midnight. Bastien shot to his feet and rushed to the door, casting unlocking sigils as he made his way there.

He'd only keyed one person's magic to this address and he knew she would only be here if it was absolutely essential—in dire straits or worse.

When Bastien flung open the door Sabine stormed in like a whirlwind, sigils blazing around her, the crackling energy lifting her auburn hair. As she slammed the door behind her, she twisted and twined her fingers around, so much faster than that of any warlock he'd ever known and secured his door with various protection, locking, and warding spells.

"How far do you wards extend?" she asked him, whirling to face him, dark eyes liquid with panic in the night.

"To the street," he returned quickly. "I have several layers but the first extends to the street."

"Good," she said, pushing back her long waves. "We'll sense him if he follows."

Fright burrowed in his bones. Even though this was entirely expected he said, "He found you again?"

She nodded. "And threatened to kill Winnie if I did not leave—though I did warn her that my leaving would not deter him in ending her life and had advised her to also leave when she safely could."

"Is she well?"

"Yes. He won't go after her tonight. He'll be searching for me. With that said, I need to leave tomorrow. Somewhere he can't find me. Somewhere he can't follow." She sighed. "It's either that, or get rid of him and I have no grand plans in my ability to do that. Do you?"

Bastien shook his head. "No, but Idris might. He's familiar with curses."

Despite the fact that it was true, it pained him to bring up the librarian. Especially in part due to the fact the warlock hardly resembled any librarian he'd ever seen before. The man was built large and muscular, not to mention much taller than Bastien himself. Truthfully, he expected Sabine to fancy him and was somewhat surprised that she didn't—or didn't seem to.

"Well, if Idris cannot help us, I must leave. Do you have any place in mind?"

Bastien's stomach lurched when she asked—because he did. It felt like the cruel hand of fate had just twisted the rug out from under him and was slowly drawing him back to what he'd been trying to flee. Telling him that he couldn't escape his prison, that it was his fate. But what he'd fled might be the only sanctuary now. There was no way the horseman could follow there.

Fuck.

It all seemed to be pointing back there. As if an oracle was guiding his life by pulling on his puppet strings—seeing the future and pushing him on the stage. He was—once again—to be a pawn.

He loathed it.

But he vowed that he would only be doing it one last time. And perhaps to save her from this demise, she need not die unnecessarily. She could serve the greater good.

"If it comes to that, I do," he said finally with reservation.

"Lovely," Sabine said, kicking off her boots and quickly casting a cleaning spell on her person, the red magic winding around her and dissolving quickly.

Cleaning spells could be used up to three times before they failed, the build-up of magic like a plaque that needed to be removed. They were great in a pinch, but unreliable if one were on a long voyage without soap or water. It certainly helped on pirate ships—from the comparisons he'd heard from the mortal world—but it was not infallible.

Bastien watched as Sabine wandered around his flat, acquainting herself with it as if she owned it. Something about her very presence stirred something in his heart and following heat licked down his spine and roused his cock. He liked her. Worse so, he liked the way he made her feel, and that was very dangerous with his Midnight Malady in mind.

"Do you mind if I stay the night, and then tomorrow, if Idris does not have the answers, you advise me to this mysterious haven you have alluded to?"

"Of course. I just have one problem."

"Oh?" she asked, turning from her browsing of his various teas. She stretched her arms above her head, crossing at the wrists and cocking her head. "And that is?"

"I only have the one bed."

"That is fine, we can share."

"No—I…I should take the floor."

Sabine arched a brow. "If anyone should take the floor it is me as I am the intruding guest, but as I am not willing to suffer the floorboards all night, I insist we share the bed."

"I don't want to presume anything or tempt any nature of sexual proclivities."

"Don't be daft, I was just chased through the streets. The last thing I'm thinking of is fucking anyone. I just wish to get a comfortable sleep."

Bastien blinked. He'd never met anyone so bold and outright as Sabine Van Arsdel. It was simultaneously charming and alluring—not to mention, unexpected. He delighted in it.

"Okay," he responded simply.

Bastien then turned to his drawers and pulled out a long white undershirt with long puffed sleeves—it was the sort that was caricature of a pirate, but one he knew spoke of wanton embraces. Handing the shirt over to Sabine, he pointed to a door.

"The restroom is through there if you'd like to change."

She caught the shirt and strode past him with an ease that had everything inside him utterly alive. When she shut the door behind her, he scrubbed his hands over his face, trying to ascertain where his head was.

Air.

He needed air.

Stalking over to the front window, he cracked it open and inhaled the crisp night breeze, taking in the star-flecked sky. Beyond, he took his sharpened eyesight and scoured the city-scape, scanning over the roofs and the balconies of all the houses and flats, following the roads and lampposts, eyeing every passing carriage and drunken lout hollering into the night. Normally, he used this ability to sight for someone to slake his thirst, but tonight he was searching for the ghostly rider who was hellbent on capturing Sabine.

He was nowhere to be seen.

Just then, the door opened behind him and Bastien turned to find Sabine stepping out and he froze. Swallowed. Blinked.

There she stood.

In his shirt.

And only his shirt.

Her legs were completely on display, and though she was short, it still only fell to mid-thigh. Her golden skin was smooth and shapely, the definition of muscles to her calves. Her fingers tucked the too-long sleeves in her palms, the neckline falling low on the generous swell of her chest, the faint light tracing the shape of her nipples.

Fuck, she was stunning.

All sultry dark eyes, unbound waves, and soft skin he just wanted to taste—

She cleared her throat. "Are you well?"

Bastien shook himself out of his reverie—she was the reverie. "Yes, of course."

She smirked at him like she was calling his lie.

Watching him, she peeled back his covers and climbed

into his bed. He wondered if she was still wearing her undergarments. And then immediately banished those thoughts. She had just been chased through the streets; she didn't have interest in that—she'd said as much herself.

Bastien closed the windows, ensured the locks were all latched, and casted a couple extra wards for good measure. His wards were his specialty—and he assumed speed was Sabine's, from what he'd observed.

His heart beat an anticipated rhythm when he approached the bed. Sabine watched him with a foxlike smile, daring him to balk.

He wouldn't.

Bastien, dressed in only loose pants and an even looser shirt, slid into his bed and laid on his back staring at the ceiling. Pointedly aware of Sabine's warm presence only an arm's reach away. He was so painfully aware of her that it made him ache.

He wondered what she'd feel like under him. The warm feel of her skin beneath his hands. The way she'd sigh as his nose traced down her throat. How her hands would clutch his shoulders as she moaned his name. The way his fangs would sink into her—

No.

He stiffened. His gums aching, his throat parched.

Pinching the bridge of his nose he breathed in and out slowly.

He had more self-restraint than most who were afflicted with Midnight Malady, but that was only due to the blood bond he'd forged—as many of the other blood drinkers he'd considered his kin had done—with their mistress.

A necessary evil, but at this moment one he had very complex feelings with. For several reasons. One of which was the warlock who lay beside him. The warlock who'd turned onto her side, hand pressed to her cheek as she gazed at him.

"What are you thinking?" she asked softly. There was curiosity in her voice, but also concern. "Your eyes make it look as if your mind is quite busy."

He turned his face to her and smiled. "Are you staring at me?"

"A little."

"Pervert."

"I've been called worse."

There was a pause as he held her gaze. As he took in that wall behind her eyes. The one that kept her from feeling everything too much—too deeply. She had her wit because it was her personality, yes, but also, she used it as one would hold a shield.

He wanted to be the one she set it down for.

And that thought alone scared him.

But not enough to scare him off.

"Is this the part where you ask me a question?" she prodded.

"Such as?"

A smile curved her mouth. "Something to the effect of 'who hurt you?' or 'what's worse?' perhaps."

He laughed. "I was actually thinking there's more to you than meets the eye."

Sabine threw back her head. "Oh, darling, as if that's the first time I've heard that. Delightful to hear, surely, but rarely do those who say it make it mean anything."

"I do not follow."

Sabine situated herself so she was propped on her elbow. "People say it when they've underestimated you, but more in my case, realize I'm more than just a pretty face. However, more often than not, I am just worth the pretty face to them and I am less substance." She twisted her lips. "I am often the side show, never the main act."

"A circus reference?"

She shrugged.

"Do you truly think this way?"

"It's what I know," she said softly.

Bastien reached out and stroked a lock of dark red hair back from her face. Her dark eyes followed his touch, warily and wondering.

"I think one day, you'll know different."

She inhaled quickly and then he let his hand fall.

For a few moments it was quiet before they both took to their respective sides, tension thrumming between them, but neither acting upon it.

Later, they both fell to sleep and the horseman did not find them.

Soft gray dawn light filtered in through the curtains and Bastien was made agonizingly aware of the woman in the bed next to him. Agonizing, because his face was nuzzled into the crook of Sabine's neck and her leg was thrown over his hips, pressing into his very hard cock—made worse by the fact that he now knew for certain she wasn't wearing underwear as the smooth heat of her core was on him,

Bastien held his breath as the thrum of her pulse ghosted across his lips and the urge to bite consumed him. Her vanilla and cinnamon scent utterly divine in his lungs; the way the slight spice clung to her skin and the sweetness lingered in her hair. The fantasy from last night came alive again and he felt his teeth sharpen.

Inhaling quickly, Bastien slowly disentangled himself from Sabine's drowsing form, and slid from the bed. She did not wake, she instead settled deeper into the bed, pulling the covers up to her throat.

Bastien swallowed. Perhaps that was for the best.

He let Sabine sleep an hour more while he made tea. Luckily, he'd fed last night before her arrival so the worst of his thirst was adequately quenched. But moreover, his sanity was clearer—thus, his thoughts.

When Sabine had dressed once again—in a pair of leather pants and a crimson crushed velvet blouse—they headed off. Due to the morning's chill, Bastien had grabbed Sabine a spare cloak and she wrapped the black fabric around herself. Unfortunately, something predatory in him enjoyed seeing her in his clothes—something animalistic and possessive.

Sabine walked slightly in front of him—he gathered that she was the type of woman who could not, and not be caged, like a firestorm. He hoped she never diminished herself to fit into anyone's predesigned box.

But then the reminder of what he'd planned to do to her entered his mind and a sick roil went through his gut. There wasn't going to be a box left to push her into.

They arrived at the café at Sabine's regular time—she'd filled him in on her regular morning routine—and found Idris sitting by the window, an open book before him.

Idris looked up when Sabine and Bastien entered, the bell above the door jingling. His smile positively glowed when he caught sight of her, but banked as he met Bastien.

Despite Idris towering over Bastien and having many pounds of muscle over him, he didn't register him as a threat—not truly—but it was difficult to tell that horrible instinctual part of him that.

The other warlock rose when Sabine and Bastien approached.

"Sabine, I didn't know you had company. Good to see you, Mister Emmons," Idris said cordially.

"It's a complicated situation," Sabine responded. "One I actually wish to speak with you about."

"Oh?" Idris glanced around at the nearly empty café. "What of it?"

"Do you remember our conversation about the Hallow Curse?" she queried.

"Yes, of course. What—? Oh!" Idris seemed to register something in the rigidity of Sabine's features. "Sabine, it can't be true."

Sabine's brows drew together in irritation, defensiveness rising in the set of her shoulders. "I am cursed," she said quietly. "And I do not deserve it."

And so, she casted protective spells and revealed to Idris what she'd revealed to Bastien. What little he knew. That she'd killed her former lover because it was necessary and now, he was hunting her down. Idris blushed when she mentioned the stipulated roles and how she'd become the Coquette, and Bastien didn't miss how Idris glanced at him— assessing his preconceived competition.

When she finished, Idris deflated.

"Sabine, I am so sorry. For my comments and callous words. How I must have made you feel. Please know you have my utmost apology in regard and I will strive to rectify this."

"While that is much appreciated, I simply want to know if you can help me." Sabine's eyes flickered about the room—she was quite bold to be speaking of murder in a public space, but fortuitously they'd casted sound dampening sigils. "Do you have any information or perhaps know of any texts surrounding this curse and how I might get rid of Nicholas—aside from waiting it out?”

Idris shook his head. “No, there is no other alternative. It is a demon's justice to be given the month to hunt and what is dead cannot die. I am sorry, but the curse must play out.”

Sabine sighed and lifted her face to the ceiling. “Well—” she turned to Bastien, “let's move onto your alternative. Where are we going?”

Bastien's stomach dropped.

This was it.

This was the unwinding of fate and the cruel knife she wielded. It was what he didn't want to do, but what he had to do—both for her safety and his continued existence.

But it was going to be the worst betrayal and it would kill her.

“We're going to board a ship.”

Hours later, after multiple stops and Idris tagging along, guilt coloring every word, the three of them were on the dock waiting to board. Sabine had gotten word earlier that Winnie had caught a train and was going away for a few weeks to visit family. That had been a brief yet heartfelt and tearful departure, but it was necessary.

Although, it was at Idris's insistence that he join them.

“My magic is not strong, but my mind is,” Idris had announced with defense. “I wish to help you thwart this evil.”

“That is truly not necessary,” Sabine had argued back. “I am not some injured doe in need of saving from all the fearsome men.”

"I am fearsome?" Bastien had murmured quietly in a playful tone.

Sabine had lightly smacked his waist in response and returned her attention to Idris—but there was amusement there. Bastien considered it an honor to have riled her.

"I did not mean to offend—again," Idris despaired. "I simply wish to rectify which I identify as a grievous wrong. If you should not, I fear I may wallow in my inadequacy in your absence."

"Mr. Swan, are you extorting my fairer emotions and hoping to glean coercion to my decision due to my feminine sex? Because I assure you, I am more than capable of deciphering blackmail, and you, my friend, are toeing that very line. Or do you think me a simpering dolt?"

Bastien had to cover his mouth to spare his laughter from Sabine's tongue lashing. Fuck, did he love how she knocked his ego down a peg. In self-flagellation way, he wanted her to do it to him.

A flash of her dominating him heated his blood. The idea of her having her way with him in the bedroom, all lusty red—

For fuck's sake.

He'd returned to Idris stumbling over his words, defending what he'd said, but holding strong to his insistence.

"Mister Emmons, does this place house a library?"

Bastien blinked. "Yes, a vast one."

"One that guests may access?"

"Yes…"

Triumphantly, Idris turned to them. "I know how this curse works. I am educated in finding out information as a librarian. If there is any way to end this curse early, I can discover it. I will spend the duration of the stay attempting to figure out how to do so."

Sabine's resolve had wavered and Idris knew it. He'd latched onto her weakness immediately and with a few more exchanges she'd agreed.

Bastien had soured feelings about the matter but he banished it all as he stood with the others preparing to board the ship.

It was far too close to twilight for his likes, the night glowing violet and orange over the water, the breeze scented with brine. Sabine was practically vibrating with nerves, casting glances over her shoulder, fearing Nicholas's attack.

There was a specific warlock Bastien was avoiding and his eyes scanned the crowd for him, but it seemed that he was not among the masses. Likely, he was going to wait for a later ship, but if he wasn't, Bastien wanted to be prepared for his presence.

Salem caught Bastien's eye and nodded. There was a petite, dark-haired female next to him toying with pink protection sigils between her black-gloved fingers and the sight of her made Bastien's stomach sink. He didn't recognize her, but he knew her for what she was.

What she was going to be.

Because it was exactly what Sabine was supposed to be.

And he was just acting the role of a sycophant.

A whistle sounded breaking Bastien from his fugue, and with gratefulness he registered the signal and they boarded *The Tithe* with haste. Sabine strode ahead of him, and as they ascended the access from the dock to the ship, Bastien was immensely distracted by the sight of Sabine's ass in her tight pants.

Fuck, she needed to wear a potato sack.

The other bonded were likely to notice her and he was not willing to share—in any form.

An ostentatious throat clearing sounded behind him and he glanced back to see Idris and his cocked brow. Bastien shrugged—he wasn't going to deny being caught.

Once they were all on board, some of Sabine's evident anxiety faded. She crossed to the starboard side of the vessel and stared down at the dock as the final boarders got on. Bastien's gaze flickered to the horizon. The sun was sinking quickly—far too quickly.

Fortuitously, all parties made it on and minutes later *The Tithe* was setting out to sea. Idris offered to take all their luggage to their quarters in an attempt to be as helpful and least burdensome as possible. It was then that Sabine and Bastien were left alone—in relative terms.

Night fell across the sky and the water was bathed in violet; white-fire stars reflected upon the surface. Voices were excited and chatty behind them, curiosity thick in the air—all the newcomers were enchanted by the tales of the masquerades and luxury to be abound. Already, a fiddle was starting up and the thump of footsteps led to dancing.

As the moon awoke, Sabine and Bastien stood at the stern, watching Vale Wood grow smaller and smaller, the problems there turning insignificant against the issue their ship sailed toward. That concern was like an infection and its plague was spreading more and more virulent as they traveled, the contagion more deadly as more souls were brought to it. They were all becoming part of this parasitic machine, dependent on their host—and their host was their mistress and she kept them all beneath her control.

Now that dark had truly fallen, new dangers came out, and with it—as expected—was Nicholas.

Sabine let out a small gasp and seeming unconsciously, she reached for Bastien's hand and squeezed it. He caught her slender fingers and didn't let them go. She just clutched tighter.

The horseman raced down to the dock, halting where it began to hang over the water. Bastien watched while that brimstone and fury horse clopped and whinnied. The rider was filled with hatred and even across the ever-expanding sea, Bastien felt that loathing penetrate him. Those Hell-red eyes bored straight into him and Sabine promising violence. They were far from the coast, but it was undeniable and he shuddered.

"He can rot in Hell," Sabine hissed.

Bastien laced their fingers together. "We'll make sure of it."

They watched Nicholas's frustration from *The Tithe*, silently celebrating their small victory.

THE
SEA

OCTOBER 3, 1867

Nicholas was seething as Sabine slipped through his fingers, while hers twined with Bastien's.

On *The Tithe*, they were offered a slice of reprieve, and they were not the only ones to feel some version of the freedom. Dancers were twirling and stamping a merry jig to the tune of a fiddler's song and rhythmic clapping. Sabine did not feel the draw to that music as she had to the melody at the Harvest Ball.

What came as a surprise shortly after was that Idris was not ocean savvy in the slightest. Waves crashed against the hull, rocking the ship, the mass of it creaking with every pummel of the water. This, had an adverse effect on Idris and he was promptly sea sick only hours into the journey.

Sabine felt pity on the warlock, but decided it was a bit of karmic justice for imposing himself on the voyage. Even if he did make pathetic hacking sounds into the whitecaps.

Beside Bastien, reassured by his presence, Sabine let some of her fears evaporate. Nicholas couldn't cross running water—or an ocean for that matter—so they were safe. However, there were concerns regarding their destination.

"What if Nicholas opens a portal from Hell to where we're going?" Sabine asked Bastien quietly.

Bastien leaned his back against the rail. "He can't. The entire ground of the island has been sanctified—it's holy."

"Please tell me you're not indoctrinating me into a religious cult—that's very mortal leaning."

"No, there's no religious connotation. The holy grounds are a convenience, not a necessity. And do not worry, as with the rest of Midith, we know there is no god—seraphic beings are undeniable, but we are not like the humans and their beliefs and hubris."

"I don't hear any denial of cults," she teased.

"Bastien!"

A voice sounded behind them and Sabine heard the telltale sound of a hand clapping a shoulder just as Bastien stiffened and the two of them turned. Bastien held himself rigid, his face an apathetic mask and Sabine's heart skipped a beat in unease.

Sabine took in the new figure with a critical air and found him lacking. And judging from Bastien's response this was a less than wanted presence.

The warlock had meticulously styled honey-brown curls atop his head and eyes like shards of aquamarine—sharp and jewel-bright. He grinned and the smile was too wide and too white, even with his fair complexion. As tall as Idris, but half as built.

His presence was domineering, but not in an authoritative way, but rather in an imposing fashion that felt like a cloying sludge that Sabine wanted to wash away.

"Reynard," Bastien said through a forced smile, casually shrugging off the imposing warlock's hand. "I didn't think you were on this ship—I didn't see you board."

"Ah, I was with my guest. She is simply *insatiable*," he said conspiratorially, rubbing shoulders. Bastien looked less than pleased. Reynard chuckled before continuing, "you know how I am."

"And where is she now?" Bastien asked—deflecting.

"Resting," Reynard responded. Slimy.

Sabine mentally noted to check on this guest of his. She felt a strong surge of protectiveness rise up for her, particularly because this Reynard reminded her far too much of Nicholas. An ill wave crept over her, an uncertain future making itself known. Was she running from one evil directly into the arms of another one?

If that were true…

Fury rose within her and she directed this newfound alertness at Reynard, however, if Bastien had made her a fool—well, she'd certainly have more than words for him. Red flashed between her fingertips, unbidden, and both males noticed. She mentally cursed and flashed a saccharine smile.

"Be kind to her, or I may find you *resting*—in the dirt," Sabine quipped.

Reynard's gaze whipped her like a cut. She held firm

in her smile, tying her hands behind her back and twisting her fingers. Bastien tilted his head and cocked a brow.

It all stitched together like a quilt of tension and silent communication met them all.

Reynard seemed to get the hint fairly quickly and left Sabine and Bastien alone once again. She threw a sarcastic wave at his back with a flash of red. Sabine reeled on Bastien, grasping the sleeve of his Bordeaux corduroy jacket and pulled him close.

"Bastien Emmons, I do not like that warlock."

"He is no friend of mine."

"Does he think you are?"

Bastien looked past her at Reynard. "No," he said, not looking at her. "He knows very well I am not."

A pit formed in Sabine's stomach, a sick pool of ichor taking the place of its former acid.

"Is that girl—is she safe with him?"

Bastien returned his gaze to Sabine. "I can't promise that."

Sabine's lip curled in fury. "Then I will."

With that, Sabine let go of Bastien's sleeve and crossed the deck with furious purpose. She'd seen where he went—to the private quarters—and due to the tracking sigil she'd casted—a very complex spell which was rare to master—she knew exactly where he was.

Sabine followed the tracking directly to one of the many cramped cabins and pounded on the door. Almost immediately the door swung open and there Reynard stood with a girl—who physically appeared a few years younger than Sabine—clutching a white silk cravat.

"Can I help you?" Reynard asked in a tone that indicated very much he did not want to help, nor offer assistance.

Sabine didn't dignify him with a response and she didn't care if that made him an enemy of her. Immediately, she felt Bastien's strong and silent presence behind her.

"Are you well?" Sabine asked the girl.

The girl's bright green eyes widened. "Me?" Her dark hair was snarl about her head, lips plump and perhaps even swollen.

"Yes," Sabine responded firmly.

The girl's eyes flickered to Reynard and the warlock's nostrils flared as the set of his shoulders squared. She cowered under the weight of his aura, fingers tucking into her blouse's neckline, her knuckles red.

"I—I'm fine," she said, then cleared her throat. She had an accent, not Vonorian, but from the same continent, more eastern. "All is well here."

Sabine was not convinced. "What is your name?" The girl started to move and Sabine stopped her. "Don't look at him, look at me. You do not seek permission to speak."

"Who do you think you are—" Reynard began but Sabine cut him off with a silencing sigil.

"Elizabeta," she finally said.

"Elizabeta, do you feel safe with this warlock?"

"He is my lover. He has guided me to all the new in this world."

"This world?"

"The world of magic."

Sabine inclined her head in understanding. "You are from the mortal plane."

"My magic manifested this past spring and my family cast me out for being a witch," Elizabeta explained. "I left before they could call the church upon me and found the nearest bridge over the Danube. The Watch let me Travel when I displayed my magic." Elizabeta flashed a yellow sigil.

Portals existed all over the globe between the Magic World and the Mortal World, accessed by bridges where one jumps from to land in the other. Every bridge portal was guarded by the Watch and only they allowed Travel as only warlocks and their spouses and children were allowed entry to this side.

"Since then, I've been trying to find my place in this new magical world." Elizabeta stepped closer to Sabine and Reynard—the latter of whom no longer had the silencing sigil upon him but was respectfully remaining quiet. "I am unused to having so many freedoms as a woman. He grounds me."

Elizabeta's eyes brightened with the expanse of hope yawning in front of her, the understanding of freedom that had never been tasted before.

"If you ever need anything—" Sabine's gaze cut to Reynard. He sneered at her but she didn't back down. "Please find me."

Appreciation glittered in Elizabeta's eyes before a flash of wariness overtook it. "I do not require a savior, but the sentiment is sweet, nonetheless."

"I see."

With that, Sabine nodded and departed, Bastien wordless on her heels as a silent guardian. Above deck, sea spray thick in the air, night descending to the deepest of indigoes, she exhaled.

Sabine understood. Elizabeta's protector was also her predator. He provided her with a comfortable lifestyle, but there was a threatening undertone—to do what he said, *or else*. It seemed Elizabeta couldn't shed all her roots, especially the deepest ones ground in women being subservient to their husbands.

Meanwhile, Sabine had not been raised with such values, however, she did have some experience with the concept as her dearest friend had parents who'd lived what Elizabeta did. Her father developed his magic late from mortal parents and he and his wife departed London for Vonor. There, they'd had their daughter and she'd become one of the most proficient warlocks of their generation as well as the talented mind who'd discovered a cure for Ember Fever—one of the few immortal diseases.

A pang of longing struck her.

She missed Lucia.

Rubbing her chest at the hurt there, she stared across the tenebrous waves, troubled not by what may lie beneath them, but across.

"Bastien?" Sabine started softly.

"Yes?" he responded, his voice a low, gentle rumble.

"I like you, so I must ask. Do you plan to kill me at this haven you speak of?"

"I beg your—no, no, of course not."

"Good," she said with a delicate smile. "Because if you do, I will turn into a demon and haunt you for all eternity, darling."

OCTOBER 3, 1867

I will turn into a demon and haunt you for eternity, darling.

Those words roared in his ears and thickened his cock. He had no idea why but the threat of those words, the sinister lilt of her voice, that saccharine smile…it stirred his blood and sent desire coursing through every inch of his being.

Turning into a demon was entirely possible, too, which made the threat all the more visceral.

When spirits possessed so much evil or anger, that hatred and loathing festered into an amalgamation that turned the universes attention on one. The attuned attention then soured and festered in a person until which time it transformed one. Those spirits then developed horns, tails, reddened eyes, ichor tears, wings, or runes carved into flesh. Those spirits were then Made demons.

Other demons—as those who attached themselves specifically to curses—were known interchangeably as ghosts.

True demons were a different breed. Hailing from circles of Hell, subservient to the rulers of their chosen sin and the torments there. There was no deity of Hell, but there were princes and kingdoms. Such places were inspired by a Dante, who'd performed the Staying and written literature about his time.

Bastien looked at Sabine, took her in and realized how his heart insistently tugged to her. Begging to be united and tangled. He wanted limbs and tongues pressed together. He wanted to be inside her.

The vibrant and wanton feelings shocked him, but nonetheless they were there. However, more concerning is that the automatic ache in his gums when presented with desire wasn't there. In fact, it was such an afterthought that it was hardly there. He'd never—in all his years of having contracted Midnight Malady—had he been able to separate sexual attraction and his thirst. They had coexisted to a point of codependency where one could not be present without the other.

Until her.

Sabine.

Bastien licked his lips.

"Bastien," she whispered. She'd inherently picked up on the mood, how he'd shifted. It was like the rolling of the ocean had taken them and were carrying their feelings on the unending current.

Their feelings were out of their hands now. The stars and sea had taken them and they were utterly at the mercy of them. Like an eldritch creature playing with the puppet strings of their lives.

"Sabine," he returned.

Without thinking it over thoroughly, he reached out and pressed his hand to her jaw—gently, oh so gently. She leaned into it, and her lips parted. He rubbed his thumb on that sweet swell of her lower lip and a small gasp ghosted across his fingertip.

Fuck, how he wanted to taste that small sound falling from her tongue. He was ravenous for it.

Sabine reached out, holding her hand against his heart. It sped up beneath her touch, his cold skin coming alive against the fiery heat of her—the promise of passion.

He leaned forward—

And stumbled.

The ship rocked violently against the ocean and a chorus of alarm went up. A very evident groan of despair came from the side of the ship where Idris was continuing to lose every single content of his stomach—Bastien pitied him, he really did. Even if he did desire Sabine's heart, too.

Bastien steadied Sabine just as a crack of thunder crashed in the sky and the pressure of the sky changed. Suddenly aware of the rapidly cooling temperatures, Sabine shivered and Bastien ushered her to their cabin.

"Come, it'll rain soon. Let's retire to the cabin and order tea and warm blankets," he suggested.

Sabine nodded, a wash of—disappointment?—flashed across her features. Bastien tried not to get his hopes up in that regard. Nonetheless, they slipped below deck and found their cabin number—a cramped, four bunk space.

There were two bunks to each wall and only enough

space for a small table and chest between. All their belongings had to fit beneath the bunks where padlocked nets kept them contained. Light sigils hung in the air in multi-variety hues, every color of the rainbow courtesy of the crew and their own unique magics.

Each warlock casted with their own signature hue. Bastien knew many warlocks whose magic manifested as red, but none the vibrant ruby of Sabine's. His own magic was an ethereal silver and it flashed above their heads here. He could pick out green and blue, purple and orange, pink and yellow, and so many more. But upon closer inspection that green was peridot, the blue cornflower, and lilac, tangerine, quartz, and dandelion.

Sabine sank onto the right-side bottom bunk and Bastien took the left. They hadn't discussed who was sleeping where, as Idris was also staying with them—so someone had to take the top spot.

"What do you—?" Bastien started before the sound of shouting had him breaking off.

He recognized the signature accent of Elizabeta and the more unsettling familiar growl of Reynard. It seemed Sabine did too because she stood up like a shot and raced for the door and down the hallway where Elizabeta and Reynard's quarters were.

Bastien chased after.

Reynard and Elizabeta's door was ajar and Bastien could see clothing being flung from one side of the room to the other, rapid-fire obscenities tossed with them.

"You do not tell me with whom I may socialize!" Elizabeta shouted, emphasized with a pair of black pants flying across the door.

"I fucking brought you along here, you ungrateful bitch! I promised you a life in the fucking lap of luxury, so when I tell you to sit and be my pretty little whore, you do it."

"You're a prick!" she screeched.

"And you're a vapid sycophant."

"I told you not to use words I don't know! They make me feel small and silly and stupid!"

"Well, that's because you are! A little foreign girl like a lost little bird, taking from the first fucking hand that fed it—thinking it was love."

"Fuck you," Elizabeta snarled.

Sabine threw open the door, filled with all the fiery rage of her passion. Elizabeta's eyes were liquid-filled, blurry with tears. There was a red mark on her cheek and her dark hair was even less tidy than before.

"That is quite enough here," Sabine said tautly, ire oozing off her frame. "Elizabeta, come with me." Sabine held her hand out and Elizabeta hurried to her. Sabine gently pushed her behind where Bastien flanked her.

Sabine advanced on Reynard fearlessly; despite the way he towered over her. She stared up with all the pent-up aggression of a hellhound. "I will not be listening to this vitriol and disgusting manner of speech. She is your fucking guest and I'll be damned if you intend to lay one more insult upon her person. I do not care in which the regard you hold for me and hurl insult at, but you will not even whisper the most fragmented of ill phrase toward this warlock or I'll ensure your tongue can never do so."

"You threaten me, impudent witch?" Reynard sneered.

"Don't try to diminish me with such human terms, all warlocks are equal—any and all sex. Calling me a witch just speaks to your mortal roots you are so desperate to bury. Or am I wrong and have misjudged your former upbringing and undeniable parentage?"

Bastien couldn't help it, his jaw dropped.

Sabine had verbally eviscerated Reynard before them.

And Bastien knew Reynard would never forgive the humiliation.

Reynard hissed an indecipherable swear at Sabine and she did not even flinch when he got in her face. She simply casted a small sigil—so fucking fast—and pressed him back a step.

"Personal space, if you would," she said without inflection or fear. "Your hurt feelings are something you should sort out yourself and perhaps reflect on the deeper inferiority you struggle with."

Reynard switched tactics and snapped at Bastien. "Leash your fucking bitch or I'll do it for you. You're supposed to bring a subservient little pup, not a spitfire."

Bastien crossed his arms and leaned against the doorframe. Then he said so casually it probably didn't register, "Tell me to quell any of her urges and I'll rip your fucking throat out—that is, if she doesn't do so first."

Reynard's eyes and nostrils flared. "You think she'll let *her* stay?"

Drusilla was the very last of his concerns right now—she was integral to such worries, yes, but he had more personal issues at stake. Even if the blood bond with her was related to many of them.

Those who were afflicted with Midnight Malady could blood bond to someone who also suffered from it. This bond provided a mutual extension of life with the disease, as the prognosis before fatality was ten years. The issue at hand was that the bond was only a power imbalance situation. Someone was always of the authority and the other was always one of submission. This blood bond—this covenant—had one mistress who thought herself a goddess, who forced them to bend to her will whether they wanted to or not.

Like a spider queen and her web of vows, they were forced to be loyal unto her until their dying breaths.

To their mistress.

Drusilla.

Bastien had bonded to her out of desperation.

As did Reynard.

And Salem.

And every damned Midnight Malady sufferer on board.

Bastien curled his lip. "I don't give a fuck if she lets her do anything. Sabine is *my* guest and I will treat her as such. She is under my protection."

"And Elizabeta is under mine."

"No," Bastien said with finality and such cold calm that even both women stilled. He stopped leaning on the frame and approached slowly—like a hunting cat. Even with his height on Bastien and the dangerous airs he possessed, Bastien was far more lethal—and they both knew it. "She is still your guest, but your guardianship is no longer needed. We'll reconvene at the island, goodnight, Reynard."

"You—"

"I *said* goodnight, Reynard." And Bastien threw a silver silencing sigil at his pompous fucking face.

As they left with Elizabeta in tow, Bastien caught Sabine from the corner of his eye flipping Reynard the middle finger, tongue out.

Warmth glowed in his chest. The way petite Sabine had no qualms about verbally eviscerating a warlock more than a head her height and more than a hundred pounds more on his frame. The way her ferocity and fierceness were emphasized by her utter fearlessness and protective instincts…

He found himself smiling as they made their way to

their cabin, but then a new fact struck a nerve.

Bastien was entirely too sure that he was falling in love with Sabine Van Arsdel.

104

OCTOBER 4, 1867

Sabine stood on the deck with a cup of cinnamon coffee clutched in her hands and the morning breeze in her hair.

Without magic the cabin would have been cold and damp. However, with four warlocks sequestered into their tiny quarters they were able to conjure enough magic to stave off the creeping wet from the sea and the chill from the October ocean air.

The night had been punctuated with Idris's rolling out of bed to lose his stomach to the turbulent waves, and

Elizabeta's soft sniffles. Bastien and Idris had taken opposing bottom bunks while Sabine and Elizabeta had the tops. Sabine was just thankful that their noisy bunkmates were on the opposite side and Sabine and Bastien had silencing sigils hovering on their side. Though it had taken an embarrassing amount of time to get Idris a tonic for his stomach and a second for slumber.

There was nothing for Elizabeta's hurting heart.

Sabine made herself useful and helped across the deck—offering a hand, making conversation, assisting with wards—and began familiarizing herself with their vessel. The voyage was expected to be five days, as long as the weather permitted, so Sabine sleuthed as much as possible.

She wasn't an idiot; she knew something was amiss— she just didn't know how far it spread. That was why she was speaking with everyone to gauge the potential. Sabine was painfully aware that wherever this ship was going to, it may be a temporary haven, but it certainly wasn't a permanent sanctuary.

On the foredeck, a petite warlock with pretty pink magic sidled up to her.

"You're very fast," the pink magic warlock said conversationally. The warlock herself was slowly tying a clumsy ward together, while Sabine was fastening multiple wards in a crimson net with ferocious speed.

"It's my specialty," Sabine replied with a coy smile. "I'm Sabine."

"Veronica," she introduced, dark eyes glittering. "Who are you here with?"

"Bastien. You?"

"Oh!" She seemed startled. "Mister Emmons! He's a fine gentleman. I am accompanying Salem."

Sabine quirked a brow as her fingers continued

working. "Should I be concerned with your response, dear? You seem awfully surprised."

"No! No, it's just that I thought that poor sea sick fellow—Mister Swan—was his guest."

Some of Sabine's nerves unwound. "Idris insisted on joining us."

"Mm, I see. And are the three of you…?" she trailed off meaningfully.

"Oh, seven hells, no. That principle is not for me, though I am not one to dissuade anyone from their proclivities nor passions."

Sexual and romantic relations involving more than three parties was not unheard of, but it was relatively new to the magic world—and completely obsolete from society in the mortal one. That wasn't to say sexual encounters of three or more didn't happen in either world, but that in one it was a hushed secret, and in the other it was simply less talked about aside from certain circles.

"Awe—" she fake pouted, "such a shame. Mister Swan is delightful on the eyes and surely Mister Emmons would be open and eager to the suggestion."

Sabine finished tying her wards and then leaned her back against the ship's rail. "Are you saying Bastien desires the male and female form?"

"He does."

Sabine smiled and couldn't help the rush of heat that sparked her blood. "Interesting. And have you met him before? Have you been to this island?"

"Oh, yes. Several times. This is my third visit."

More of Sabine's anxieties quelled. If Veronica had come and gone from the island multiple times, then at least Sabine wasn't being led to her doom.

"Tell me about it," Sabine pressed casually, resting her

elbows on the rail behind her.

Cool.

Aloof.

Certainly not in any terms prying for information.

Definitely not that.

Veronica's next spell wobbled—a tell. "What do you want to know?"

Sabine shrugged as the wind played with her long tresses. "What should I expect?"

Veronica twisted her lips. "A debauched getaway." Sabine's brow rose as Veronica continued. "Drinks, parties, games, masquerades. It's a time of artistic libations and general depravity in a secluded fashion."

"Artistic libations, hmm?"

"Mmhmm," Veronica murmured suggestively. "The way they make you feel…" Her eyes rolled back.

Sabine's cheeks flushed. She was no stranger to sex, but the way Veronica seemed to be memorizing something—it felt deeply personal. The responding rosy hue on Veronica's face indicated exactly what Sabine assumed.

"Hmm, I assume you and Salem are beaus, then?" Sabine queried.

Veronica's dark eyes flashed open. "No. Salem claims no sexual desires for any*one* or any*thing*." Veronica's brows narrowed in consternation. "Have you not given Bastien a taste?"

Sabine's brows rose slowly and comically. Veronica's words had a visceral effect on her, triggering her mind into conjuring fantasies in which Bastien was kissing down her throat, along her jaw, over the swells of her breasts, and then further down where he rested between her thighs and he *tasted*. And he *devoured*. She crossed her legs in response, seeking friction or reprieve from the sudden arousal that had blood rushing beneath her skin.

"Nothing of the sort," Sabine said. "Though I do intend to change that, I think. Certain thoughts—if I may be so bold to state—have made themselves known and if this place is as you indicate, then I intend to take full advantage."

Sabine had spent so long, nearly the full year, grieving her old life and bandaging the wounds of Nicholas's betrayal. But now, she was fortifying herself, this reprieve, the balm she so desperately needed. These promised freedoms and opportunities of debauchery and delight acting as a tonic to her soul. Time had worked much of its ability, but it couldn't make magic. This hideaway where Nicholas couldn't touch her would be that final stitch over her hurt.

"Well, if that is your intention," Veronica whispered. "Prepare you strength now—you'll require it."

With that, Veronica winked and departed, still working on her warbled pink ward. Meanwhile, Sabine lounged against the rail and watched the crew and guests explore the ship—there were about two dozen people on board, most of which were not working.

There were warlocks on the riggings, flashes of spells catching her vision as they guided *The Tithe* through waves. The captain, a dark-haired man with a short beard and blue eyes, seemed just and fair as he ordered members to duties and conducted all that involved his role. He didn't stand out as particularly cruel, nor kind; he simply existed and those on board respected him. Nearby, a woman with an elaborate blonde updo in a fanciful pink dress fluttered around a thin male with sandy hair and glassy eyes that tracked her every movement. Others simply watched the waves.

Sabine had spoken to many, but none had been as revealing thus far as Veronica had been. Most had spoken of the feeling regarding the island, or their lives aside from their destination, or simply the weather. It felt as if there was a big secret and everyone was holding their breath around her. It was as if it were a bubble but Sabine didn't know where to poke for it to pop.

Suddenly, Sabine saw Bastien emerge from below deck and the charming smile he tossed her, the glittering silvery eyes…

A taste soon, indeed.

OCTOBER 5, 1867

Sabine had struggled to keep the thoughts off her face for the past day. Her overt attraction and awareness of Bastien was like a palpable thing that she required. It was like an itch she desperately needed to scratch.

The entire previous day was spent comforting Elizabeta and Idris for their specific auges, and pointedly ignoring Reynard and his venomous glares—and attempts to see Elizabeta. Due to Reynard's persistence, Bastien spent much of their time apart, conversing with who Veronica indicated as Salem and a few others to busy the displeased warlock. Sabine saw less of Veronica, particularly since the girl had a fancy for food and had relegated herself to the kitchen where she assumed she was harassing the staff there.

But now, the thoughts were prowling through her mind like a panther stalking prey.

Sabine was staring out over the water at the rear of the ship, midnight waves crashing against the hull, crushed diamond sky soaring above her. The brisk ocean breeze cooled her flushed skin, but did nothing for the dampness between her legs. And that frustrated her—particularly because with three other people in their quarters she couldn't take such matters into her own hands and find pleasure there.

No, instead she was left with the sea and its expanse of nothingness.

She wondered if the waters were enough to keep Nicholas away.

"If anyone could command the sea, it would be you and your face of wrath."

Sabine turned to the voice and found Bastien beside her, an impish smirk on his lips. His silver eyes glittered like star-fire and Sabine had the wild thought of wanting them to consume her like a supernova burning in the abyss.

"I will take that as a compliment rather than the impulse to question if you're calling into question my looks. But to answer the question you have not asked—I am frustrated. At what? Nicholas. The curse. Confounding feelings."

Bastien leveled his gaze at her and raised a brow. "Care to elaborate?"

Sabine sighed. "Nicholas was my lover once upon a time. Last year he'd betrayed me after we'd been circling each other for some time, skirting our feelings, never admitting out of fear. But when we finally did and we were together…" Sabine cleared her throat. "It was only a short while, especially after I discovered he truly wanted my dearest friend and I was a placeholder." She shook her head and scoffed. "But the worst part wasn't that. It was that he'd cursed her fiancé and attempted to kill him—and all of us."

"Sabine…" Bastien whispered, his voice devastated. His face crushed with her pain. "I didn't…know."

She gave a dry laugh. "How could you? It's a dirty little secret one keeps under their bed and pulls out only in times of darkness. The fact remains that I am a murderess and he has cursed me because it was my hand that had slain him."

There is only me, and I am your ruin.

The final words Sabine had spoken to Nicholas rang in her head. The words she'd thought were final. But he came back since…and he'd thrown vicious words at her—ones far worse than any she'd tossed.

Sabine let out a breath and shook out her hair. "He had us all tricked, Bastien. And it was almost too late."

Wordlessly, Bastien reached out a hand and rested it on hers upon the rail.

"I remember I was angry—so angry," she admitted, spite entering her voice. The memory of the wrath filled her, how she summoned the cut and severed him skull to groin. Bloodlust slaked. "I wanted him dead. I wanted to be the one to do it."

Bastien let out a small sound but did not interrupt.

Sabine hardened her gaze. "So, I did."

Bastien cupped her jaw, thumbing her lip. "You are a marvelous creature."

"Despite being cursed?"

"Even in light of being cursed." He grinned devilishly. "And what an apt title Coquette is."

"And I think Lover fits you perfectly as well."

Bastien's eyes widened ever so and his lips parted. It was bold, but she had no intentions of taking the words back. In barely one breath to the next she'd admitted to purposely killing her former lover and voiced her intentions towards Bastien—albeit not directly.

As if a clock ticked down one single notch, a breeze kicked up and stirred her hair as Bastien dipped down and kissed her.

His lips crashed upon hers, parting her mouth and tracing her tongue with his own. He tasted of apples and smoke, and something darker—richer. Her arms wound around his neck, tangling her hands in his black hair as his fingers pressed into her back and jaw. He tipped her head back, delivering worshipping movement to her mouth, lips slanting along hers.

Sabine let out a small keening sound as she pressed her body firmly to his, her heart thundering. Bastien returned with a sound low in his throat, almost like a whimper. Sabine grew intensely wet at the sound.

"*Bastien*," she murmured against his mouth.

"*Sabine*," he whispered like a chant. A prayer.

She felt his fingers dip beneath her ivory blouse, fingers skating over the warm skin on her back. She shuddered in delight.

When they broke apart, Bastien rested his forehead against hers and she felt his breath ghost across her lips.

"I need you to do me a favor," he said as if catching his breath.

"What do you need?" she asked, equally breathless.

"Trust me. Please trust me, and don't believe anything at the island. Just know I will protect you."

"I'm going to need more than that," she said, hands coasting up his chest.

"Not with so many keen ears and eyes around," he said lowly.

"Are we safe there?"

"Safer than in Vale Wood with Nicholas."

Sabine nodded. "You'll tell me more when we're there? When we're alone?"

"I promise."

"Good," she said, hand sliding up to his throat. "Just don't forget what I said about haunting, love."

She kissed him swiftly—dominatingly—then pulled back. She tilted his head back despite him behind taller than her, baring his throat. Sabine kissed a line up to his jaw.

"Don't fuck me over, because I'd like a chance to fuck you."

Bastien made that sound again and Sabine thrilled at the reaction she elicited in him. She felt his jaw flex against her nose as she skimmed across his smooth chin.

"You're killing me," he practically moaned.

"Mm, but what about *la petit mort*?"

She nipped him playfully and his fingers tightened into the small of her back—pressing her into him and the thickness between his legs that prodded her abdomen.

"Fuck, Sabine."

Sabine was used to being bold. She'd never watered down her personality nor words on topics of sex or other "less polite" matters because they might lead to some discomfiture. Sabine would've never survived a day in the Mortal World and all their restrictive customs upon women.

"When we have time alone, darling," she said, pushing him away and backing away to their quarters. "Until then…" she skimmed her fingers over the edge of her low neckline, "use your imagination."

HOLLOW
PLACE

BASTIEN EMMONS

OCTOBER 7, 1867

The Tithe docked at twilight.

When the island rose up on the horizon just hours ago, peaking through the fog, Bastien had called Sabine to see. She'd been delighted by the appearance of the island and the large mansion on the hillside. It was nearly palace-like; reaching columns and large windows with accompanying balconies. Gothic fences rose from the ground, encapsulating the one property on the miniscule island. Trees with bare branches like skeletal fingers holding onto the last rusty leaves lined the cobbled path up to the mansion. The path terminated at a tree line that led to a dense forest—the Mad Woods.

At the bow, Bastien wrapped his arms around Sabine, the sultry warlock leaning against his front, her hands tucked into the cage of his arms. He dipped his lips to her ear, memories of that kiss flooding his mind—the way she smelled of cinnamon and vanilla and tasted like decadent sin.

"Do you remember what I told you?" he asked.

She kept her voice low. "To trust you."

He tightened his hold. "Please don't forget it."

Sabine had nodded.

Now, they were stepping off the ship and onto hallowed and warded land.

Nicholas hadn't been able to reach Sabine while she was on the ship over the water, and now Bastien hoped he was right that the blessed island would be enough to keep him at bay.

Though, the fucking island had begun to claw at him. The bond chafing under its too close restraints—and Bastien resented it.

Idris was trailing behind them with Elizabeta at his side. The female warlock had taken to helping Idris on the voyage, enjoying being his nursemaid to keep her mind busy. Through that, they seemed to have forged some sort of connection, and Bastien feared Idris had made himself an enemy of Reynard.

Reynard himself was at the rear of the group, his hateful gaze burning holes in their backs.

Seven warlocks with Midnight Malady greeted them, frenetic light in their eyes. A few of them hadn't fed in a few days and the mania and insanity was setting in—Drusilla must have been employing a punishment and self-restraint exercise on these sufferers. Everyone was finely dressed in evening wear with low necklines and snug fits, all silk and velvet and satin.

Bastien recognized all of them—Draco, Mortimer, Rosemary, Stefan, Pearl, Lestat, and Compton—and they were all utterly unhinged and devoted to Drusilla. And all of them were sporting black-tipped fingers and pointed ears. This was a message as much as it was a threat and Bastien had the conceited thought that it was all aimed at him. Though, it may not be as conceited as he imagined, seeing as he'd been silently rebelling against her for years and refusing all her sexual advances in that timeframe as well.

"Welcome to the Hollow," Pearl said with too white teeth, bared in what should have been a smile.

The island was the Hollow, the dwelling was Hollow Place.

They were all led up the hill to Drusilla's mansion as night descended above them, stars sprawling over the fingertips of trees. Sabine was wary next to him. No one else seemed to notice it, but the way her gaze flittered with cat-like awareness paired with her surefootedness on the uneven ground spoke volumes about her instincts.

A flash of pride and guilt went through him. Bastien had originally brought her here for nefarious means, but he'd grown remorseful of them. He'd vowed to himself—and silently to her—that he was going to get her out of it. The only thing was, this den of beasts was safer than back on the mainland with Nicholas and his curse.

"All of you follow me and you will be shown your lodgings," Lestat said dryly.

As they ascended the ivory steps, torches and sigils glowing around them, Mortimer interrupted them. Specifically Sabine and Bastien.

"Not you two though, she wants to see you first."

Bastien set his jaw and nodded. Sabine, sensing his sudden rigidness glanced at him and quickly deduced this wasn't a good thing. She straightened her shoulders and met Mortimer's look with a withering one of her own.

"Sure," Sabine said with sugary sweetness that was so at odds with her expression. "I would love to extend my thanks for her generous hospitality."

Mortimer flashed her a surprised look and then shifted to Bastien. Bastien revealed nothing.

"Take us to her then."

Bastien's statement was punctuated by the opening of the tall wooden doors, revealing the sprawl of a checkerboard foyer and shimmering crystal chandelier.

It was futile to ask what Drusilla wanted—she wouldn't have divulged it to them. She liked to let them linger on her word and wonder what her intentions and impulses were. That, mixed with the bond, gave her even more power.

As they got closer to Drusilla, the bond turned into a garotte, and Bastien fought an internal battle to fend it off. On the surface, he showed no evidence of this struggle. He was cool, collected, and apathetic.

They were escorted through the halls and into the west wing of Hollow Place, following walls of heart's blood red. When they entered a party, his eyes darted around at all those present—dancing, gossiping, drinking—and met them with an iron stare that said "back off" in no uncertain terms. Mortimer led them past into a solarium and Bastien took in the verdant dark leaves of emerald that Elvira—whom he'd once thought was his ally—was attending to.

Then there was the garnet velvet chaise which Drusilla lounged upon.

Drusilla was draped in white silk with chestnut curls cascading down a pale shoulder. Her irises were dark, limpid pools of striped tiger's eye, thickly fringed in black and lined in gold. Lips red as blood curved in an arrogant, toothless smile as she sat up with intrigue.

"Bastien," she cooed in her husky voice. "Welcome home. And who is this delightful morsel you've brought with you?"

Without prompting, Sabine strode forward directly next to Bastien. "Sabine Van Arsdel," she said with confidence that Bastien did not feel. "I wish to thank you for your generous hospitality and refuge of tranquility. My, if it wasn't for your genuine kindness I would have been lost to the plights that await me in Vale Wood. Not to even speak of my heavenly virtues."

Elvira slowly turned, surprised by Sabine's presence and airs. Bastien met her surprised look with a pleased smirk.

I quite like her, Bastien mouthed.

I can see why, Elvira mouthed back.

Drusilla cocked a sculpted brow and then stood to her full 6'2" frame, bone white silk rippling in waves over her luscious curves. Her heels clicked as she took measured steps towards Sabine. Sabine, who didn't flinch at his mistress's imposing height.

The bond became painful as she neared and when she was an arm's reach away, she paused and the sharp stab of her influence dulled to a manageable burn.

"She is an utter delight," Drusilla said, a hint of her old accent slipping in—something akin to Elizabeta's. "And I've missed you, my sweet." This, she directed at him.

Drusilla took Bastien's face in hand and kissed him once on each cheek, her lips cool and promising venom behind her teeth. Bastien stood prey-still as she delivered this absolution on him. He wanted to scrub his skin with acid.

When she released him, she transferred to Sabine and

when she took her face in her hands, he was shocked that she met Sabine's lips with her own.

Pure, unadulterated jealousy ripped through him. The wicked possessiveness stole his breath and he had to fight the claws at his sides from tearing out Drusilla's throat. His teeth ached at the idea. He'd never had such a visceral reaction against his mistress before.

Drusilla broke from Sabine and Bastien had to pointedly fight his urges before she realized them. Quickly, he schooled his expression.

"Please, go out and enjoy the party—it is a casual affair this evening. Tomorrow, I'd like to meet with you all in the parlor in the late morning before the masquerade tomorrow night." Drusilla's voice was sickly sweet, dripping poisoned honey.

"You are so very kind," Sabine said, reaching for Drusilla's hand and squeezing it. "We will be prompt on your schedule."

Bastien saw the subterfuge for what it was. He realized how Sabine saw Drusilla's game before she'd even stepped onto the board. Like a fucking genius in the puzzle of all Hollow Place's machinations.

A sinking feeling crept into Bastien's stomach.

Did she see through him too? Had he fucked all this up before it had begun? Surely, she wasn't playing him, too?

Bastien looked at Sabine, but she just had that coy sugary look on her face. She did not look at him.

"Your punctuality is agreeable."

"Well, we should make haste to this party, then." And with that, Sabine quickly, flashed two cleaning spells to freshen them up and turned on her heel with Bastien in tow.

Sabine was in a vermillion corset over a black silk blouse and waist-height black leather pants. Bastien himself was in a teal corduroy jacket, matching pants, and a half-buttoned black shirt. It was agreeable attire for the theme of the party this night, though would not be suitable for the upcoming masquerade.

She took his arm and led him out into the party they'd passed through. When she looped her hand in the crook of his elbow, she tightened her grip on him. With that pasted-on smile as they walked out, she whispered to him.

"Act normal, but when we are alone you have an incredible amount of explaining to do."

Bastien swallowed. "That's a fair request."

"Oh, darling," she bit out through a gritted teeth smile, fingertips chewing his arm. "This isn't a request—it's a demand."

He didn't know the story his face told after that. The two of them took a turn about the room and Bastien watched the faces filled with sanguine hunger watch Sabine. She was a vivacious morsel and he could tell they wanted to taste her—but few in the way in which he wanted to.

Stefan and Rosemary had their heads leaned together, mouths dark with a mixture of wine and blood, the damning chalices in their hands. A blonde he didn't recognize had her hands roving over a male he only vaguely knew, but even so, she only had eyes for them—that same thirst present. Music and titters surrounded them but he was hyperaware of all the eyes—more importantly, *Sabine* was aware of all the attention.

She watched with curiosity and suspicion, taking in everything and forgetting nothing. Bastien realized that even though he knew she was clever, he hadn't anticipated this degree—and that wasn't anything towards her character, it was on his.

"You remember what I said on the ship?" she

whispered, not looking at him.

"I do."

"If this place kills me, I'll do worse than that."

It was fucked up of him, but her violence turned him on beyond belief.

OCTOBER 7, 1867

The rooms were papered red and the carpets were something akin to crushed velvet. It was dark, just before midnight, but low golden light from the wall sconces offered ambient lighting. And such lighting highlighted the fact that there was only one bed.

It was generously sized with deep crimson covers and fringed in gold with a similarly styled canopy. The scent of cinnamon, incense, and something heady hung in the air, clinging to the coverlet. Heavy wood furniture dominated the room despite the fact the suite was massive.

Evident rather quickly was the presence of Bastien and Sabine's things, but not Idris's.

"Where—?" Sabine began meaningfully, gesturing to their luggage.

Bastien scrubbed the back of his neck in nervousness. "He's safe. They like to keep the assigned rooms to couples and then keep single individuals in separate quarters."

Sabine raised a brow. "Did you indicate to them that we are a couple?"

He hesitated for a fraction of a second. "It's not hard to guess."

Sabine stepped closer to him. "You are confirming us as a couple without the discussion?" Her brow was arched to the point it bled into her tone.

"I believe I misspoke. To be very clear, love," he said softly, brushing a lock behind her ear. "I would like to be, but…it is *safer* for them to presume we are. If they believe I have staked my claim."

"As if I'm a possession?"

"To them. To me?" He brushed his thumb over her jaw. "You are much more than that."

Sabine inclined her head and inhaled softly. "You don't get to charm me with silver-tongued words, Mister Emmons," she chastised, even while he continued brushing his fingers across her face. "You're hiding things."

"I am," he confirmed, leaning down and lightly grazing her throat with his lips. She shivered and then he continued. "But I do not want to. I just cannot say at this moment."

Her thoughts utterly spiraled. Became depraved and utterly licentious. She had a wicked fantasy of him taking her here against the wall, hand wrapped around her throat, while her nails dug furrows into his back. She wanted it, but oh, she wasn't just going to bed him simply because the desires were there—not when she didn't know what was happening at Hollow Place.

Sabine, not to be completely controlled by her lusty thoughts, grasped Bastien by the jaw and pulled him from her throat, staring him dead in the eyes. "I do not want to die here."

"I won't let you."

She leaned in close so her lips brushed his. "Good."

And then she broke from him and stepped back.

"Where are you going?" he asked, blinking away confusion.

"Bed," she returned, digging into her belongings. "I am more than fatigued and it has been a long journey. I would like a bed that doesn't move."

Sabine grabbed her night clothes and departed for the adjoining washroom and stripped off her corset, blouse, and pants, and slipped into her black silk negligee. When she returned, she found Bastien sitting on the arm of the brocade couch, jacket discarded. He lifted his head when she approached and immediately his eyes brightened.

She wagged her finger and tsked. "Sleep."

Bastien groaned, shuttering his eyes, and nodded. There was a hint of a smile on his lips, despite his attempts to hide it.

Before she climbed into their bed, she casted several sigils in her deep red magic—wards and inactive defensive spells, an illusion set with a trigger, and one for heightened hearing. Once they all hung in the air, she tucked herself in and was asleep the moment her head hit the pillow.

Bastien sighed and got into his sleep clothes before

finally climbing in next to her, leaving a wide berth between
them.

OCTOBER 8, 1867

"Finally found land, did you?"

Sabine whirled and standing there through the haze of mist and smoke was Nicholas.

"How are you here?" she gasped.

Her heart lodged in her throat as she took him in— pale, fair-haired, light-eyed, youthful, appearing thirty, though he was more than double that. Bisecting his face was a scar, that should not have been a scar at all, that ran from the center of his skull and below the collar of his ruffled shirt.

The wound was the death blow she'd given him, cutting him directly down the middle. It should have been a raw and angry thing, bleeding and peeling back to reveal viscera. But it wasn't.

"I'm in your head, lover," he crooned, stepping closer as if gliding over the smoke that congregated around his feet. He was gray—he always was until his eyes turned to brimstone orbs—and his visage wavered.

"You're not truly here," she said with more strength than she felt. "So, why bother me?"

Nicholas cocked his head to the side. "Because I will be here. I will hunt you, my sweet."

Her lip curled. "Do not deign to use terms of endearment on me, they only serve to stoke my wrath."

"Good, I like it when you're angry—it's passion."

"It's hate," she spat.

"Semantics," he dismissed with a wave.

Sabine took in more of their surroundings; the eerie white-gray nothingness of it all. It was a dreamscape in the most nightmarish sense. No beasts or demons, but pure absence. It was only the two of them, as if occupying a space that did not exist—perhaps it didn't.

"You figured out I cannot cross running water," he chuckled darkly. "Clever."

Her nostrils flared.

"What you didn't figure out is how to get rid of me," he taunted, approaching her.

Suddenly, from one moment the next, between blinks, he was before her. She jumped back but he wrapped a coil of her hair around his fist and tugged her close.

Sabine yelped as pain barked in her scalp, stinging further as he brought her to his face. Strands of dark red fell across her eyes and mouth.

"But you cannot get rid of me, Sabine. This only ends when I drag you to Hell."

"Or the thirty nights expires and you've already lost a week."

Nicholas's lip curled back and a vicious sneer. "I see you've done some research."

"A bit," she snarled.

He tightened his grip—he still smelled like evergreen and it made her angry.

"You were always such an insolent little bitch. Never knew when to shut up and listen. You should've never been allowed to whore about as you did. Like a fucking prostitute you were discarded when something better came by. Even fucking B—"

He broke off as she slammed her knee into his groin.

Sabine then ran from him, off into the mists of gray-white and channeled all her energy into waking up. She forced herself through the oblivion and into her consciousness. For good measure she casted defensive spells, unknowing if they'd work in this limbo state.

She heard an indignant screech and then thrashed awake.

The covers were thrown from the bed as all her limbs flailed. Sabine let out a wild gasp, sitting up as if possessed. Bastien came awake with a wild start and suddenly his hands were on her, rubbing her upper arms, even with the sleep fogging his eyes.

"Sabine? What's wrong?" he queried, panic lacing his

words.

Her hand was on her chest as she breathed in and out rapidly. Sweat slickened her skin and her hair stuck to it. Beneath her hand her heart was racing, pounding like a war drum.

"Sabine?" he asked, applying more pressure to her arms.

"He was in my head," she managed.

"What?"

"Nicholas. He was in my dream—only it wasn't truly a dream."

"He dreamwalked?"

"You've heard of it?"

"It's uncommon, but yes—it's a demonic ability."

Sabine drew in a sharp breath. "So, you think he's devolving into a demon?"

Bastien hesitated. "I think so."

"What does that mean?"

"It could mean that once the curse has run its course, he can return to hunt you as a regular demon would with no timeline restrictions. It could also be he would be more vulnerable and we can kill him before the curse is done. Or I could be completely wrong and he's just a vengeful spirit and will remain as such."

Sabine exhaled a shaky breath and nodded. "Right."

She counted to ten in her head and measured her breaths.

Bastien sidled closer and Sabine was only distantly aware of Bastien being utterly shirtless—again—next to her. He put his arm around her and his skin was significantly cooler against her flushed flesh. She leaned into him, absorbing his comfort as he massaged soft shapes into her arm.

"He can't touch us here. The ground is hallowed and the ocean separates us."

"But we're not wholly safe here either." She paused, lifting her head to his. "Are we?" It was less of a question and more of challenge.

"No. And not just for you, for me, too. Things feel different this time. More tense."

"Between you and Reynard?"

He laughed softly. "That, among other things. Reynard is the last of my concerns. He holds far less power than he postures about."

"And you?"

"I hold more than I acknowledge."

"Because of how Drusilla feels about you?"

He froze. "What are you saying?"

"Bastien, she's infatuated with you."

"You know this from one encounter," he said flatly.

"I am incredibly perceptive."

"I have rejected her advances many times over, but she is still intent on pursuing me. The others welcome her to their beds, but I have been the last holdout."

"Why?" She hadn't realized it right away, but Bastien had completely taken her mind off of Nicholas. He had prevented an anxiety-induced spiral.

"Resentment mostly. I hate what she holds over me—how she controls us."

"And how is that?"

Bastien had resumed his drawing on her skin at some point. He continued doing so and sighed. "Secrets. Black mail. Influence."

"And you cannot break from her?"

"I am trying."

Sabine sensed there was more to it than that but she

did not press. Magical bonds existed and do did blood contracts, he could be any combination of the sort or none at all—she wasn't aware enough of the world to pinpoint it. For now, it was enough and she did not want to fight. Instead, she tangled her arms with his and guided them down.

"Just hold me," she whispered. "And if you think I am having a nightmare, please wake me."

"I will," he told her softly.

Bastien paused his smooth circling on her skin only long enough to pull the covers up on the two of them as they curled together.

As Drusilla had requested, Sabine and Bastien arrived in the parlor with Idris in tow—having retrieved him from his own lodgings.

The parlor was filled with sunlight, filtering in through glass windows and fracturing off sun-catchers in gemstone hues. Monstera leaves cut shadows across the ecru walls and warped over the eggshell chair rail, carving new florals on the wood. Pale wicker furniture dotted the space, dusty pink cushions on each seat and covering the ottomans and floor cushions. A fine white tea set was placed upon the low table, tiny purple flowers spotting the cups and matching sprigs of lavender stood poised in a vase.

With a cup pressed to her lips, Drusilla perched on her chair in a white lace dress with scalloped sleeves. Her long cascade of dark hair was falling down her back, and those tiger's eye eyes were watching them.

"Good morning," Drusilla greeted warmly—though it

didn't reach her eyes. "How was your rest?" When she removed the cup, she left a burgundy smudge.

"Most pleasant," Sabine answered, taking a seat on one of the other wicker chairs. Bastien and Idris followed suit. "It was refreshing to not rock with the waves."

"That I can certainly agree with," Idris inserted.

"Will anyone else be joining us?" Bastien asked pointedly. He did not wait to be served the tea and instead poured it himself.

A flash of anger flickered across Drusilla's face before she composed herself with another sip of tea. "Just the four of us for now."

"Mm," Bastien hummed noncommittally.

Drusilla's lips twitched.

Idris's brows drew together as he watched this exchange but he was smart enough not to say anything—he was a scholar after all, even though he hardly resembled it. The chair looked comically small as he wedged his bear-like mass of muscles into the spot. Even so, he moved gracefully enough that the cramped space did not hinder him.

Drusilla, not to be not hostess-like, turned to Sabine.

"So, how did you come to meet our dear Bastien?"

Sabine's hackles prickled, but she shoved the reaction deep down. "Art class," she answered sweetly. "We were short a model and Bastien happened to volunteer."

"Really?" Drusilla cocked a brow and side-eyed Bastien. "And what next? Were there sparks flying? Love at first sight?"

Idris choked into his cup and Bastien pasted on a look of disinterest. Clearly, she was prying and he wasn't giving in to her. Sabine took his cue for what it was.

"Awareness, certainly, but nothing as so magical as that."

Drusilla clocked Sabine's deflection and turned her attention to another point of their conversation. "So, you're an artist?"

"I am. Charcoals and oil paint are my referred mediums."

"Do you paint portraits?" Drusilla inquired.

"They are my favorite subject."

"Splendid!" Drusilla said, setting down her cup and clapping. "You must paint us some portraits then! I will summon for the supplies."

Without Sabine accepting the request, Drusilla was already summoning someone with a tassel pull and a bell chime. A short girl of maybe twenty scurried in with wide eyes. When she approached Drusilla, she drew close and the mistress quickly whispered in the girl's ear. The girl nodded and disappeared as quickly as she'd appeared.

In silence and within moments the girl returned once again with art supplies in tow and a second girl carrying an easel.

"Is this enough, Mistress?" the first girl—the blonde one—asked in a soft, pretty voice.

"It is, thank you, Agatha, you may go."

Agatha dipped a quick curtsy and slipped away. The second girl copied the action but Drusilla's sharp tongue caught her.

"I did not pardon *you*."

The second girl froze and turned slowly, her blue eyes wide and full of fear. "My deepest apologies, Mistress. I should not have assumed so—"

"No, you should not have," Drusilla said brusquely.

Sabine rallied herself to defend the blue-eyed girl and shifted in her chair. Whether by sensing her ire or by simply knowing her, Bastien's hand lashed out and caught her wrist.

Sabine turned to him; lip curled. Silently, he shook his head. That anger flamed within her hotter but Bastien doubled-down on his instruction.

Still furious, Sabine backed down and stared Drusilla down. The mistress's attention was wholly on the girl, predatory light in her eyes—like a lion and a gazelle. Silently, Sabine vowed to intervene should Drusilla raise a hand.

Tension plagued the room and practically rattled the cups in their saucers. Everyone held their breath, but no one as tightly as the girl.

"What punishment should be fitting, Mistress?" the girl asked.

Drusilla did not react. She simply held an iron stare. Then, finally—surprisingly—she spoke.

"Nothing. You may leave."

The girl deflated and curtsied once again before practically evaporating from the room.

Sabine uncurled her fists, but crescent moons still dug into her palm from her nails.

"Shall I paint?" Sabine said, finally breaking the pressure of the room.

Drusilla transformed before her eyes, a cloud of darkness disappearing behind the light of the sun as delight encompassed her face. She took up her cup and sipped it.

"Yes! Please do! If you would be so kind, I would most enjoy being the first recipient."

Sabine glowed with false exuberance while repulsion plagued her bones, and walked over to the easel where it had been set up. She glanced around the room and then pointed. "There, I need that lighting. Is there a particular seat you would like to take?"

Drusilla rose to her grand height and gracefully walked to the brightest patch of filtered sunlight. She pulled a chair from the corner and sat on it sideways, arm resting over the back and legs crossed.

The sunlight cut across her face casting one half in perfect clarity and the other in ominous shadows. It was a perfect depiction of duality. Just like the hand of false benevolence she extended here at Hollow Place.

"How is this?" she asked.

"Perfect," Sabine answered.

And then began.

She examined Drusilla carefully and selected the oil paints she'd need—ultramarine blue, ochre, chestnut, lilac, vermillion, ivory, heather gray, raw sienna, umber, titanium white, rose, lamp black, and viridian. They glistened on the palate in seemingly nonsensical shades, but Sabine knew how they'd all come together in undertones and shadows.

She started with a swath of titanium white and once the base was set, she was able to work her non-spell magic across the canvas. The brush swiped through the puddle of dark paint and then it carved a new shape across the blankness.

Sabine came singularly focused on the task at hand, her vision tunneling in her passion. She became completely unaware of Bastien, Idris, or anyone else in the room besides an odd sense of other's present. Beyond that, she was lost to the art.

Drusilla, for all her heinous self that had bled through from the small interactions, was a perfect subject. Her face, half in light and half in dark became what Sabine saw her as. That shadowy half became all those repulsive thoughts Sabine felt—the jealousy, the vindictiveness, the spite, the arrogance—and the light became the offerings she gave—hospitality, joviality, performance, affection.

But in the eyes, they switched. Those tiger's eyes

stripes could not hide it all.

Sabine was never one to curb her emotions or thoughts, but especially so when it came to her art. Art was expression, freedom, and human—or rather, warlock— emotion. It would not be quelled. It would be shouted from the rooftops and screaming from the page.

Eventually, after more time than she had any concept of passed, she finished.

Breathing a sigh, she stepped from the canvas and saw it in a new light—as the viewer and not the artist.

It was an exact likeness in soul.

When Sabine gave her the nod, Drusilla swanned over and took in what Sabine had created. Drusilla cupped her hand over her mouth as she stared. The other reached out, but didn't touch the canvas.

"Magnificent," Drusilla whispered in awe. "Absolutely magnificent." She whirled. "You must do more."

And again, before Sabine could say anything Drusilla was summoning guests and Sabine was relegated to the easel.

Over the course of the morning and afternoon Sabine painted. Her palette was covered in so many different colors and shades; her fingers were splattered and stained. Drusilla plied her with drinks and Sabine surprised herself by being all too willing to accept.

The more she drowned herself in her passions, the more that light side of Drusilla appealed to her with an odd sort of charm. A charm that at the current moment she didn't care to dissect.

It was hours, Idris and Bastien staying close by, refilling their cups and seemingly not conversing with each other, but simply tolerating the other's presence.

Slowly, the afternoon evolved and more guests joined the parlor and enjoyed the company and painting. Sabine was one of the rare sort of artists she'd encountered that didn't mind being watched as she painted. She didn't get any self-consciousness—she was self-assured in her talent and she did not wither beneath the weight of their eyes.

She utterly bloomed with pride—and perhaps some ego—at their praise and delight. Sabine became so caught up in it all that much of her hesitations bled away and she caught herself smiling.

And Drusilla was smiling back.

OCTOBER 8, 1867

Sabine was being charmed by Drusilla just as Bastien had and his stomach was in knots at the prospect.

Her venom had melted off her tongue and the knife of her gaze dulled. That bloody charm had softened the warlock to his mistress and he hated it—he hated her for it. For poisoning Sabine's mind like she had his.

Eventually, the fawning tapered off as everyone decided to spend their days elsewhere and eventually that evening Bastien found himself alone with Sabine in their rooms.

As was Drusilla's style, garments and masks had been

delivered on the bed for them. Bastien's jacket and pants were satin, shiny, charcoal black, with a deep red shirt and a mask of the same red lined with onyx leather.

He'd gotten dressed while Sabine had taken her belongings to the bathing chamber. For now, the mask dangled from his fingertips by its strap and he waited for Sabine, perching on the edge of the bed. When the door clicked open, he perked up in interest.

Sabine stepped out and his groin and jaw ached. She was in a gown of amber—curve-hugging, and silky, with ripples and drop sleeves. With her gown came a coil of pearls around her neck and studs in her ears, as well as a pair of ivory elbow-length gloves. Like him, her mask was in her fingertips. It was pointed up at the edges, the whole of it filigree designs that would fall across her cheekbones like snow.

"What do you think?" she said in a sultry tone and she slowly crossed toward him. "Do I look delectable?"

That was exactly the word he was imagining.

Bastien cleared his throat. "You do."

Sabine's mouth curled up in satisfaction as she continued walking toward him. As she stood directly before him, she cocked her head and analyzed him.

"What are you thinking?"

Suddenly, he was thinking the only thing that made sense in the moment. That he had a secret and he no longer wanted to keep that secret from her.

"I need to confess something."

"Uh oh," she said with half as much concern as he thought she should have. "Do you have a secret lover here or something?"

"No, worse."

"Oh," she said, the forced flatness of her words

belying her true concern. Sabine took a seat on a chair across from him. "Okay, I'm listening."

Without considering anything further Bastien barreled on.

"I have Midnight Malady."

Sabine stilled. Her eyes widened almost imperceptibly. But she did not run and she did not scream. Though what he did notice was heartbreak.

Those with Midnight Malady had to drink blood every three days to survive. If one did not, they would eventually succumb to the disease and insanity. Already, his sanity was slipping as he was due to feed this night, but he hadn't yet as there were specific places, times, and people who were willing at the masquerade.

But the blood drinking was a double-edged sword because one day the consuming of blood would be his death. Those with Midnight Malady never lived longer than ten years.

Unless the sufferer was blood bonded.

Like him.

"How long have you had it?"

"Three years. Almost immediately after I completed the Staying."

"How have you not had the nightly madness?"

Those afflicted with Midnight Malady fell to bloodlust and insanity each night, made worse without feeding. Daytime was a balm, a sanctuary. The only thing that had halted the madness was the blood bond.

Everyone here had been as desperate as he.

"Remember how I mentioned Drusilla holds something over me? It is a new treatment here. But it comes at a great cost. It is not something I like to speak about."

Sabine's mouth parted; heartbreak written across her

face.

He knew what she was thinking. And it just served as a reminder that there was a countdown on his life, even if it wasn't the actual disease that took him. He'd secured a lesser of evils fate by bonding to Drusilla—cursing himself in a way not quite like Sabine.

"My dearest friends research immortal diseases," Sabine said, surprising him. There was steel in her voice—completely unexpected. "They have discovered the cures for both the Wasting and Ember Fever. Surely, it's a matter of time before they discover how to treat Midnight Malady."

Something surged in his chest. Something warm and full.

He realized distantly that the feeling was hope.

He had hope for the future—that he had one. *Could* have one. Perhaps even with Sabine. If she ever forgave him for this.

Tears pricked Bastien's eyes and he cleared his throat. "I have contacts who are researching cures, but nothing concrete, yet."

So far, the only treatment remained the blood bond.

Sabine softened and stood. She crossed to him and sank to her knees, clutching his hands. She was so warm.

"I've never trusted anyone as much as I do them, and I'm certain they can and will help," she whispered.

He nodded as his eyes flickered from her dark gaze, to her lips, and then to her throat. He kept watching the pulse jump in her neck along the pearls, the way she breathed and how the line of white spheres slid over her skin and moved over her breasts.

Seized by emotion and wanting, Bastien slipped one of his hands from her clutch and cupped her jaw. Sabine seemed to understand immediately and her long lashes fluttered down on her cheeks as she closed her eyes. She moved in just as he did and he tilted his mouth against hers.

It was slow and decadent. The kiss slid languorously, Bastien's lips catching her lower one and tentatively tasting her. His tongue was gentle as it prodded the seam of her lips and she opened to him. She tasted of cinnamon and vanilla as their tongues danced. Blood rushed through him, igniting in his groin and gums.

Suddenly, the ever-present ache in his gums whilst in Sabine's presence sharpened and he felt his fangs slip into place.

Bastien broke from the kiss just as the points of his teeth scraped her lip.

"I'm so sorry," he gasped. Covering his mouth. He felt alarm running through his nerves.

Sabine reached out and pulled his hand from his mouth, baring his fangs for her to see. She took them in curiously and cocked her head. Once again, she had both his hands in hers.

"Do—" she cleared her throat. "Do you want to bite me?"

Bastien jolted, but with his hands in hers he didn't move far.

"What?"

"Are you in control? Will you be able to stop?"

There was no fear in her voice. It was plain curiosity mixed with a dash of excitement. Bastien was baffled. Did she…did she truly want this?

"I am, but that isn't my greatest concern," Bastien began.

"Then what is?"

"Have you been bitten before?"

"I have not."

"Do you know the…side effect?"

"I have heard whispers."

Bastien flushed. "You may become…aroused."

Those with Midnight Malady had an aphrodisiac-inducing bite. When they bit their—for lack of a better word—victims, they became aroused. Most often he avoided highly erogenous zones, electing for wrists or inner elbows, but the throat or the inner thigh had an intensely pleasurable effect on the recipient. So much so that a bite of the sort almost always ended in a sexual encounter of some manner.

Sabine shifted, but he noticed the distinct way her thighs flexed in her dress. The way she pushed her knees together. Seeking friction.

Bastien shuttered his eyes at the knowledge he now possessed of an already aroused Sabine.

"Perhaps…" she began, a gloved finger tapping her lip. "If it is too much for me to handle without reprieve you may use your hands to give me relief. If you are comfortable with that solution."

Bastien would be more than happy to oblige Sabine's needs. He'd been fantasizing about her, about that sweet spot between her legs and here she was welcoming him to it.

"Are you sure?" he asked.

"I am very sure."

"And you are also aware you may experience other lowered inhibitions?"

Sabine smirked. "I look forward to it."

Bastien moved towards her slowly, stalking her like prey. Delight simmered in her eyes. Carefully, Bastien brushed her dark auburn hair back from her shoulder, exposing her throat. He took in the smooth golden column of her neck, eyes zeroing in on the excited throb of her pulse. Gently, he lowered his mouth to that point and kissed it once before he opened his mouth and sank his fangs into her.

Her blood bloomed in his mouth, hot and sweet and slightly spicy. Exactly how he imagined she would taste. He moaned as he sucked and gathered her up in his arms, pressing her against him. Sabine let out a soft keening sound of pleasure and Bastien's hand flattened against the small of her back.

Sabine ground against him, seeking friction. Her hands went to his abdomen, pawing at the buttons on his shirt. Bastien fisted a hand in her hair, tipping her head back, pressing his fingertips against her scalp and massaging gently.

"Please," she begged, her hips gyrating.

Bastien hummed as he drank.

"Please, Bastien. Your fingers. I need them." She gasped. "I need you."

Requiring no more direction, Bastien's hand slid to her calf and slipped beneath her dress. His fingers coasted up her knee, gently swirling before ghosting over her inner thigh and then seeking her core. He found her bare beneath the dress, her sex wet and smooth.

Bastien moaned against Sabine's throat as his finger plunged inside her. Sabine's core instantly clenched around him with need. He withdrew his finger and thrust it in again, turning it into a crooked motion as he massaged her sweet center. The come-hither motion had her desperate. Bastien kept pumping that single digit in her as she began rolling her hips, the undulating motion giving her some of the friction she so craved.

As he drank, his mental clarity brightened, and Sabine became more insatiable. He added his thumb, pressing and swirling on her clit and she gasped.

"Oh, fuck. Yes, Bastien—right there." Her voice was thready and begging.

His other hand was occupied in her hair, tugging it to give that slight sting of pleasure he sensed she craved.

Bastien continued his mission of driving Sabine to orgasm, curling that finger and pressing harder with his thumb. And he gathered very quickly that it was the right choice. Wetness covered his hand and she started fluttering around his finger.

He knew she was close and so, he swiped his tongue over the wounds, adding a little more of his erotic saliva and suddenly he felt her tighten and she exhaled sharply.

And then she came.

She moaned, deep and raw as she contracted around his finger, her hips still riding out the waves of her bliss. Bastien pulled his fangs from her and licked her throat, placing kisses over the bite as she came down from the high.

Sabine shuddered as she finished her completion and when she drew back to look at him, her eyes were heavy-lidded and liquid. Her breathing was rough.

"That was..." she clearly searched for words, "spectacular."

"It was," he managed, slowly disentangling from her. He knew his cheeks were flushed with her blood.

"Well," she said, smoothing her hands down her dress's skirt. "Shall we depart?"

"We shall."

Bastien washed his hands and then the two of them donned their masks and left the suite behind.

OCTOBER 8, 1867

Sabine felt as if she had bees buzzing in her blood and nectar on her tongue. Her mind was wondrously fogged with pleasantly warm and honeyed thoughts. Everything was golden and soft.

Bastien's hand in hers was like fluid flowing water. So soft but nearly intangible. She giggled at the thought of a hand being untouchable—a hand was the most touchable thing of all. Sabine giggled again and she noted absently that Bastien glanced at her.

Fuck, he was lovely to look at.

Those striking eyes, that shock of black hair, those lips…

Sabine fanned herself as they crossed the checkerboard floor of the masquerade.

The marble flooring was dark brown and cream tiles, the walls warm wood with carved florals draped in long gold curtains. The chandeliers were dripping amber and gold above them and a warlock blessed with topaz magic had hung sigils in the air to brighten where the fixtures couldn't.

Warlocks milled about in finery and masks of every hue and variety. She noticed a female in a bold peacock blue dress, her entire ensemble taking on the motif, complete with a feathered mask, and beside her was a man who wore the sly red of a fox, the mask of the creature's likeness and whose eyes flashed just as devilishly. Others were more subdued than the animalistic couple. Another woman wore a gown of petal pink and her mask was a riot of pastel wildflowers that contrasted nicely with her ebony locks, which in turn was a juxtaposition to her companion who had a dress of midnight blue and splattered with silver constellations, her mask full of diamonds like stars in the sky, set delicately against her pale features and platinum hair.

Bees and peacocks and foxes and flowers and stars.

Sabine giggled and eagerly reached for a glass on the grand tower of champagne. She sipped delicately and then reached for a chocolate covered strawberry. The flavor of both bloomed across her tongue like pure sunlight.

She felt so light!

"Sabine?" Bastien said warily. Why was he wary? It was so good. Life was so good.

"Mm?" she asked, a blissful smile on her face.

"Are you…intoxicated?"

Intoxicated didn't seem the correct word, but nonetheless, Sabine understood.

"I am…experiencing effects."

Bastien inclined his head. "I see. Might we try some water?"

Sabine pouted but let Bastien tow her towards a different refreshment. There, they found Idris who was speaking with Elizabeta. Idris was garbed in hunter green—Sabine didn't think him much a hunter—and Elizabeta was draped in a pastel shade of rose—though the shade did not resemble the flower in any manner; or rather the gown did not resemble the color's namesake. No, unlike a rose, this gown slithered over Elizabeta's slight curves and some rouching added emphasis to her hips.

The two of them had water glasses in hand and turned with their approach.

"Oh, hello, Sabine!" Elizabeta said cheerily. She saw a sparkle in her eyes—joy?—as she reached a black gloved hand to gently squeeze Sabine's arm. "How are you this eve?"

"Requiring hydration," Bastien answered for her as he plucked up a glass. "Drink. *Please*." The please was so soft Sabine positively melted like butter beneath the request.

"I must do as bid!" she chimed. And then downed the water.

The effect wasn't instantaneous, but something was. As the water settled, she felt it trickle through her blood and then slowly seeping into her brain. She felt it cleanse her thoughts and reign clarity within her psyche. As it continued, some of her soft glow faded.

Sabine blinked.

"What…?"

Bastien leaned to her ear. "I think you experienced an uncommon side effect of a bite's first exposure and the combination of that and your climax gave you a heightened and lingering euphoria."

"And water made it vanish?"

"It gave your body the opportunity to realize and correct itself."

"Oh." Sabine pressed a gloved hand to her lips.

Yes, indeed. It did clear some things up, however, it didn't banish the active awareness surrounding Bastien.

No, in fact the clarity simply made painfully aware the attraction she wanted to act on. Bastien had given her a terrific orgasm and she felt inclined to return the favor. In fact, she was fantasizing about it—thoughts of tugging him to a shadowy alcove, pinning him with dark, sultry eyes as she sank to her knees before him and slipped her fingers into his waistband—

Fantasy suddenly became reality as she excused herself and Bastien from Idris and Elizabeta's presence—what her false reasons were, she could not recall—but quickly, she took Bastien's hand and lured him to the fringes of the milling crowd. She took in the edges of the room and found what she was looking for. An empty, darkened corridor.

Sights set, Sabine continued pulling Bastien along. He did not argue, nor speak in general, and she wondered what he was thinking and why he was not sharing it with her.

Finally at their destination, her core slickened with desire, Sabine urged Bastien forward. He glanced at her with a mixture of curiosity and suspicion, but it seemed something in her expression had eased his worries.

Properly secluded, the music and chattering became a distant hum and Sabine brought her previous imaginings to life.

Hands sliding down his chest, Bastien's silver eyes widened. Sabine bit her lip as she began sinking down, down,

down, all the way to her knees. She was face to face with his groin, and there was a very impressive erection pushing against the restraints of his pants. She looked up at him, her lip still caught between her teeth as his own lips parted.

"Sabine, what are you...?"

"Shh," she hushed him, scraping a nail down his hard cock. "Just enjoy."

He hissed in pleasure, jerking with her touch, and she grinned.

Sabine's hands went to the button on his pants and slipped it from its hole and with a few wriggles she freed his large and aching cock from the confines of his trousers. He was thick and long, blood throbbing hot beneath his silky skin. She took him in hand, gripping him firmly, and pumped him.

"Fuck," he hissed, hands tangling in her hair.

Sabine licked her lips and then she swiped her tongue over the head of his cock, licking away the pearl of arousal that beaded there. Bastien let out a near suffering moan at the touch as the salty sweet taste of him spread over her tongue. She opened her mouth and then took the head of him inside her wet heat, sucking and flicking her tongue along his slit. He twitched with her ministrations and gripped her hair tighter.

She loved it.

Bobbing her head along his shaft, she took him deeper, still sucking. Slowly she let herself adjust and took more of him. She was determined to take all of him down her throat.

The sounds he was making were indecent; wanton, masculine moans, and such vocalizations had her core aching for him and her nipples painfully tight against the bodice of her dress. She could listen to him groan for her forever.

Once she took him down her throat, her chin against

his sac, she loosened her throat even more and then put in the work. She moved him in and out of her throat, feeling his cock flex with the pleasure. She suppressed the gag that threatened from his movements and kept sucking him, letting her tongue slide against the underside of his cock, alternating between scraping with her teeth, and cushioning the sharp edge with her tongue.

"Sabine, fuck, you take my cock so well."

She hummed her agreement and he let out a choked sound.

She repeated the hum.

Bastien's fingers turned to claws and suddenly he was thrusting with her movements. She let him do it as tears leaked from her eyes and saliva leaked from the corners of her mouth. Still, she loved it. She loved that he was making such a mess of her and she loved that she knew he was getting unimaginable pleasure from it all.

Their movements became frenzied and suddenly Bastien moaned sharply.

"Sabine, I'm going to come."

In response, she reached up and clutched his ass, the other going to his abdomen, encouraging him to do so in her mouth.

Bastien shuttered his eyes and then with a groan he came. His hot, salty climax slipped down her throat and she swallowed it while he continued throbbing in her mouth. She didn't stop sucking until she knew that she'd taken every last drop.

Pleased with her work, Sabine slipped him from her mouth and rose to her feet. She removed her glove, wiped the mess from her face with her bare fingers, and then returned the glove to its previous position. While she'd done so, Bastien had tucked his manhood away and refastened his pants, but stared at her with a mixture of awe and something else.

"You…are a magnificent woman," he said, perhaps dumbstruck.

"I would love to hear that again," she demurred.

"Then allow me to repeat it." He swept her up in his arms and pressed his lips to her ear. "You are a magnificent woman."

She giggled. "You're just silver-tongued."

"Oh, on the contrary. I think it is you with the silver tongue. Or perhaps gold after that miraculous display."

"Naughty, naughty," she chastised, pulling back to look him in the eyes.

"Says the warlock who just—"

"Must what had been done be rehashed so hastily?"

"I wouldn't mind a reenactment." He wiggled his brows.

"And here I thought you were a mild-mannered, respectful gentleman."

"Now what gave that impression? Because I must rectify it immediately to prevent such delusions from ever presenting themselves again."

Sabine laughed. "The water."

"Ah, I see. Never shall I fetch a lady water, even if she is parched of thirst. Never especially if I should find one lost in a desert."

"Never. That would be rather gentlemanly of you, and we wouldn't want that."

"No, we wouldn't."

Sabine grinned. "Champagne?"

"Are you asking me to get champagne, or is champagne something that makes me a gentleman?"

"The former."

"Well," he said, offering his arm. "By all means, lets allow my rakish behavior indulge us in some liquid courage." He leaned in slyly. "Not that you need any courage tonight."

"Mister Emmons." She playfully swatted him and this time it was his turn to chuckle.

Sabine thought the rest of the party continued in a less spectacular manner, particularly after that dazzling bit of fellatio she'd performed. She sipped her champagne, but thoughts in her mind kept returning to how Bastien felt in her throat, the way he tasted. She very much enjoyed it and she knew she always performed enthusiastically. Even so, it was like she'd fallen from a high and she was lingering in the desolation depths of its foil.

Bastien led her around, but they did not dance. They spoke to others—friends and acquaintances—though they spent the longest with Idris and Elizabeta. Conversation with them passed comfortably, but Sabine would have been lying if she said she was entirely pleased by it.

No, in truth, she was still very much painfully aroused.

She shifted, clenching her thighs together, seeking friction. She wanted Bastien—desperately. But she would not ask, that was not her behavior. Especially as Bastien had already given her to climax earlier. Even still…she wanted *more*.

She was hungry for it.

"Would you like to get some air?" Bastien asked her after Elizabeta and Idris departed for a dance.

"I would love to," she said, fanning her flushed skin.

The redness was not from the heat of the room, no, it was from the heat roaring in her blood.

Taking Bastien's arm, the two of them stepped out of the ballroom and found themselves on a stone patio. Bastien led her off to the left, where moonlight cut across the pavers and sliced the darkness. It was in the darkness they tread, cool in the night air, the chill nipping her skin in the most pleasant way. There were no stars tonight, but the moon was bloated in the sky—though not full.

Sabine found herself leaning against a balustrade overlooking the black ocean. The moonlight cast ripples across the waves, like gilded paint on a charcoal swept canvas. Her fingers itched for the materials to depict the image. The idea took her as the rest of the scene came to mind—the carved fingers of the skeletal tree branches, the soft hush of the grass, the muted stone. All of it she could paint.

"You are restless," Bastien commented.

"How can you tell?" she asked, not looking at him.

"I can smell it," he said suddenly, his lips brushing over the back of her neck.

Her eyes shuttered in response. The ghost of his touch lingering. The heat mingling with the October air. It was divine. She arched into his touch.

"I can smell your desire," he continued, voice husky. His hand flattened against her abdomen and his fingers splayed across it. Her core clenched at the possessive touch.

Her breath was shaky as her lungs drew in.

"And I want to taste you," he whispered, flicking his tongue against her throat. "Here—" His fingers slipped south and then his hand cupped her pussy through the gown and she mewled.

She was so fucking sensitive.

"Mm, I would kill to hear that sound again."

"Then do your worst to a murderess, Mister Emmons," she said sultry—decadently.

Bastien spun her around and effortlessly hoisted her bottom onto the ledge of the balustrade. She immediately grabbed the rail and Bastien sank to his knees and hooked her legs over his shoulders. With that, he disappeared beneath the skirts of her gown—though it was also somewhat hiked up— and revealed her soaked core.

When his lips skated over her inner thigh, her fingers plunged into his hair. She was so sensitive and every ghost of his lips was like lightning struck right from the sky, rattling her bones like thunder. He teased her for a moment, as she balanced there—both proverbially and physically—on the edge of losing herself. Her mind raced as his fangs scraped ever so, and her eyes rolled back in her head. He then repeated this teasing torment along her other inner thigh, so high northward that his nose skimmed her clit and she let out a mewl of aching bliss.

"Please," she begged. "More."

He chuckled softly and then slowly he swiped his tongue through her center, diving right into her slit and fully tasting her. She groaned and tugged him by those ebony locks deeper against her, urging for friction. As he nuzzled against her, plunging his tongue in and out of her cunt, he delivered that delicious friction she wanted and she threw her head back, ecstasy crawling over her skin in the most divine way.

The night air kissed her exposed skin like the most salacious and tentative of affections, the chill only heightening her enjoyment. She had no worries if anyone would hear nor encounter them—she was in an orb of their making, like a snow globe or crystal ball.

Sabine's hips undulated against his movements and

suddenly he licked higher and sucked her clit into his mouth. She let out a breathy sound that had her mind flashing blank. Her mouth fell open and she pulled on his hair harder. As he continued licking and sucking her clit, she felt an orgasm begin to bloom. She felt herself climbing higher and higher, so close to the crest of the wave. She knew bliss was going to shatter her and she chased it.

"Bastien," she moaned softly. "I'm so close."

He practically purred against her as he devoted his mouth to the apex between her thighs. Sabine flew to the edge of her climax and then suddenly it took her and powerful pleasure slammed into her and had her writhing. She moaned as Bastien continued to feast, hands raking through his hair, hips rocking against his face, hands cupping the cradle of her thighs. She broke apart, light fracturing beneath her eyelids, his name like a prayer tripping from her lips.

When she finally came down from the orgasm, she sagged against the stone and Bastien reemerged, lips glossy with her arousal. Sabine grinned and as he stood, she tugged him forward and kissed him. She could taste herself on him and it sent remanent tingles through her nerves.

High from the multiple orgasms, the mutually beneficial oral sex, the recent blood-draining-euphoric-saliva-inducing bite, and the simultaneously intimate and depraved atmosphere, Sabine wanted to let her inhibitions loose and discard of her concerns.

Yes, her woes still existed—as did the peril of Nicholas's undead return—but at this present moment in time, he could not touch her and she could do with a few days of innocent debauchery.

And so, when she and Bastien returned to the party, she pulled him to the dance floor, movements flush and pressed together in graceful sweeps and dips, they did.

For days, Sabine lost herself to the near-magic of Hollow Place.

And Bastien followed her into it.

OCTOBER 12, 1867

The days began to bleed together as did the guilt and longing Bastien felt towards Sabine. He was falling for her. Hard. Intensely. Devotedly. And she was fucking up all the carefully laid plans.

No, not carefully laid. Who was he fooling? It was hasty and barely put together at best.

Feelings were such pesky nuisances.

Sabine, he'd realized, had been under such intense stress that she'd finally cracked. He'd watched the moment the decision lit her eyes and then she'd disrobed of her inhibitions as easily as one doffed a housecoat. Dance took her body and drink took her lips—just as often as she shared both with him. For a selfish moment he allowed himself to enjoy it, but when Drusilla had looked at him approvingly it had soured any intimacy he felt in the moment. Now it was spoiled and corrupted.

The night he'd taken her sweet pussy in his mouth, they'd retired to their room where Sabine collapsed in a heap of amber layers. Arms flung akimbo about her head, legs dangling from the bed, she gave a pleasant, drunken sigh.

"Does this experience have to end?" she'd murmured.

Bastien hadn't responded, guilt riddling him with rot, but he was saved from the obligation of answering because moments later soft snores filled the room as intoxication lulled her to slumber. Having hung his head in his hands, he took a deep breath and then crawled into bed next to her.

Over the next days, Sabine participated in a life of leisure and Bastien encouraged it. What he'd noticed—though not spoken—was that with her imbibing, Nicholas had not visited her dreams. He wondered if it was a coincidence or if the liquor had acted like a deterrent—a toxin or poison of some sort?

He didn't know.

All this was running through his head as he sipped the coffee that Drusilla had procured for them that morning. In fact, Drusilla herself watched Bastien over the lip of her own cup, eyes hungry for more than one thing. He tried very hard to ignore it all.

Beside him, draped over a chaise lounge, lazy sunlight dappling her form, Sabine luxuriated in the recent buzz from a feeding. Bastien's body sang with her blood. It had crossed his mind that a bond could be developing between them, but he'd dismissed it—that was foolish and impossible. There had been no exchange.

Dark eyes, heavy lidded, and pouty lips, full and flushed, lent a thoroughly debased look to the warlock. All of which was countered by the white silk dressing gown she wore, golden limbs exposed through the parting of it.

"She is taking to this life well," Drusilla commented so innocently, Bastien knew no innocence had a part of it.

"Most people enjoy luxury."

"She seems different though. Perhaps we shall keep her around awhile."

Bastien bit his tongue, refraining from an overprotective outburst. Reynard sidled up to Bastien and he held his breath, praying he didn't lash out. The thought of slicing his throat was overly appealing.

"The drinks are doing wonders for the fodder's influence," Reynard murmured, bumping shoulders. He wanted to tear that shoulder from its socket. "Don't you think, Bas?"

Bastien's lip curled. "I think the drinks are doing what they've always done."

"Indubitably. But these ones are *special*." Reynard's grin was lecherous.

Grim comprehension slid down his spine.

"Are they laced?" he hissed.

Reynard playfully swiped the side of his nose.

Son of a bitch.

"Who?" he growled.

"It was Salem's idea. Drusilla was more than thrilled to acquiesce."

His eyes flitted to Sabine. Her cheeks were flushed, her eyes glassy with thrill and drink and more. Her long auburn hair was mussed from her vigorous hand brushing, fanning the heat off her neck. The neck he'd bit not so long ago.

All this time she really wasn't in her right mind. All this time she was coerced. All this time she was drugged.

Nausea rolled through Bastien. All the food and blood he'd consumed readied to rise in his gorge.

Never had the tithes been drugged.

Yes, they'd been plied with alcohol, but never a completely mind-altering substance. This had changed the game.

Bastien charged for the hallway where Elizabeta caught him at the edge of the room, all blurred edges and slow eyes. She grasped and fumbled for his sleeve.

"I know what he is—what you all are," Elizabeta hissed, so quiet, Bastien almost didn't hear. "Back home we lived in fear of them—the vampire."

Vampire. It was a mortal term he'd heard once or twice before. A mortal word for a blood drinking monster that didn't exist. But perhaps it was fitting. Perhaps someone carried the tales of Midnight Malady affliction to the mortal world and the legends spread. He could surely adopt the term. Wear the name with all the inherited terror it wrought.

"You monsters have brought us here as prey." Elizabeta's lips pulled back from her teeth. They were red. "But the lambs you thought you sought have claws and it's too late for us all."

She cackled as she pushed him away and stumbled for a cushion.

Bastien muttered a curse and tore from the room. He stalked the halls until he found Salem in his preferred room, all light and airy as a cigarillo parted his lips and smoke coiled from its tip.

He crossed the checkered tile in two large strides and slammed both palms into Salem's chest.

Salem's surprised exhalation produced clouds of nefarious smoke. Bastien pushed through it while he hauled the other warlock up by his shirt collar.

"I can explain!" Salem gasped, already knowing why Bastien was in a rage and forgoing a useless excuse. "It was to help."

"Explain," he growled.

"It's a trick," he wheezed. "The first dose was the only one of any potency. I've been weaning it since. It barely has any effect anymore."

Bastien's grip loosened. "But she doesn't know that."

"No, and I'd like to keep it that way."

Bastien let Salem drop, his lacquered shoes hitting the marble with a barely audible tap. Rubbing his neck, Salem cleared his throat.

"There is a bit of a…let's say revolution beginning here."

"I'm listening."

"Many are displeased with Drusilla's machinations, worsening since—" Salem broke off.

"Since when?"

Salem's eyes flickered around the room, nothing and no one catching the sunlight cutting through the nine-foot panes. No one hiding beneath nor behind the grand piano. It was just them in the large expanse of gothic elegance.

"She's become secretive. Belinda swears she heard demonic murmurs on the eastern edge of the island."

"Impossible."

"I thought so, too. But Draco has gone missing and only a spray of blood on the sand was found."

"But Hollow Place is hallowed. It has been blessed."

"By a less than sanctimonious priest—whom was actively working with the demons of the Heartrender Curse."

Of course, Drusilla would employ an evil priest. It was exactly like her.

"So…the holy soil is deteriorating?"

"It seems so." Salem sighed. "This is supposed to be a haven, Bas. That was what was promised. But now, it's like a cult pining to have a queen. I mislike it."

Bastien threaded his fingers through his hair and resisted the urge to yank it all out at its roots.

"What can I do to help?"

"Stay out of it."

"But—"

"No. Dru's eyes are already too close on you. She is intrigued by Sabine—keep her attention there."

"So, use her as bait?"

"Is that not what you brought her here for?"

"Perhaps things have changed."

Salem's dark brows rose. "You are falling for her—oh, Bas. This is not good."

"I fucking know," he moaned.

"This has never happened."

"I'm quite painfully aware."

"This changes much."

"Oh, you think?" he bit out sarcastically.

"You should leave this place."

"We cannot," Bastien despaired.

"Why not?"

Bastien sighed. Without betraying Sabine's secrets, Bastien explained an unhallowed being was chasing her and they needed to wait him out on hallowed ground or running water.

"There is an entire ocean beyond you."

"Wow, Salem. I truly haven't thought of that. Why, what would I do without you? In case you haven't noticed,

Nostradamus, I do not have a ship at my disposal."

"Okay, first of all, why must you bring up mortal philosophers? It's truly dreary. And second, surely you could bring yourself to…acquire a ship."

"Nostradamus was a warlock actually; he just hadn't performed the Staying."

"Pish."

"And do you think I could sail a ship alone?"

"Perhaps a canoe."

"You are comedic," Bastien said flatly.

Salem lit another cigarillo, his first one still smoking sadly on the floor, ember dimming.

"Let me help," Bastien pleaded.

Salem took a drag, eyes flickering from Bastien to the floor. He exhaled the cloud and began. "For now, do not be suspicious. Keep Sabine close—and safe—but let Drusilla's attention be captured by her. When it is time, I will let you know."

"Time for what?"

Salem took another drag.

"To end Drusilla's reign of terror."

Back in their room, Sabine flopped against the covers, her dark red hair fanned out behind her head.

"Does this delight ever have to end?" she murmured dazedly.

Bastien knew now that it was not just the stress cracking that had turned her so languid, but a touch of sedative. The guilt that wracked him was unlikable and foreign. He was unused to feeling this sickening feeling. Guilt did not come to him easily, nor often.

But when it was about Sabine…she changed everything.

"Sabine," Bastien began. Her eyes flittered to his, showing her attention. "There is something I must tell you."

Sabine sat up, her hair gliding upwards like a silken cascade.

"Yes?"

Bastien opened his mouth. Closed it. Opened it again.

"Everyone here, everyone you've met who has been here before?" he started while she nodded. "Everyone has Midnight Malady and we are blood bonded to Drusilla."

"Then what am I doing here?"

He hesitated.

Every ounce of the drunken, languid coquette left Sabine's frame, melting away to reveal the wrathful goddess beneath. Her eyes were molten pools of rage as she bit out three words that staked him.

"You have betrayed me."

OCTOBER 12, 1867

Deception was one thing Sabine could not forgive. Nicholas had deceived her under the guise of romance. Stealing away her heart and crushing it when it got in his way. He hadn't wanted her like she'd wanted him. Just like Bastien hadn't wanted to save her like she'd needed to be saved.

Sabine was no idiot. She understood immediately once he'd confessed to the vampiric Midnight Malady infested island. It was like a religious cult. A fucking blood bond, to boot! She'd quickly deduced they were not here simply to enjoy debauchery. They were here to feed the demon-sick warlocks. To be their feeders until they ran dry and their desiccated corpses could be tossed to the sea.

Well, Sabine had no interest in that.

She leaped off the bed and threw herself to the French doors opening to the balcony. In her stupid dress she tossed herself off the rail and scaled down the trellis of climbing roses. Thorns scraped her as she descended, but she found footing and made it to the ground in seconds.

As she tore across the muddy landscape, her black-gloved fingers twisted with crimson magic, foisting speed on herself, and defense at Bastien—who was in pursuit. She was barefooted, mud squelching between her toes as she ran into the gray night. The scent of the earth was ripe and wet, the churning of the ocean a brine that assaulted her nose.

Thunder cracked overhead as they sky opened up and sheets of rain descended from the heavens. Hair slicked to her skull, drops falling from her lashes, she did not stop. She made for the east side of the Hollow, along the wrought iron fence bracketing the woods, cutting her off from the sea.

"Sabine, no!" Bastien called from behind her. "Please listen!"

"Fuck you!" she called back, tossing a cutting sigil behind her.

The groan of a branch cracked against the night as Bastien cursed. Apparently, her sigil had landed.

"Sabine, please it's not safe over there! Those succumbed to madness are bound to the woods."

Lies.

Embarrassment and despair coursed through her like a vicious tide. She was angry—so fucking angry—that she saw red through the haze of rain and tears. She didn't know where she was going, only that she needed to get away.

She ascended a hill, hem of her dress soaked and muddy as lightning lit up the sky. Bastien's longer legs were quickly eating up the distance between them. Still, she was not going to go quietly. She was damned if she would.

Right at the edge of the woods, where briars and brambles tangled with the fence, Bastien caught her. He pushed her against the cold iron bars, both hands caught in his clutch and hauled over her head, as she bared her teeth.

"You are a bastard! A foul, odious toad!"

"And you are still a divine vixen."

"Do not try to flatter me! The cow led to slaughter needs not be praised for being as it is."

"You are not a cow," he said softly, fingers tightening on her wrists.

"Oh, how painfully observant of you."

"Nor are you being led to slaughter."

"Do not deign to fool me. I am no tot. I can deduce why we have been brought here."

"I would not try to offend you by denying such claims, as they are true. But I have changed."

"Oh, have you?" she spit, laughing without humor. "Was it before or after you tongue-fucked me? Or I tongue-fucked you?"

Darkness left her eyes; hollowness was taking its place. He'd stripped something raw within her. He'd emptied her and he was desperate to fill her back up.

"Before. Long before."

"When?" she commanded, low and lethally.

"When I asked you to trust me."

Something entered her gaze once again, but he knew they weren't out of the woods yet.

"It does not change the fact that I am here to be drank from and likely tossed once I am no longer of use—no matter if you've decided I'm suddenly worth more."

"I knew right away I would rescue you from that fate, no matter how."

"Gallant."

"I mean it, Sabine. I have become part of a resistance here. One that seeks to overthrow the mistress's ways. One that we must wait out until it is time and until Nicholas cannot touch you."

"I am tired of being used for someone else's gain. I thought you were different."

"I am."

She scoffed. "Then why am I being held against my will, nearly tied to an iron fence?"

"I am—"

She raised a knee with a sudden, violent jerk, slamming it into his groin.

Bastien roared in pain and released her, falling to the mud. She took off, wearing imprints of his fingers on her wrists like cuffs. She cast an illusion sigil, but Bastien's proficient ward sliced through it and in a handful of smooth steps he caught her once again, crashing into the mud together.

"You are here," he rasped half in pain, half in exertion, silver eyes glowing as lightning slashed the night. "In the mud, beneath me, because I am in love with you."

"You what?" she managed, chest heaving.

"I am in love with you."

And just like that, she melted and her gaze caught on his mouth. He saw where she was trained and there was a question in his eyes. She gave the answer.

His lips crashed down on hers.

Their tongues clashed as electricity speared the sky, casting them in brilliant illumination that was as white-hot as their sudden passion. Sabine tore at the buttons of his shirt, shredding them from their threads and shucking off his shirt. Above, he pressed his hips into the cradle of her thighs, welcoming him into the apex of her. The hard ridge of his impressive cock pushed against her, eager for her heat.

Her hands roamed down his back as his hitched her legs around his waist. His mouth kissed a trail down her throat, nipping with the subtlest hint of fangs. Tugging the neckline of her dress down, her breasts swelled against the strain and popped out. His mouth immediately found her peaked nipple, flicking his tongue against the aroused tip. She moaned and surged up against him.

Bastien's fingers dug into the mud as his pelvis undulated. Sabine, hungry beyond belief, yanked down his pants and freed his length. She palmed it desperately and then guided it to her slick center.

"I take a tincture," she rasped.

Bastien groaned when he felt her pussy, unguarded from the elements. She hadn't elected to sport any undergarments—again.

"Sabine," he whispered like a prayer.

"Inside me," she commanded.

He slid inside her with one swift stroke, stretching her and filling her with perfection. She gasped as he slammed fully inside. Then, as his mouth paid respects to her breasts, he began fucking her in earnest.

Bastien railed against her, a tempo to the thunder as he drove into her mercilessly. His teeth dragged over her pink nipples and his cock dragged over her sensitive clit as he fucked in a rolling motion. He was hitting a place inside her, so tender and tight she began to see stars.

Rain slicked their skin as Bastien hauled her bodily against him, lifting her so that she was seated upon him.

"Ride me, love. Take what you need."

Sabine did as bid, viciously bearing down on him as she sought the friction her greedy clit demanded. She fucked hard and fast, gasping into the night air as the storm swirled around them. She was streaked in mud and he bore similar marks; dirt carved like scratches that matched the true scratches she was delivering to him.

The orgasm began coiling low within her. Tight and hot, the pressure built until her vision blacked out. Her mouth opened to the moon as the climax crested through her and she shattered. She moaned and keened as she came and then moments later Bastien followed her over the edge, spilling inside her. She felt him throb as he surged in their final waves of mingled climax until they slowed in their rhythm.

Rain still slashed the night as she took him in, beholding the silver eyes that had pleaded with her. That had seduced her. That belonged to the man who said loved her.

Bastien's lips parted.

"I meant what I said," he whispered.

"You must prove it to me then," she whispered back, unready to unlock her heart just yet.

The two of them disentangled and made their way back to their suite. Sabine was unwilling to perform a walk of shame and so they both reascended the trellis, mindful of the rose's thorns, and clambered over the railing. On the balcony, Sabine stepped out of her ruined dress and padded muddy footprints to the ensuite bathroom.

With speed and efficiency, she filled the tub with scalding hot water, coils of steam rising from the surface. Before she climbed in, she took a wet cloth and scrubbed the worst of the mud and grime from her skin, repeating the action in the sink until she deemed herself adequate for the tub.

She sank into the deep water as Bastien entered the room. She pointed at the sink, skin already pinkened from the temperature.

"Clean yourself somewhat before you even consider joining my bath."

"Is that an invitation?" he asked, ruined shirt hanging in tatters, showing of his sleek and carved abdomen.

"Do as I say and maybe you shall find out."

It was an invitation, she revealed after he'd scrubbed and climbed in. Immediately, she began kissing him, their flesh clinging to the chill from the outside fuck as they warmed. Her teeth pulled his lip, and his fingers snaked beneath the water, finding her pussy still wanting.

As Bastien fingered her and worked her up again, she rode his hand until he bent her over the edge of the tub and fucked her from behind. Fisting his hand in her long-soaked locks, he bared her throat and kissed it as he utterly destroyed her core. She clenched around him as he rammed into her, water sloshing over the edge of the tub.

"Come for me again, pretty vixen."

She clamped down on him as the orgasm stole through her, his name on her lips as she came and came and came. He kept fucking her through the waves and then after a few erratic strokes he came, groaning her name like gospel.

After, they truly did wash. He helped her scrub the mud from her arms and legs and when the water turned gray with filth, they drained it and refilled it once again, repeating the process once her auburn waves were refreshed. With the third fill, they luxuriated in the heat, enjoying the citrus oils tipped into the water. It mixed in a lovely melody with his smoke and apples and her vanilla cinnamon.

Sabine leaned against Bastien, tracing swirls on his forearms as he cradled her to his strong body.

"How often do these cultish soirees occur?" Sabine asked.

Bastien stiffened for a moment before answering. "Approximately once a season."

"How very pagan."

"Paganism would encourage these events more often."

"Perhaps that was the wrong term. But what would you call leading lambs to slaughter on account of solstices and equinoxes? Druidic?"

There was a lilt to her voice.

Bastien seemed to pick up on it and squeezed her.

"You're fucking with me, aren't you?"

She shrugged and let out a little giggle as he tickled her ribs.

"Perhaps."

"Imp."

"Toad."

Bastien nipped her throat in retort.

"I must ask you a favor," she began nervously.

"Anything."

"I need you to put me first. Not because I ask, but because you need me to be first. I cannot handle always being the second choice. I cannot survive the humiliation of being a stepping stone. So, if you cannot do so, let me leave."

The storm lashed against their windows, thunder cracking the clouds and lightning spearing the dark. The wind howled, yet they stayed perfectly warm within the bath.

He wrapped his arms tighter. "Never. I will always put you first Sabine. I swear it."

"Okay."

"Soon, you will see this love is true. And I will pleasure in proving it to you."

"You sound masochistic."

"I am masochistic in my mindless obsession of you."

"Should you be cast as an insane, caustic villain in a bad gothic romance with that sort of devotion?"

"Absolutely not." He paused. "It would be a great gothic romance."

"Hmm," she demurred. "Well, I always did prefer the villain."

"I will be your villain—forevermore."

"Romanticism at its finest."

"Watch me burn down this manor in your honor so that I can fuck you on the ashes and call you the queen of all."

"Well, with an offer like that how could a lady refuse?" He tugged her in for a kiss. "She cannot."

"That is the honest to Hell truth, isn't it, darling?"

She sighed. "You're going to break my heart, aren't you?"

"No," he said, lips ghosting across hers. "You're going to break mine."

They slept and they fucked and they repeated this cycle until dawn broke through the parted curtains. The horizon was timid in the aftermath of the storm, the morning hesitant to rise against the fury of last night's heavens.

But like Sabine and Bastien, it began all anew.

OCTOBER 14, 1867

Sabine's fingers crested the leather and cloth spines of various texts as she perused the shelves with Idris. Like her, he had been participating in the debauchery, but unlike her, he had not yet discovered the truth.

Sighing, she took a book of immortal diseases off the shelf—now since outdated—and leaned against the stacks, her draping sleeves hovering around her wrists.

Shifting uncomfortably on her thigh-high booted feet, Sabine attempted to train her attention on the words before her and not the knowledge that two of Drusilla's followers were in hearing range. She wanted to tell Idris the truth.

The library was large and expansive as promised, shelves were towers, every tome untold knowledge. It was all mahogany wood, checkerboard marble, and heavy reds. Curtains were of wine velvet; sofas were a matching shade. On the sparse tables were golden lamps spilling pools of amber that highlighted ink blots and mysterious gouges in the surface. Rugs were in various states of decay and value, questionable stains marring many of them.

"Have you read this one before, Sabine?" Idris asked, brandishing a book detailing the circles of Hell. "It's simply fascinating! It even details how one would traverse all the circles of Hell and survive."

"I endured Lust and that was certainly enough for me."

Idris's cheeks flushed with color. "What would you think my cardinal sin to be?"

Her leather pants squelched against the wood as she adjusted, the laces on her hips offering peeks of her skin, luckily not where thin scratches and fingerprint marks marred her flesh. The love bites that tattooed her ribs were covered by a white blouse with a red and black corset cinching it all together. Her velvet jacket was folded over a chair.

She contemplated Idris's question for a moment before deciding.

"Gluttony."

Idris's brow quirked. "Gluttony?"

"It is a common trait for the scholars. Lucia's sin was Gluttony. Her husband's was Greed. Both are to be expected. Just as passion linked to Lust is the ideal for artists."

"It is odd, isn't it? How we associate gluttony with food and drink, however, it is just an overconsumption of one thing. To consume it in excess."

"Exactly."

"Is that trait how Professor Turner discovered the cure?"

"I would presume so, yes," Sabine confirmed as she closed the page describing treatments.

Slowly, she walked over to Idris. She sidled close, giving an outside air of intimacy, but it was clear in every line of her face that there was no softness. She was brusque in her expression and low in her voice.

"I must tell you something, but you cannot react in a negative manner. React as if I were an engaging, flirtatious creature."

Idris adjusted immediately. His eyes were hard but his smile coy. "Done," he said with a heart-faltering grin.

Her hand went to his forearm, fingers on his pulse.

"Do not react. There is a plan, so do not worry. Everyone here has Midnight Malady and we have been brought as sustenance."

Idris stiffened, but covered it by brushing a lock of her hair from her face. "How was this discovered?"

"Bastien told me. He is part of it."

"That bastard—"

"He is atoning for his sins," she interrupted, feeling his heartbeat race beneath her touch. "The point is, he is determined to thwart these threats because we are stuck on this island. There are no more ships for days and I cannot return to land. Nicholas would find me."

"What can I do?" he pressed, fingers skimming her draping blouse sleeves.

"Pretend. I shall inform you as I discover more. Do not let anyone know what I have told you. No one. Not Elizabeta. Not anyone."

"Understood."

Sabine leaned into him, pressing her lips just shy of his ear. Her breath brushed the shell as she whispered, "Now, pretend to enjoy the debauchery and do not drink anything—it is drugged."

"Because of course it is," he murmured sarcastically.

OCTOBER 14, 1867

Drusilla stirred her black tea with a brass spoon, tipping amber liquor into the cup. She was humming to herself, softly, demurely, utterly at odds with the waspish exterior Bastien had come to know.

She was tormenting him, he'd decided.

Psychological warfare.

Surely some doctor of the mind had studied this kind of behavior. It would behoove one to have this knowledge in their arsenal.

Tinkling filled the air as the mistress tapped the bee-tipped spoon on the rim and set it on the waiting saucer. She sipped daintily, all fingertips and elegance. A mouthful of the boozy tea later, she lounged back on her preferred couch, dressed in her preferred white, dappled in her preferred sunlight. It was an irony, he realized, that she so sought the sunshine when the legends of the vampire were destroyed by its very rays.

"I think we shall call open season on Hollow Place," Drusilla announced, staring blandly at a potted monstera.

Bastien blinked. "I beg your pardon?"

"Open season," she said, turning unblinking tiger's eyes on him. "Begin with a party and then send the tithes into the night. Then a hunt shall begin."

"Are you out of your mind?" Bastien demanded, standing to his full height.

Drusilla stood too, towering over him. "Mind your tone, boy."

"We are not animals," he hissed, staring up at her. "We do not kill for sport."

"Who says?" She gave a fake pout, burgundy lips shiny with cosmetics.

"Drusilla. You cannot be serious."

"Oh, I am deadly so.

"They are fellow warlocks! Is it not bad enough we bring them here to feed? Now you wish to kill them?"

"We are better," she growled. She leaned down to him. "Better. Stronger. Faster." A finger slid down his throat and he shivered in revulsion. "More passionate."

"And more prone to insanity," he retorted with his lip curled.

"The addling of the mind will be dealt with."

"And there is the small fact that our condition is fatal

as we do not know truly how long the bond lasts. Or have you forgotten that with your capricious airs?"

"Watch you tone, boy."

"The others will not agree with this."

"They don't need to agree. They must obey. And you have no choice because I own you." She falsified sadness. "What happened to my enthusiastic acolyte? You used to be thrilled with the prospect of embracing Midnight Malady."

"I have been disillusioned."

She reeled back as if hit, her chin jerking up. "Ever since last season you have been combative. It is something we shall work out of you."

The rage that lashed through him had his fists in balls. "You will not touch me."

"Fine, fine, I'll allow that little redheaded bitch to do it."

"Do not call her that." His voice was low and lethal.

Thoughts of Sabine filled him. Her touch, her scent, her voice. She was intoxicating and enchanting. Her veneer of confidence that hid the vulnerability was the most exquisite of treasures. Her trust in him, however misplaced, was delectable.

Drusilla's brow rose. "My, my."

Fuck.

"You love her."

"No."

"Liar."

Bastien's lips tightened into a hard white line.

He filtered through his mind, harkening back to how his mind once thought. How he was a materialist, eager to over consume and luxuriate. How feats and opportunities thrilled him. How he'd once thought himself invincible. Then how he'd tried to drown himself in a false nature.

It had only been recently that he'd changed so. Not entirely shorn of the coat he wore, but enough that donning it once again found it ill fitting.

Regardless, he sank into his former self.

"I have been coming to terms with the potential end of my immortality. It has made me rethink certain things, including impermanence."

"Continue."

"Things are made more beautiful when they are temporary. The wine is sweeter when there is no more of it to go around. I have been drawn to the things that are no longer long-lasting."

"But your girl has performed the Staying."

"That may be true, but she has a fleeting nature to her. Something that you cannot hold onto. Too wild."

"Like a filly," Drusilla demurred.

"I suppose."

"So, you do not love her. You just wish to contain her. Control her." Drusilla stepped forward. "You wish to possess things which are a challenge."

Bastien swallowed and neither confirmed nor denied this. It was a lie, but he held it within his teeth, a guard against the venom Drusilla liked to spread. The coat was snug and altogether too loose, but he stayed within it unless Drusilla let up.

"Then I may be able to help you attain her. And once you have and she no longer holds the same allure, you will come crawling back."

Revulsion roiled through him. None of it was true, but he didn't dare say any of it to her. This may have been the only out he could circumnavigate.

"It is settled. I will arrange for the little warlock to belong to you and then you shall tire. Once that time arises, the discussion of open season will be reassessed. No arguments right now."

Bastien bit his tongue and acquiesced.

"And do not forget," she called as he began retreating from the room. "Attendance at tonight's soiree is mandatory."

"Understood."

When he was excused from Drusilla's presence, he found Sabine and Idris in the library, poring over stacks of tomes. Sabine's hair was tied at the nape of her neck, frustration knitting her brow.

"I presume the search does not bode well?" Bastien interjected.

"Less than favorably," she retorted.

"None of us are infallible."

"Aside from me, of course, darling."

"Right, how could I be so mistaken?"

"Your failings will be overlooked this time."

"Bless you," he said jokingly. "How might I repay this kindness?"

Sabine looked up, a feral light in her eye. "Oh, I could consider a thing or two."

A stack of books slammed on the table.

"Pardon the interruption," Elizabeta announced, a smear of dust-streaked sweat marring her brow, her dark hair frizzing. "But I may have found more promising texts."

She seemed to have no recollection of her drunken-drugged ramblings to him of vampires, but even so, an unsettled jolt went through him.

"This one—" she pronounced, lifting a book that appeared to have been recently cleared of dust with a green ribbon tucked between its pages— "seems most fitting of your plight against your ex-lover. Though, I admit I am not educated on curses. They did not exist back home how they do here."

It was a volume on holy wards.

"You told her of your curse?" Bastien asked, shocked.

Sabine shrugged, blasé. "Keeping it secret or not doesn't much change the fact it exists. Either it will take me or it won't. More people knowing of it doesn't give it any more power."

"But it is risky."

"How so?" Sabine asked, cocking her head.

Bastien opened his mouth. Closed it.

Sabine curved a smile then blew him a playful kiss.

Elizabeta flipped to a page. "This details hallowed halls and how through corrupted machinations, the blessings can wear away into nothingness and all protections will cease."

"Unfortunately, this is common knowledge, Bettie," Bastien informed, leaning over to read the spines on her pile.

Fading protections were drilled into those who'd lived in this world longer than a handful of months. It was why, despite Drusilla's depravity at Hollow Place, she was diligent about maintaining the wards and blessings. None needed a demon swarm among their shores.

Elizabeta's fair cheeks flushed in embarrassment. "Well, I see I must inform myself."

"Not to worry, darling," Sabine soothed. "I shall take you under my wing and happily assist you in the inner workings of the magical Earth." She leaned in to whisper conspiratorially. "I am still learning the odd ways of these Vale Wood folk, though. Vonor is much more lush."

"That is because you're biased," Idris interjected in his flat Midith accent.

"Biased does not mean wrong, schoolboy," she teased back.

Idris blushed and jealousy raged through Bastien.

He had to remind himself that it was he who had Sabine beneath him in the storm. It was he that she rode through the night. Not Idris.

And it was he, who'd saved Sabine from the darkest part of the forest. The part where those gone insane from Drusilla's torments and the affliction were kept and pitted. Like a gladiator arena, but death was promised. It was a sick little secret of the mistress's, and sometimes her favorite bonded accompanied her to the carnage as a treat—as she so called it.

He had not wanted Sabine to fall in with the ones so resilient to Midnight Malady that they did not perish after the insanity stage. It was wrong and unsettling.

"I know it does not cause certainty about ending the curse, but I'd like to try," Elizabeta said. "Perhaps we could combine some of the rites within paired with sigils to create some sort of…hallowed sphere around you?"

Bastien cocked his head in interest. "Go on."

"As I said previously, curses in the Mortal world are not as they are here. But there are ways to ward them off. They are less physical, but there are physical talismans that will ward them off. Perhaps that sort of framework will provide an answer."

"It's brilliant," Bastien commended.

Elizabeta's face reddened and she ducked her head.

"I shall bring these to my suite—with the mistress's permission, of course."

"Of course," Bastien replied.

"How are your living arrangements treating you, dear?" Sabine asked.

Elizabeta hugged the single book closer to her chest. "It is all right. Reynard is displeased about it, but I am lucky to be sharing with a few other ladies. There is not much privacy, though, and these women have no such qualms about nudity. It is…affecting."

Sabine giggled. "You'll come to learn many mortal customs are very chaste and reserved. It is something to become accustomed to, but I am sure you will adjust in time."

"Right."

"And what is your plan this night in regards to him at the mandatory soiree?" Bastien asked.

Elizabeta pondered this. "Perhaps I can enlist the assistance of those present?"

"You want us to tell Reynard to fuck off?" Sabine bared her teeth in something that wasn't a smile. "It would be my pleasure."

OCTOBER 14, 1867

The gown was crushed velvet in a shade of dusky mulberry. The sleeves draped from her shoulders in short swoops, following a romantic line across her décolletage. It was cumbersome, but Drusilla had insisted. Her dark auburn waves were left loose falling to the small of her back.

Beside her, Bastien was in a black silk shirt with a subtle filigree pattern and plain trousers.

Together, Sabine and Bastien maneuvered over the black and white checkered tiles, conscious of those that were considered tithes, and who had been coined vampires.

Near a swath of plum curtains, Bastien and Sabine joined Salem and Veronica, whilst Idris guided Elizabeta around the hungry vampires. They'd switch off who'd pair with her every now and again, but they'd agreed she'd not be alone for fear of Reynard sinking his claws into her and doing Heaven knows what with her.

Sidling up to Veronica, Sabine clinked her glass against the other warlock's and sipped delicately. Like Sabine, Veronica had dark brown eyes, but that's where the similarities ended. Veronica was fair of skin whereas Sabine kept a golden hue from her mother's home country. Veronica's hair was long and dark, her lips a rosebud and nose a gentle slope.

She worried for the other girl. She was built so small—not frail, not like Elizabeta—it was alarming to imagine her being fed on by the likes of Reynard. But, she had Salem, and he seemed harmless enough.

"So, how does this compare to the previous three times you've visited?" Sabine asked the other woman.

Veronica smiled, twisting her pink magic between her fingertips. "It is different this time, but no less thrilling."

"And how is it for you when you return home?"

Veronica got a faraway look in her eyes. "I long for Hollow Place when I am not here. I miss the luxury and indulgence of it all."

"And you do not fear for your safety?" Sabine hedged, attempting for a casual air.

Veronica gave her a queer look. "Why would I? The mistress assures all protections for us."

Sabine blinked.

Was she mistaken? Did Veronica not actually know what happened at Hollow Place? How could one attend so often and know nothing of the vampires? Was she lying about her attendance record? Did they somehow use an illusion sigil to erase their memories? But no, she seemed to know Salem, Bastien, Drusilla, and others.

"I meant back in Vale Wood," she amended hastily. "Do you not worry about those who may seek to indulge here and threaten you to get the information?"

"What a morbid thought," Veronica said consideringly. "But something I hadn't contemplated. You've opened my eyes to this particular risk. Thank you, Sabine."

Conversation lapsed into less pointed topics and when enough time had passed, Sabine guided Bastien away into the privacy of an alcove. Idris and Elizabeta had joined Salem and Veronica in their absence and she could just make out Elizabeta's long curls from their vantage.

Partially closing the curtains, Sabine leaned toward Bastien.

"Is Veronica not a tithe?" she whispered into the quiet.

Bastien frowned in thought. "She is."

"But she has been here before? Is that unusual?"

"I've never seen her before."

"Bastien, she has been here before. She's told me so. Twice. And she knows exactly who you are and what you're like."

"That's not possible."

Unease coiled through Sabine. "Are you usually of sound mind at these events?"

"Most often."

"Then could she be using an illusion to change her appearance or alter your memories? Is there a spell for that?"

Sabine was talented, but she was not so cocky to believe that she knew every cast.

"I—I…" For the first time, Bastien looked truly unsettled.

"I don't know."

"Do you trust Salem?"

"With my life."

"Then he may be in danger."

Sabine peeked out from behind the curtain and her stomach dropped as her blood ran cold.

Where Elizabeta, Idris, Salem, and Veronica were standing was empty, replaced by a burgundy chaise lounge, which Idris was sprawled across, eyes closed, punctures in his neck.

"Motherfucker," Sabine hissed, ripping the curtain aside and dashing into the ballroom.

Beside Idris, she dropped to her knees and pressed two of her fingers to his throat—there was a strong pulse next to the thread of blood winding a path down his Adam's apple. She searched his head quickly and found a sticky lump. Her fingers came away bloody.

She brandished her red hand. "Still trust Salem with your life?"

Bastien's face went white and then screams took up the room.

One word could be heard over the cacophony.

Demons.

From the direction of the forest rang a large bell, doling out a warning to those who hadn't heard the screams. Shouts went up outside, easily heard in the clear night through the open doors and windows.

Sabine dragged Bastien through the tide of vampires and tithes to their suite. In their dim room, she yanked off her dress and pulled on the clothes she'd worn earlier in the day—the leather laced pants, the white blouse, red corset and black jacket. When she stuck her feet into her thigh high boots and laced them up, she noticed Bastien was threading a belt across his hips, arming himself with salt, holy water, and other amenities to fight demons.

"While I am not complaining about the stop here, it does not seem like you to have a wardrobe change."

Sabine slid a blade into her boot. "I have had one too many dresses catch aflame during conflict; I was not aiming to be set fire again. Also, have you ever fought in a dress? There was a reason I swore off of them prior to coming to this Hell-forsaken island."

"Fair point," Bastien said without argument.

He handed her vials of holy water which she stuffed into her pockets. While there was no god like the humans of the mortal world believed, the power of Heaven certainly had its effects on the denizens of the underworld.

Armed, the two of them ran from the manor and out into the night. Explosions of color lit up the sky along the beach, bathing the landscape in magic, individual sigils flashing like fireworks. Warlocks of both vampire and tithe variety battled against demons, the creatures of the underworld everything from humanoid, to beast.

A vampire with frost blue magic slammed a destruction sigil into a demon with tusks and glowing yellow eyes, while another warlock crashed to the shore, demon mounted upon their chest.

It seemed the demons could only venture along the fringes of the island, the wards failing, not failed. But how long would that last?

The scent of sulfur was thick in the air, screams turned the void night into a hellscape, the magics a sick kaleidoscope of fantasy.

It became painfully clear which warlocks were proficient with their magics, and who was not. In the absence of talent, holy water sufficed—splashed on, dipping blades into, crossbow bolts doused. Even so, wobbly spells crashed through the wind amid zephyrs of power, certain casts obliterating demons where they stood.

Sabine didn't hesitate, and with her proficiency for speed, she had whipped two cutting spells out of thin air. The crimson magic glowed, casting her in a bloody glow as she sent them at a scorpion-tailed and a violet-skinned demon. They both shrieked from the wound.

Bastien, holding his talent in wards, crafted a net of safety about them as Sabine took on the offensive. Bastien wove protection sigils, chaining them together, while tossing out the odd violent spell as they carved their way through the fray. His fingers were deft and elegant, like a pianist's and battle was his melody.

An enraged roar hit the night as Drusilla's burgundy spellwork sliced the hand from a demon. The mistress was righteous fury incarnate. Her height lent her a domineering air that her austere features enhanced. Her jaw was set, teeth bared, tiger's eyes hard. Her fingers like claws shredded spells as hellfire and infernal runes lay waste to her haven.

While Sabine defended the false haven of Hollow Place, she kept mindful of Salem, Elizabeta, and Veronica's whereabouts, the three of them, though, were nowhere to be found. Worry wove its way through her, both for the girl she swore to defend, and for Idris, who was completely unaware of the current conflict.

She prayed the wards and hallowed ground held.

There seemed to be only the first ten yards of the island available to the demons, anything closer and agony tore through them before they began to char. It was easy to demark the line by the frame of casualties and for the most part, the warlocks stayed on the safe side.

The fight began dwindling, the demons either falling

or disappearing back to Hell, having realized the effort wasn't worth the risk. As the last few demons were slain, Sabine caught a flicker on the edge of her vision.

Bastien growled behind her.

Fear turned her cold.

No…

There, tracing the edge of the safe line, was a hellhorse and a mounted rider.

Nicholas grinned at her, a wicked, pale thing, as hellfire licked at his calves, his steed huffing steam. The two of them shared the unsettling red eyes, both of them trained on her.

Reaching out a finger, Nicholas traced the invisible barrier, his fingertip turning black with the threat.

He was directly on the edge of the barrier.

Sabine's heart raced, thudding painfully in its cavity. Panic poisoned her blood, her mind flooding with it. She stilled, hands shaking.

Nicholas was here.

He was here, where she was meant to be safe from him.

"This will not hold for much longer, my sweet," Nicholas taunted. "An adequate attempt, though."

Sabine's lips pulled back over her teeth. "You will not take me."

"We shall see," he said in an eerie sing-song.

Nicholas then turned his horse from its canter and opened a portal to Hell. A fresh waft of brimstone struck her as Nicholas crossed into the underworld.

Sabine felt animalistic terror seep into her veins. She fled the scene of battle and rushed for the manor as Bastien's footfalls sounded behind her. She didn't know exactly where she was going, only that she needed to get away. Away from

Nicholas. Away from the fear. Away from it all.

As Sabine crossed the main entrance, she slid across the marble floors, skating across the checkboard in her boots. She caught herself on the banister, confused by why the floor was so slick, only to find the sea of scarlet splashed across the foyer.

A body was splayed across the marble.

Dark hair.

Unseeing eyes.

Chalk white skin.

Elizabeta.

Sabine ran for the girl, gathering her in her arms. Her throat had been slashed in one ruthless blow, the gore of her trachea exposed for the violence it was. Her head hung lifelessly from Sabine's elbow, dipping far too low than what it should have.

Pain echoed in Sabine's chest. The grief melding with guilt. She said she'd protect her, but instead, she'd failed. She had no idea who'd taken her life—it could have been anyone on the island. The only person it couldn't have been was Bastien as he was with her the entire time.

Footsteps clipped on the floor and Sabine turned to find Bastien in the doorway, face stricken.

"Sabine…"

Sabine looked at her hands covered in red and the sudden urge to peel off her skin overtook her. In a dissociative state, Sabine set Elizabeta down and shakily cast a cleanse.

She wicked away the blood with a cleaning spell, only for more to stain her again. She tried again and again, but still the red returned.

Terror soaked through her as her breathing became fast and shallow. She tried wiping the stain away but nothing worked. She let out a whimper, her jaw aching as she casted and casted.

Bastien was there, suddenly. Holding her.

"Love, you're clean. There's no more blood," he whispered.

No, no, he was wrong. She was covered in it. Stained in it.

Bastien took her hand and pressed it to his lips.

"There's no blood."

But no, he was right.

She looked at her hands again, speckless and pristine. There was no trace of blood on her person. Not a single drop.

Sabine shook as she looked up as Bastien, fear heavy in her eyes.

"But I saw it."

"What have you done?" an aghast voice sounded from across the room.

In the archway leading to the ballroom stood Drusilla and two nameless vampires. Shock was a mask across her features, a perfected façade in the face of a perceived crime. A shaking hand went to her claret lips.

"You…you killed her," she said in mock despair.

It took all but a second for it to click in Sabine's mind.

And then it did as Drusilla commanded the two nameless vampires to take Sabine away.

She was being blamed for Elizabeta's death.

"Drusilla, this is insanity," Bastien protested, holding Sabine tighter. "Sabine found her body."

"She was the only one covered in this young warlock's blood!"

"Because she found her!"

"She will be dealt with. Until we can investigate, she shall be held in our detention."

"With the lost causes?" Bastien was unequivocally

horrified. "They'll rip her apart!"

"Don't be absurd. She will have a locked cell."

Hands locked like shackles on her upper arms and towed her away. Sabine cast desperate looks at Bastien over her shoulder as she was hauled out of sight.

But the last thing she saw was Bastien's shocked face morph into indisputable fury.

OCTOBER 14, 1867

"You are mad," Bastien accused venomously.

Drusilla simpered and crossed the floor, heedless of the pooled blood and still very much dead warlock. The hem on her dress dragged through the scarlet, streaking in her wake.

"That is quite unkind of you to say."

Rage boiled within Bastien. "Sabine has done nothing wrong. Nothing but hold my attention, and you cannot stand it."

Fire lit in Drusilla's eyes, her lips curving back over

her teeth. "Who are you to blame? Me? Why would I? It must be her. We have no proof otherwise."

"It's all our word against yours then, isn't it?"

"Oh, it's 'our' now, is it?"

"I was with her the whole time," he said, slowly enunciating the last two words with impact. "She was looking out for Elizabeta's welfare, not looking to take her out."

"A trick, surely."

"I would stake anything on her innocence. I would claim any responsibility her freedom receives."

"And how can I be assured you'll be responsible for her?"

Drusilla snapped her fingers before he could respond. Immediately, Agatha made her appearance and made a slight sound as the sight of Elizabeta's body.

Bastien knew beyond a shadow of a doubt that Drusilla was Elizabeta's murderer. He didn't know if it had been done directly by her hand, or by her word, or some other means. But the mistress was responsible for this warlock's death—the catalyst of it.

Bile burned bitter in his throat as he inclined his chin at her.

"I would swear a blood oath," Bastien answered finally. "To show my responsibility and belief of Sabine's innocence."

"Mm, no," she demurred. "Those bonds are difficult to break—if not impossible—and I do not want you tied to her in such an unbreakable way. No, you'll marry her."

Bastien felt the wind fall from his lungs. He blinked in shock as nothing but complete confusion flooded through his brain.

"Marriage is quite unbreakable."

Drusilla gave him a trying look. "Have you not heard

the term divorce? I know you're a young pup, Bastien, but honestly, pick up a book."

"To me it is."

The mistress rolled her eyes. "You'll dispel your youthful fancies and fantasies one day. Reality and wisdom come with age."

Bastien knew Drusilla had aged beyond her appearance, but he didn't know the exact number. She had committed the Staying many years before she'd contracted Midnight Malady and she'd lived with the disease far longer than seemed possible—all thanks to her various blood bonds. He didn't understand the science—or perhaps it was magic—behind it, but surely Sabine's talented professor friends should know the answer. Perhaps he could offer himself as a case study in his attempts to properly woo Sabine. Would that even be effective?

"If you wish for Sabine to live, those are my terms."

Bastien glared. "Fine. Then may I fetch her at once?"

"No, dearest apologies. There is paperwork to be sorted for the ceremony—not to mention an officiant to acquire—so in the meantime, she shall languish in the prisons. It should only be a day or two, perhaps three." Drusilla patted his cheek in mock affection. "You'll see sense soon."

And then she walked out of the room, leaving him alone with a dead body and the smears of gore dragged by her gown.

Agatha returned with several maids carrying buckets of hot water and towers of towels. It was part of Drusilla's masochistic ways to forbid cleaning via spells; it all must be done by hand to "build character" even though every maid was just as adept a warlock as he.

Bastien was still standing there.

When Agatha nudged him gently towards his suites, he went in a daze, finding his way through automatic movements alone.

He was set to be married.

And as much as he cared about Sabine—deeply—he wasn't certain it was reciprocated, and surely forcing her into a marriage wasn't conducive to developing genuine feelings. It would only foster resentment and that pained him in ways he didn't want to admit. The idea of Sabine abhorring him tore his heart apart, had his ribs crushing under the immense pressure of fear.

Somehow, Bastien found himself in his scarlet suite, staring at the mussed bed where he and Sabine had been staying. Seeing her discarded gown on the floor carved a mark into his sternum, the rest of her belongings strewn about twisted his lungs around his throat.

He couldn't breathe.

He couldn't see.

Panic laced his blood and it poisoned his veins. He fell to the floor, head between his knees.

He couldn't think.

For a while all memories eluded him.

For a time, he existed in nothingness.

But finally, he pulled himself together and he rose from the floor to make his way to the prisons.

Unfortunately, his plan was foiled when he opened his door and was greeted by two guards, one of which was Reynard. He gave Bastien a slimy smirk and twirled his orange magic menacingly. The other guard was a red-haired vampire with long curls, all luscious curves and sultry eyes. She was one of Drusilla's favorites—Suzette.

"Apologies, Bastien," she said in her thick brogue. "Mistress's orders."

He nodded, hung his head defeated, and retreated inside.

When he tried the balcony, he was met with a similar sight—Pearl and Mortimer.

He was trapped.

OCTOBER 15, 1867

Sabine landed on the packed dirt floor without ceremony. Drusilla's cronies slammed the cell door closed behind her with an odious clang that pierced her ears.

Looking up from the ground, her elbow smarting from impact, Sabine glared. They didn't spare her anything but disdain. And then they left and she was alone.

She got up and brushed herself off, ensuring her jacket wasn't torn. As she pressed herself against the bars, she peered out and found her cell was on a walkway and below was a crumbling stadium, stairs leading down to a packed dirt area.

She was in an amphitheater.

The stones were white, limewashed and dirt-streaked. Around her were towering trees. Ancient masses, leafless and stark against the moon. Her cell was cramped, perhaps six feet by six feet, and maybe two feet more above her head. The ceiling was unforgiving stone, no windows, no bars, no light to be found.

Immediately, she tried the lock but it was held tight and wrapped in orange and blue sigils. Sigils that had been formed with more dexterity and proficiency than she was capable of.

Sabine sighed and sat on the cushion-less bunk and stared out into the night. She didn't want to waste her energy until she had a plan of escape.

While she plotted, grief pooled within her. Grief and guilt in equal measure. She was meant to protect Elizabeta and she'd failed miserably. And what of Idris? Where was he in all this? Was he still alive? It was all her fault he'd even come here—he'd fancied her, and albeit the library was a draw, it was her doing. Then there was Salem, was he trustworthy?

She had answers for none of it.

While in thought, a shadow passed her doorway and she stilled. In silence, she held her breath and watched, then slowly, that shadow drew closer. She shivered but didn't make a sound.

A vampire drew into her view, but it was wrong.

Its eyes were dark, wholly swallowed by the pupil, leaving only a thin ring of blue. Its ears were pointed, knife sharp, and its fingers tapered into black claws, fading from its natural, once flesh-tone. It cocked its head to the side in a jerky, almost insectile fashion. Wraith-like in its emaciated frame, it glided closer.

Sabine couldn't determine its gender on sight alone, and even then, felt no comfort in calling it anything by mortal means. It was no longer a face of humanity. It was a predator. A mad thing without ethics or morals. In its face, sophistication lacked, for all it was, was hunger—ravenous, endless hunger.

And she was its prey.

This was one of Drusilla's bonded who'd gone mad. Who was so far past the brink of saving that it was forsaken. One Bastien had told her was now used for cruel entertainment.

Sabine pressed herself against the cell wall, instinct driving her as far away from the thing as possible.

This is what Bastien meant when it wasn't safe here. Not that he was trying to trick her. He was trying to protect her from whatever *that* was.

"Hello, tender morsel," it said, wrapping its clawed fingers around the bars. It pressed its face between the gaps, eyes eerily reflecting the meek moonlight. "What a treat you are. What have you done to be committed here?"

The voice was definitively male. Serpentine and low, something in the realm of seductive—if only the one to hear were without sight—but closer to sinister.

"I've done nothing."

"If you've done nothing, that means you've done something to Drusilla, which means you've done nothing." It smiled—too much teeth. "Did you steal one of her favorite toys or playthings?"

Sabine didn't answer and stayed unsettlingly still.

"Ah, you did." Something akin to joy entered its voice. "Was it Reynard? The cruel brute? Or Bastien? The wicked artist?"

She flinched.

"Ah, yes." Licking its lips it pressed closer into the cell, squishing and squeezing. "Artistry and romancer-y, that the Emmons be. She was always partial to the Emmons boy, no matter how many times he rejected her. Over and over, under and under, always no, never yes. Possessive, actually. She seems to think of him as a challenge. Yes. That one day she'll wear him down. Down, down, down."

She didn't answer again.

It sighed, then examined its nails. "I was one of her favorites, once upon a time, like a storybook, I was. One of knights in shining armor, playing games like I was king—king, king, king of the castle."

Curiosity, despite her fight or flight, piqued. She kept herself apart, arms crossed as she raised a brow.

"Then what are you doing here?"

It shrugged. Licked its lips. "I took a lover. Once, twice, thrice. Forever and nevermore. But that lover ended up being more than physical—that's the thing about the mistress, oh mistress. She's fine with lustful affairs, but emotional? It's too much, too much, too much for her.

"My lover was killed and it was made to look as if I'd done it. That it was me, me, me, like I'd been the one to have it done. But 'twas not, forget me not, and all that lot. She was mine and mine was hers. But not Drusilla's, never hers."

Fear shot down her spine. That was concerningly similar to Benedict and Lucia's story, and a bit too close to home regarding hers. Save for the very evident insanity.

She couldn't imagine how Benedict felt in those nebulous seven years. The prison sentence. Alone. Having been framed for the murder of his fiancée—her best friend. The lengths he'd gone to, to fix it all. To break time...

She'd been imprisoned all of a half hour and already she was going stir crazy. How had he managed seven years? It was enough to drive one to insanity, surely.

"And you didn't fight it?"

"He had not one shred of proof," a new sinuous voice interjected, a feminine one.

An even slighter frame slid into view, the same attributes as the male, but her hair was long and blonde, mixed with detritus and dirt.

"Irving's crime was love," the female explained, just as madness touched. "Mine was rebellion. Love of his and lack of mine, true crime, it was indeed. Laws made and remade, all it takes is once a word from a lady, one whom calls herself mother, lover, owner, taker."

Sabine's brows knitted.

"How many of you are there?"

"Dozens and ones, and twos. Only as many as can hold," Irving chimed. "You could be one of our ones, tender one. So many ones, you should be our one, yes, our only one."

"One is good, one is well, one is fair," the female chirped, nodding frantically. "Yes, ooh, One, please join us. Join us for a tasty, tasty treat."

Sabine retreated back against the wall.

A third vampire descended.

"Taste, one taste," it begged. "Please little one, one, one, one, one, one." The ones degraded into a wail and the maddest one shook the bars of her cage, begging to be let in, or her to be let out. "Just one!"

A fourth vampire leapt at the bars, chittering maniacally. It was missing an eye, its hair was a wild snarl about its head, dark and matted, flesh bone white.

"Bite. Bite. Just one bitty bite," the fourth vampire

snapped. Its fangs seemed alarmingly long.

Sabine, overwhelmed, having had enough, quickly fashioned three cutting sigils and sent them with accuracy through the bars. Three yelps went up and skittering feet on dirt followed. The only one who still stood was Irving.

"How long have you been suffering this madness?" Sabine inquired.

"Too long, One. Too, too long. I am afraid to die, but living is so terrible. Please, One, help me. Just a little drink. I have been here a handful of winters."

Five years then. Irving had been here for five years.

It should have been impossible, but with Drusilla's blood bonds, evidently, much they knew about Midnight Malady they'd been mistaken about.

Irving slid down the bars and laid upon the dirt, facing her, eyes so desolate. An aching sadness poured from him and tugged at Sabine's heartstrings.

Quickly, Sabine came to a decision. The start of her own plan. Her own escape. She'd become too dependent on others during this ordeal with Nicholas, and now that framing with Drusilla had hit a head.

"What if I could help you? And in exchange you help me?" Sabine quested.

Slowly, Irving picked up his head and watched her. "How?"

"I know the warlocks who've cured the Wasting and Ember Fever—quite well, actually. I can ask them to discover the cure of Midnight Malady. And then you'll be free of this disease and Drusilla."

Irving eyed her warily. "There is no cure for the Wasting. You dare jest with me? I am no joke to be laughed at. No jester at court—" his voice began to rise in aggravation.

"I promise you I am not having a laugh at your expense."

"There is no cure for immortal diseases."

"You haven't met Benedict and Lucia."

Irving hesitated. "Even should your friends not be fiction; the malady is more complex. The cure should not be so simple as simple is or as simple does."

"They are brilliant," she reassured. "If you help me eliminate Drusilla and her closest loyalists, I promise I will help find the cure for you."

"Why me?"

Sabine answered honestly. "I don't know."

"You don't trust me."

"I don't." She continued the honesty. "But I trust motivations, selfish greed or not."

Irving seemed to contemplate this.

"Do we have a deal?"

"What are we doing?"

"Creating an uprising and overthrowing Drusilla's control."

"I will help you," Irving answered. "I will enlist the help of those most motivated and flush with the mistress's hatred. That will instill a bond closer to trust, closer to success, much more than just a guess."

"Then that is the deal."

"When do we begin?"

The other vampires hesitantly returned, stepping close to the bars. Sabine lifted a hand and twirled a red sigil between her fingers in a silent threat. They skittered back in fear.

Sabine tilted her head at Irving.

"Deal with you friends and we'll discuss the plan."

Irving turned and smiled menacingly at the other mad

vampires. He stepped away from Sabine.

"This one is not for feasting, beasties. This one, One, is our salvation against the Drusilla nation, her reign is set to end like we were condemned. Only she is the fallen and we are the risen."

The blonde cocked her head.

"One is our saving angel?"

"She is," Irving confirmed.

She flicked her eyes to Sabine, a sinuous grin spreading across her mouth. "Then I vow I will not take a bite from our, One."

Irving nodded excitedly. "Esther has the most self-control of any of us, none of us are as strong-willed as she— as it was she who led the first rebellion, as someone else led the second, but as you lead the third."

"Do not trust Washington, though, One. He is insatiable as the sea is untrustworthy."

Sabine looked to Washington, limned in the moonlight, glowing in an odd ethereal glow, a total juxtaposition to the feral glint in their eye. He, out of them all, reminded Sabine the most of a demon, even though he shouldn't possess any demonic traits or blood.

"I would apologize, but I have no qualms about what I am or who I'm like. Get too close, One, and I'll take a taste, taste, taste." He licked the bars of her cell.

Irving struck Washington with an open-palmed smack, holding aloft a citrus-toned sigil behind him—it was one of cutting.

"Do not make me use this, Washington. Be a fool, be a dead, dead, fool, should you make your mistake."

Washington hissed but scampered off to the edge of the stadium. Esther rolled her eyes and examined her jagged nails. Sabine wondered if it was a leftover mannerism of her pre-insanity days.

"You are most lucky, One," Irving said, turning to Sabine. "You found us, those who hate Drusilla, so much so that we will not betray you for our hoped for freedom. We know she will not set us free, free, free. Freedom from her is another prison, or one of death." The end of death came out in a hiss.

"I am most fortunate," Sabine said dryly.

"Sleep, One. We will watch out for you. You will need your strength for the battle to come, come, come."

Begrudgingly, Sabine acquiesced and curled up on the hard cot. It was cold and stiff, completely unsettling, but she cast a warming spell to at least stave off the former. Nothing could be done for the latter.

When slumber took her, Nicholas found her.

Sabine groaned as she stumbled through the foggy mists of whatever dreamland Nicholas had conjured. It was all a whiteout blur interspersed with black skeletal branches. Sabine swore it was a graveyard, but she wasn't certain.

Upon a large rock, Nicholas perched, ember red eyes penetrating the fog. He had a knee pulled up while the other dangled down. Twisting his fingers a slow violet sigil took form. Sabine readied her own defensive spell.

"Your safe haven is wearing out," he said simply.

Sabine rolled her eyes. "My patience with you is wearing out."

He acted in mock affront, putting a hand to his chest. "You wound me."

"I certainly did. But like a cockroach, you keep coming back. Don't you know how to stay dead?"

"I didn't deserve to die the way I did," he hissed, leaning forward, eyes fiery.

"Explain how not? If not for Benedict's breaking of

time, you had cursed your best friend and protégé, had his wife murdered, and undermined him every step of the way. Not to mention how you'd used me only to get closer to Lucia, and when that failed, tried to kill *me*," Sabine hissed, wrath filling her with something so vicious she was incandescent with it. "I was a pawn and you were pure evil. *That* is why I killed you."

"Have you never done something selfish, Sabine? Or are you so virtuous to think you get to dictate who lives and dies? Hmm, riddle me that."

"You're fucking delusional, Nicholas." Sabine scoffed, utterly at a loss. "Do you hear yourself? Of course, I've been selfish—taken the last slice of cake, bought myself new garments when I could've helped the staff—but never have I unjustly cursed and murdered." Sabine's spell sparked in her hand.

"I had so much influence; I was worth more than—"

Nicholas broke off because suddenly he was behind her—and still atop the stone—wrenching her back by her hair.

Sabine cursed his proficiency with illusions and used all her might to force herself to wake. If she jolted from sleep, then Nicholas couldn't touch her. Couldn't hurt her.

"I may not be able to drag you to Hell here to suffer for eternity, but I can still kill you," he taunted in her ear, his voice echoing as both Nicholas doubles spoke. "Perhaps I shall end you as you had me?"

Pure, unfettered terror stripped her to the bone, dropping her heart into a void so deep she screamed awake from the descent of it.

Sabine's open eyes found the same stone cell with Irving standing guard, a defensive sigil already readied in the palm of her hand. Despite the cold, she was sweaty, hair plastered to her forehead as her breaths came in ragged gasps.

"Nightmare, Sweet Morsel One?" Irving inquired.

Sabine pulled her knees up to her chest on her pitiful bunk, unshed tears burning in her eyes.

"Worse," she whispered. "Much worse. I can't sleep."

"How is much worse than a nightmare? Dreams cannot portent the omens of the dark dream, so the mare is the culprit, is it not?"

"It's complicated," Sabine whispered.

Irving cracked a smile and Sabine thought it was the first of the genuine sort she'd noticed from the mad vampires.

"I think you'll find I have the time—more than when the clock chimes and the bell tolls."

And so, Sabine, against her better judgement, confessed all the cursed truth to the mad vampire.

OCTOBER 19, 1867

For three days Bastien raged inside the cage of his suite while Sabine languished in her cell of Drusilla's. All his worst fears rampaged through his head. She was locked up with the mad vampires—some of whom he'd once known, but none of which he'd trusted—and he didn't even know if she was still living.

Every avenue he'd tried was thwarted, blocked by Drusilla's cronies. His meals were delivered under guarded eye, which included his blood doses. A servant was delivered, quick and efficiently once a day, Bastien drank from their wrist and they were once again ushered away.

His room was destroyed. He'd shredded the curtains in a rage, turned over the chairs and chaise. Glass was strewn from shattered decanters. He'd hoped the sounds of destruction would draw enough attention for them to check on him. He'd hurled every insult under the sun at them. Alas, it was all to no avail.

Daylight streamed in through the glass doors, a crisp fall breeze ruffling his hair as he sat with his head in his hands on the floor. Two vampires were stationed on his balcony, watching with disinterest. His heart hurt and he was so full of wrath. He knew the mistress was unreasonable, but this felt excessive.

At exactly noon, the door creaked open and Agatha entered for his daily blood feeding. He didn't move from his solitude on the floor. Her soft, slipper-clad feet swished as she made her way to him. She seated herself delicately next to him, adjusted her skirts to cover her more fully and rolled up her sleeve.

"Myself and others have been most worried about you, Mister Emmons," she began beneath her breath so the guards would not hear. "So, we took it upon ourselves to keep our ears out for anything that might be of importance to you."

Slowly, as if staving off the hope, he lifted his head. He met Agatha's gentle brown eyes, eyes that were filled with a stoic ferocity.

"What sort of importance?" he quested almost silently.

"First, one of our maids braved the forest to deem if Miss Sabine was hale and hearty—which she is."

Bastien's heart leapt with Agatha's words.

Sabine was okay. She was alive.

Agatha gestured to her wrist and Bastien took it gingerly. Carefully, he found her pulse point, the throbbing line of blue against her fair skin and sank his fangs into it.

Agatha let out a small sound of discomfort, but didn't pull away. She cleared her throat.

"The maid—which is our most capable warlock—is taking another visit this afternoon to ensure she is still in the same condition."

Bastien drank, but spoke with his eyes, urging her to continue.

"Additionally," she said. "The talk of tonight is that your wedding shall occur, but that the Mistress has something malicious planned. Unfortunately, we have not been able to glean quite what.

"Then, there is the matter of the murder. Miss Sabine is still the only suspect at large. They are not even attempting to query into anyone else."

"So, it's a set up," he murmured against her skin.

"It seems that way," she concurred, tucking a stray lock of dark blonde hair behind her ear. "Mister Swan is alive—I was unsure if that was something of note to you, as he is the Rival." Bastien cocked a brow and Agatha waved him off. "The staff talk."

"Veronica and Salem?"

"Salem is…odd. He is not acting as himself but he is alive. Veronica seems quite…" Agatha's eyes went confused. "I'm not sure. She's quite close to the mistress."

That was not good news. Veronica rubbing shoulders with Drusilla paired with the evidence Sabine had brought him about her return trips to the island—that he did not remember—didn't bode well. Not to mention Agatha not able to recall details surrounding her. Sabine may have been onto something about Veronica and illusions.

"All right," Suzette interjected from the doorway. "Time is up, please depart from the suite, Agatha."

Bastien removed his mouth from the girl's wrist and she took it away quickly, wrapping it in a pre-prepared bandage. She got to her feet, dipped quickly in a curtsy, and slipped from the room. He watched her leave while he wiped a smudge of blood from the corner of his mouth. He stared down Suzette but neither of them said anything.

Bastien continued his floor vigil.

Hours passed in silence until a knock came at his door that evening. He opened it and was shocked to find Salem standing there.

Bastien's brows knitted. "What are you doing here?"

"Your guards have let up. You're no longer under house arrest."

"Ah, so kind of you to have visited me during such a time."

"I tried, but I was barred."

"Right."

"It's true," Salem argued.

"So, what are you doing here now?"

Salem produced a garment bag. "I am here to be your best man."

Bastien's stomach flipped from both joy and fear. "So, it's tonight?"

"It is. But before you get changed, we need to retrieve Sabine."

Bastien's mood darkened, like a storm cloud crossing the horizon. "You mean to tell me we're doing this without any precautions? Meaning we only marry if we survive to and from the prison?"

"That would be the case."

"Terrific," Bastien said sarcastically.

"My thoughts exactly."

Sometime earlier—Bastien wasn't sure when, his balcony guards had left, and the ones from the hallway were nowhere to be found. Before they departed, Salem set the bag on the bed and shut the door, locking it both mechanically and by spell for good measure.

The two of them set out across the grounds beneath the twilight sky and remained armed with sigils. Tension rose between them as they navigated through the forest, wary of every sound and every crunch underfoot.

Despite the fact there were specific wards keyed to each mad vampire to prevent them from journeying too far in the forest from the amphitheater, but it was Bastien's belief that one could never be too safe. Insanity could sometimes be stronger than spellwork.

Bastien and Salem made the trek to the prison unharmed, but was startled to find Sabine in her cell, chatting animatedly to a vampire outside the bars. Their arrival made a sound and the two of them turned. Protectiveness and possessiveness formed over the vampire's face—whom Bastien was surprised to discover was Irving—while unfettered joy and relief spread across Sabine's.

"Bastien!" she called in a breathy rush, throwing herself against the bars in excitement. "I was so worried about you."

Bastien rushed over, Salem watching over him while Irving slowly backed a few steps away. Through the bars, Bastien caught Sabine's face and kissed her desperately. She looked exhausted and tasted like sweat and salt and night, but in that moment, it was the most divine flavor he'd ever had.

His tongue tangled with hers, a soft moan slipping from her lips as he captured her in the kiss and drowned her in passion. His teeth scraped her lip and she bit his back. He grinned in response, adoring his little vixen beyond belief.

His vixen. Soon to be his wife.

Bastien realized with a start that she had no idea about their impending nuptials and he had to be the one to break the news to her. He mentally prayed that she didn't blame or resent him for the circumstance. He could always offer a later divorce—even though the idea was almost physically painful to contemplate.

For now, he enjoyed his one blissful moment before he had to shatter it.

His hands went to her auburn waves, slightly tangled and unwashed, but he didn't care. She was still perfection incarnate. He so desperately wanted to push himself against her, into her, to have her eternally and carnally.

But reality was swooping in.

Bastien pulled back and met her night dark eyes.

"I have something to tell you," he began softly.

OCTOBER 19, 1867

I have something to tell you.

Those words, in her experience, were not ones you'd want to hear if you were hoping for good news. More often than not, it impended the end of something she was eager to continue. Those were words saved for a diagnosis or an opener to soften a rejection.

Sabine disassociated enough to buffer against the pain and pulled back from the bars.

"What is it?"

"They cannot prove that you did or didn't kill Elizabeta, so as a precautionary measure they've decided you may only be on the island as long as you remain in my presence."

Sabine relaxed a little. "Oh, is that all?"

"And…" Bastien trailed off uncertainly. He scrubbed the back of his neck and glanced at Salem who was carefully eyeing Irving, who was steadfastly staring at her.

Bastien cleared his throat.

Tried again.

"You have to marry me. Tonight."

Sabine's mind went blank. Pure shock ripped through her, turning her blood icy cold. Her mouth formed an O and she could have sworn anyone could see all the whites around her eyes.

"I beg your pardon?"

"It's Drusilla's condition."

She wasn't against the idea of marriage, she always thought she would one day, but not like this. This…it felt like something had been taken from her. But, at the same time…her and Bastien…she felt something for him that terrified her desperately.

"Don't you think that's a little counterproductive to her goals in pursuing you?" she asked.

"She has ulterior motives I do not trust, I'm sure."

"And I can just walk out of here unimpeded?"

"Not exactly," Salem interjected, a key ring swinging from his finger. "You're free as long as you survive the trip back to the manor."

Sabine's smile was feral. "Well, isn't it serendipitous I've befriended one of her castaways."

Irving gave her a matching smile, clapping his hands together. "Yes, One. We are friends. I will protect you through the forest, so dark and dreary, and scary and weary."

"Thank you, Irving."

"Ready for this?" Bastien asked, a thin jealous edge to his words.

"Do I have much choice, darling?"

"Not exactly."

"Then let's."

Salem released her from the cage and she bolted from it and into Bastien's arms. His scent was so reassuring, smoke, crushed leaves, apple. It was home. He wrapped her up, his face nuzzled in her neck, her face pressed against his chest. Bastien was so strong and warm, she hadn't realized how hard she was holding it together until she was about to break.

Irving approached slowly. "I shall guide One and her friends to safety. I am no leader, but the others won't bother you in my accompaniment."

"Thank you, Irving," Sabine said.

Irving beamed and waved them onward. He led them from the prison and to the forest, Sabine stayed near Bastien but readied a sigil just in case. The night was dark and chill, but there was a slight levity to it, as if even the mother of nature were giving them the briefest of respite.

Bats screamed above them, leading them all to jump. A rogue sigil spitting into the night. Every branch on every tree was another claw reaching for them; every rustle was a vampire approaching. Tensions rose high on a tightrope string, a feeling so palpable Sabine swore she could touch it.

Esther appeared from the fringes of the trees and Bastien nearly took her head off with a cutting sigil. Sabine shoved his arm away and yelled.

"No, she's friendly!"

As if she were her unleashed dog and he an

unsuspecting pedestrian.

Bastien lowered his hand, the cutting sigil having sliced through a wayward branch. Esther had bared her teeth, long fangs, wild hair a snarl, fingertips blackened, readied for battle, but instead, she reined in her rage and madness. Sabine admired her willpower.

"Others are coming, One," Esther hissed. "Washington has tried to waylay them down, down, down in the depths, but darker ones break free and pursue us still. It is time to run, run, run."

Sabine didn't question Esther's warning and took off. Sabine, Bastien, Salem, Irving, and Esther all raced to the edges of the forest, feet pounding the soil. Esther and Irving bracketed them all, serving as the slightest buffer against enemy.

Unfortunately, it left them at the mercy of the dark and from nowhere, Esther suddenly rocketed to the ground in a tangle of limbs, another set, more olive in tone, wrestling to the forest floor. Snarls took up the night as the malignant sound of unfriendly steps reached their ears. Sabine spun a speed sigil and broke into a new frenzy, the wind whipping past her, fluttering her hair like a banner.

Sabine could see the edge of the forest, the line where she was free from the woods. But before relief could take her, iron bands of arms took her instead.

She fell to the ground, rolling and screeching as she wove a cutting sigil and slammed it against her attacker. An unfamiliar shriek took up the night and she slammed the heel of her boots into anything she could reach. Fortuitously, she was released and stumbled away, only to find Bastien caught in the arms of another mad vampire, this one snapping its long fangs at his face.

All the others were in various states of combat and

Sabine took it upon herself to simultaneously throw her body against Bastien's foe, and cast a destruction sigil. The combination knocked him flat to the forest floor and her spell burrowed a hole directly through the vampire's chest leaving the scent of burned flesh.

Taking Bastien's hand, she dragged him up, mere steps away from safety. The moon cast a cool, ambient glow, an unbothered light, completely devoid and detached to their conflict.

A grunt sounded from behind them and Sabine hesitated. Then Salem's shout spurred her forward.

"Go, go, go!" He sounded as if he were in pain. "Irving and Esther are holding them off; I'm right behind you!"

Tussles continued behind them but Sabine and Bastien sprinted over the invisible line and onto the field of green. She spun on her heel in time to see Salem make it over as well. The three of them, once again regrouped, looked back and found Esther and Irving—alive—staring at them with feral joy, a gleam of bewilderment in their eyes. Other vampires were in various states of health on the ground around them, some no longer among the living, though Sabine couldn't find it in her to grieve them.

"Go on, One! We will not forget our agreement," Irving called out.

"Thank you, Irving!" she shouted. And echoed it again to Esther.

The two of them nodded and then slipped back into the woods and to their home of the amphitheater. Sabine watched until they disappeared from sight.

Her breaths were rough and she hadn't realized how scared she'd been until her adrenaline rush began to dissipate. She placed a hand on her chest and the other to Bastien's.

"Are you okay?"

"I am, well, love," he said softly, cupping her hand. "And you?"

"Good."

"Are you ready to get married?"

Her breath came in sharply, but she couldn't deny the flash of excitement.

"I am."

OCTOBER 20, 1867

Candelabras lined a path in the back garden. Long stemmed candlesticks poised in towering elegance, half a man tall. They were silver, as was the gothic arch that served as her marriage altar. It was framed by three mirrors, all ending in a point like that of a church steeple so that upon speaking their vows they could be seen from every side.

Sabine had been tended to by the maids, bathed in a hot bath and scrubbed clean, cleansed with a vanilla soap and spritzed with her cinnamon perfume. Her hair was long and soft, falling in fluffy auburn waves to the small of her back, devoid of any adornment. Her gown was glittering satin, sparkling like a thousand diamonds in the candlelight.

It was just after midnight, the night dark and cool, but she was kept warm by anxiety and a subtle sigil. The stars winked above her, the glow of the moon a silver crescent high above, coloring the sky in hues of violet and blue.

She walked down the aisle, the runner a swath of endless merlot, the fabric crushing the bed of autumn leaves beneath it. Sabine kept her head high, no veil to hide her features so she schooled her expression into one of imperiousness—one to rival Drusilla's complete air. As she breathed, she felt the dress constrict, the boning of the corset digging into her ribs, the sweetheart neckline pressing against her decolletage.

At the end of the aisle, illuminated by the flickering fire's radiance was Bastien. His black hair was ever so endearingly falling over his brow, his silver eyes only for her. He was wearing a black button up in some shimmering fabric, his dark trousers adorned with a chain, a cross dangling from one end. Silver chains dripped from his neck and she had to resist the urge to hook her finger in one and tug him close.

Every step down the aisle brought her closer to her almost-husband. Her fingers tightened in the red rose bouquet she held before her, anticipation humming in her blood. She kept her gaze focused on Bastien and not the vampires and tithes bracketing her on each side of the aisle.

All the warlocks around them had their gazes pinned to her—she knew it, she could feel it, even if she wasn't looking to confirm it. They were dressed in finery, attire completely suitable for a formal wedding even though there had been no indication a marriage would take place at Hollow Place.

When she was mere steps from joining Bastien at the altar, Drusilla stepped from behind one of the mirrors, a large grimoire poised in her hands. Sabine stutter-stepped but did not stop. Drusilla grinned, fangs showing, tiger's eye irises reflecting the candlelight in an eerie way—a juxtaposition that Sabine had admired on Bastien.

Despite the odious air of the Mistress, Sabine continued until her hands were clasped with Bastien's.

"Welcome all," Drusilla began, teeth too white in a grin.

Her chestnut hair was a dark fall in the night, lent a slight wine tinge from her burgundy gown. It was the first time Sabine had seen her not in white.

Drusilla's long fingers—tipped in mad black—skimmed a thick red ribbon from the middle of the exposed book. The words of said book unfamiliar in a language Sabine did not know. What she did know was the sort of ceremony about to be conducted.

Handfasting.

Bastien squeezed her hands gently, drawing her attention from their malicious officiant.

"It's you and me, vixen," Bastien murmured to her. "Don't forget that. Even if this hasn't been our choice, I still choose you."

I choose you.

I choose you.

I choose you.

I. Choose. You.

Tears welled in Sabine's eyes. No one had so blatantly and obviously stated such. They'd implied it with actions, even lied through words, but never had they been so clear as they were from Bastien. He'd said it and proved it through actions and words and kept continuing to do so.

Some of her walls came down, her guard softened, opening enough to let him in.

Sabine nodded softly and chose him too.

Sabine tuned out Drusilla, imagined the words she spoke were that of a moon goddess or deity of the night—not the vampiric mistress who'd coerced them.

Together, they vowed to make promises before all of their witnesses, never breaking eye contact from each other.

"Will you be present during the difficult times throughout every night and the challenging moments of each day?" the moon goddess asked.

"We will," Sabine and Bastien said in unison.

The unearthly officiant wrapped the red ribbon around their entwined hands with every promise.

"Will you be present during plights of sorrow and pain?"

"We will."

"Will you show honor and pay respect to each other?"

"We will."

"Will you endeavor to grow stronger within this union?"

"We will."

"And when you inevitably falter in your ways, will you remember the commitments you have made, past and previous? To maintain an open soul and vow here to never commit harm to those you promised to?" the night deity quested.

"We will," they both said, a shiver of power running through them.

"Are you now, of your own volition, willing now and always to make this commitment tonight, each and every day?"

"We are."

The cord, scarlet in color, wrapped around their hands represented their marriage, a glow of red and silver, their entwined magics glimmering on the surface of the satin.

"With this marriage, we conclude with the vows from each, the bride and groom."

A nod at Bastien urged him to begin.

"I, Bastien Emmons, vow to you, Sabine Van Arsdel that from this day and forevermore I am yours." His voice was a caress, every word suffusing her with hope and ardor. "I will cherish you, love you, and choose you, each and every day. I promise to embrace you through every struggle, kiss you better of every hurt, to wipe every tear you cry. I will always and forever be your husband, companion, friend, and lover for all of my remaining days for as long as you choose me."

Emotion was thick in Sabine's throat as she took in Bastien, truly took him in, and saw every one of his oaths he made. All the promises he would uphold to her. Continuously choosing her with every word and action. Proving to her that she was not his second choice. That she would *never* be his second choice.

"I, Sabine Van Arsdel, vow to you, Bastien Emmons that from this day and forevermore I am yours. I will cherish you, love you, and choose you, each and every day," she whispered and Bastien jumped when she said 'love' as it was the first time she'd uttered it to him. But she meant it. She knew in that moment that she loved him too. But she was still afraid. Nevertheless, she continued. "I promise to embrace you through every struggle, kiss you better of every hurt, to wipe every tear you cry. I will always and forever be your wife, companion, friend, and lover for all of my remaining days for as long as you choose me."

"With this, the bond is tied," night-moon goddess

announced. "You may now seal it with a kiss."

With their hands tied, Bastien couldn't cup her face like she knew he wanted, but she tilted her head to give him access and he kissed her deeply and ardently. A slow slide of his lips against hers met with a melding of tongues as they tasted and gently sucked. The intimacy of the kiss evoked feelings within her she'd thought she'd long buried and she couldn't deny she wanted more.

They broke their kiss and a roar of delight went up around them. Faces swam before her eyes and reality began to blur as she was struck with the gravity of the situation. She'd just gotten married—which should have been one of the happiest instances of her life—but her friend was still dead, she was still on the edge for murder, and she had no idea what the story with Veronica was.

Sabine searched the attendees for Veronica, but couldn't see her anywhere. Was she at the back? Everyone else was present.

Including Idris.

Who watched her with quiet sadness even though he clapped in celebration.

Idris who'd fancied her.

Who'd come to Hollow Place for her.

A pang struck her chest, the guilt eating her alive.

She couldn't imagine the pain he was feeling and she couldn't offer condolences or apologies without sounding vain or vapid. Any idea she had fell like sand through her fingers.

Music was struck as Bastien and Sabine made their way down the aisle, their handfasting ribbon to be taken away into a box and given to them as a keepsake. As a physical manifestation of the marriage.

Afterward, they were prompted to dance, feast, and—

well—fuck.

"Make sure it's consummated," a drunken vampire cat-called.

Whoops and wolf-whistles went up in answer, drunken, frenzied cheers fell upon the night, carrying to their ears and injecting insecurity into her bloodstream. She'd never been one to shy away from sex, but having people command it, to expect it as an obligation felt…superficial.

Regardless, after dancing and feasting, some hours later, Bastien began leading her back to their suite and she went willingly. Pulled by desire, she followed, hands clasped, hearts hammering in tandem.

In their suite, Sabine found the room sparse with new blankets on the bed, and a new canopy fastened to the posts. They were deep red and inviting. She cocked a brow at him in question.

Bastien grinned sheepishly. "I may have destroyed the suite in a rage when they wouldn't let me out to see you. I was hoping they'd be drawn by the noise, but alas, I was forced to live in squalor and under guard."

"Oh, you poor thing," she teased sarcastically. "You had to suffer in luxurious chambers while your delicate little wife languished in the woods."

Bastien wrapped an arm around her and pulled her close.

"Say it again," he whispered, voice intense.

"You poor thing," she teased, knowing what he was actually asking for.

"Not that," he growled, nuzzling her neck.

She delighted in the feeling. "Your wife."

He hummed in satisfaction. "That's right. My wife."

Sabine slid her hand down his front and cupped him between the legs, the hard ridge there unmistakable.

"My husband."

And suddenly Sabine was splayed flat on the bed.

Bastien began devouring her in earnest. Kissing her from throat to hips, not forgetting her breasts. He was untamed, tearing at her pretty gown, shredding it beneath claws, baring her for him. He had that gown in tatters, discarding the remains and hungrily watched her naked form.

The only thing left on her was the black lace garter. His finger snapped it against her thigh.

"You keep this on and nothing else, understood?"

She nodded, dazed by bliss.

He latched onto one of her nipples, laving it with his tongue. Sabine moaned and rolled her hips in searching, begging for friction as his hot mouth drove her wild. His hand went to her other breast, kneading the other nipple between his fingers, pinching and rolling it, ratcheting her up so tight she swore the barest brush against her clit would send her to the stars.

"You better bite me tonight," she said warningly.

"Where?" he asked against her heated flesh.

"Where do you want to?"

"Mm," he seemed to ponder. "Here," he said, tapping the inside of her thigh.

Fuck.

Yes.

"Yes," she vocalized.

"Such a sensitive wife."

Sabine tried rubbing her thighs together, aching for friction, embarrassingly drenched for him. She was ready to beg if she had to.

Bastien's mouth left her nipple only to train down her breast, down her abdomen, kissing a belt across her waist before descending between her thighs. He gazed up at her, silver eyes devilish and devoted before he kissed one inner thigh, then the other.

Her eyes rolled back in her head and she moaned, pussy throbbing for him.

"Bastien, husband, please," she moaned.

He was weak to her words and his mouth took her core.

She nearly screamed as he began licking her, tasting every secret place of her pussy before he sucked her clit into his mouth and she saw stars.

Bastien gave her pleasure so intense she fell into an abyss, the void swallowing her up and exploding through her in millions of constellations. She was writhing, hips undulating, hands tangled in his hair, pulling so tight on his scalp he must have felt pain. Yet, he did not stop. He kept licking and sucking as her orgasm crashed through her, shattering over and over.

And then he bit her.

Right there at the juncture of her thigh. Right where her blood thrummed. She screamed as he drank and sucked, his hands massaging her through the pleasure.

She realized distantly that he'd achieved giving her a climax so intense she was euphoric just with his mouth. If she hadn't discovered she'd loved him while speaking their vows, she would have figured it out right then.

Coming back down to Earth after her bliss, she became feral. Tearing at his clothes, shredding them like he'd done hers; he chuckled as she got him naked in record time.

Sabine began her worship of his cut form. The marble white flesh, cut with lines of muscles, his abdomen ridged beneath her lips, her fingers wrapping around the long shaft of him, pumping him—once, twice. He groaned and then she tumbled him over so she was astride him, wasting no time plunging his length inside her.

"Fuck, Sabine," he groaned in agonized bliss.

"I know," she returned, rolling her hips against him.

She found that sweet rhythm that hit exactly where she wanted, grinding her clit against his pelvis, racing for another orgasm. Sabine rode him hard into the bed, his hands gripping her hips, urging her on, her fingernails digging into his chest.

Blood smeared with her arousal, slickening her core and pace. She was so desperately wet she didn't know what was what.

Bastien's hips bucked up to meet her, sweat dampening their flesh as she chased another climax and he was climbing for his.

Soon, their rhythm became carnal. Fast and frantic. Both of them were moaning, keening, begging with each other's names. Then, within moments, they broke apart together. Their joined pleasure smashed through all barriers, careening through them like a cosmic event, a solar flare stronger than the sun, blinding white, brighter than moonlight.

Their passion was intense and it took several minutes for them to regain their bearings and breath. And when they did, they gazed at each other, starlight eyes and midnight gaze, bonded in such a new way, Sabine didn't know how to bear it.

Tears brimmed in her eyes.

"I love you," she whispered.

The light that glowed in his eyes was a supernova. Incomparable and pure. His smile was heartbreakingly joyous.

"I love you, too," he whispered.

She bit her lip and then kissed him until dawn broke.

OCTOBER 20, 1867

Bastien woke with a hand over his mouth and it wasn't his wife's.

His eyes flared and icy awareness shot through him, suddenly wide awake and having no idea of the time. The only thing that stopped him from lashing out and clawing out the eyes of his attacker was the vampire leaning over the opposite side of the bed, knife to his new wife's throat, an empty syringe in her arm.

"Make a fuss and she dies," Reynard said lethally calm, aqua eyes hard.

Bastien gritted his teeth, swallowed, then very

carefully nodded. Reynard released his mouth, but did not yield on the grip he had on Bastien's chest. He turned to Sabine's attacker and pleaded with his eyes.

So soft he almost didn't hear it himself, he whispered. "Don't. *Please.*"

"Come with us quietly and you'll have nothing to worry about," Veronica said placidly.

Bastien swallowed and nodded.

Slowly he got out of the bed, sliding from beneath the silken sheets and quickly bending down to put on his trousers from the floor. Once somewhat decent he stood, buttoning the fly, and glaring hatred at Reynard and Veronica.

The two just smiled back politely.

Evidently, the nightly sigils Sabine insisted upon had done fuck all.

Grabbing a dark red button-up from the back of a chair and a discarded pair of boots, Bastien followed them out of the room. The hallways were dim, the curtains drawn against the uncertain daylight, candles flickering against the wall. Bastien walked, led down a flight of stairs where he soon realized he was heading to Drusilla's favored solarium.

Irritation brimmed along his shoulders, tension running through him in a poisonous cloud.

"So, you two really have become Drusilla's little lapdogs, hmm?" Bastien quested nastily.

"Always have been," Veronica tossed offhandedly.

"I'm assuming you're proficient with illusions?" Bastien guessed.

"Memory spells," she said instead.

Shock lit through him.

Memory spells had long been outlawed due to their unethical nature and all traces of them had been destroyed or under heavy guard, access only allowed for scholarly purposes and government assets. Even then, the highest echelon of them required severe reasonings for their access.

Warlocks were more likely to decimate their own memories than do any erasing of anyone else's. The results were often catastrophic and more than one unfortunate soul was committed to a sanitorium due to severe loss of cognitive function.

So, not only illegal, but dangerous.

And evidently Veronica was skilled in them.

Had she ever used them on him? A souring in his stomach told him he knew the answer, he just wouldn't like it.

"How? No one has taught memory spells in hundreds of years and even then, that knowledge was closely guarded."

Veronica gave him a droll look. "You really don't know how old Drusilla is, do you?"

Sudden unease wound through him like a sickly serpent. He was suddenly very sure he didn't know.

Veroncia let out a witchy cackle. "Even if she wasn't four-hundred years old, do you think a little legality would stop her from learning whichever magics she wanted? Hell, that's how she came to be infected with Midnight Malady and pursued some sort of treatment, if not a cure."

"Drusilla is a scholar?"

Veronica paused and looked at him quizzically. "You don't know her at all."

Bastien seemed to have to agree.

He did not know the Mistress.

Not at all.

In Drusilla's solarium she was in her predictable white, swathed in long sleeves with some elaborate ties around the neck. Her hat was a wide brimmed thing, angled jauntily over her brow. In her true fashion, she had burgundy lipstick, smears of it over the brim of her floral teacup.

When Bastien stood before her, she smiled primly.

"How was the wedding day?" she asked conversationally.

Bastien glanced blandly out the window, estimating the evening. "I think it's still my wedding day."

"So, it is."

"Why am I here, Drusilla? Why was I woken with my wife's life threatened?"

The two vampires flanking him didn't flinch at his description.

"Ah," she said, as if enlightened. She took a sip of tea. "Yes, I just thought I'd remind you that since your marriage is surely consummated—" Drusilla cocked a brow but Bastien remained silent. "That all your vows are in effect."

"Yes, I am aware."

"Including those to me."

Anxiety shot through him, a steady hum like his blood, ringing in his ears.

"What do you mean?"

"Aha!" Her voice was delighted. "I thought you would have figured it out, but perhaps I really was too clever." Drusilla cleared her throat. "'*And when you inevitably falter in your ways, will you remember the commitments you have made, past and previous? To maintain an open soul and vow here to never commit harm to those you promised to?*' Does that ring any bells?"

"Sabine never made any commitments to you," he hissed.

"But *you* did. And since you two are now bonded, any commitments you made, she is now tied to. Reaffirmed by last night's vows." She sipped more tea placidly. "Which means neither of you can kill me." She cocked her head to the side playfully, her chestnut waves cascading to the wayside.

Regret and rage suffused him. He had been duped. He had played right into her hand and now he was at her mercy. And it was all his fault Sabine was now too.

He wanted to tear apart the pretty room with the checkerboard tile and floor to ceiling curtains. He wanted to rip the monstera plants from their pots and shred the plum velvet of the couch. All he saw was red and all he wanted was destruction.

"What was your plan, anyway?" Drusilla asked, leaning forward, elbows on knees. "Because once I'm dead that bond is gone and your bloodlust returns."

"I have a treatment plan," he gritted out.

"Oh, do you?" she said in mock astonishment. "Well, I'd love to hear what you've learned. Or does it only include that marvelous self-restraint you cherish?"

Bastien remained silent.

"That's what I thought. Toodle-oo, Mister Emmons."

He was dismissed without further direction and he strode from the Mistress's favorite room, Reynard and Veronica following in his wake. He wanted to claw the eyes out of both of them.

Reynard and Veronica stayed in pursuit of Bastien until he turned on his heel and snapped at them.

"Not only are you her lap dogs, but now her guard dogs, too? Piss off for half a fucking second. I can't go very far on this Hell-forsaken island."

In a huff, he stalked off and made his way to one of the notoriously empty ballrooms, and as expected, he found Salem there with his classic cigarillo.

"We have a fucking problem," Bastien began, anger coating his words as he crossed to Salem.

"Uh oh," Salem replied as Bastien plucked the cigarillo from his friend, took a drag, and handed it back.

Bastien savored the headrush that gave him a brief respite from the wrath he was feeling. It was his demon's-damned wedding day and Drusilla was pulling this shit? He had just married the woman he loved and the mistress was ten steps ahead of them.

"When the time comes, I need you to kill Drusilla."

"Why would I do that when that would make me mad?"

"I have a solution for that."

Salem took a slow drag of his cigarillo, dark brow raised, deep brown eyes clear. "Well, this is a new development. Why not you?"

"My lovely little marriage last night?"

"Mmhmm?"

"A ruse. The entire thing a trick. Every word I said bound Sabine to Drusilla because of my blood bond. So now she can't harm her."

"You did what?"

The small voice from the entry way was broken. Like a heart cracked in half.

Bastien turned in horror and found his new wife standing in the doorway, hand on the frame as if to keep herself from falling. Devastation wrought clear lines across her face, and the way her lips were parted he could see her breaths coming faster, restrained by the red corset she wore over the black slip dress.

Oh, fuck.

He processed the words he said. The ones she probably heard.

Oh, fuck.

He realized exactly how it sounded.

Oh, fuck, fuck, fuck, fuck, fuck.

Sabine, tears welling in her eyes, dashed out into the

twilight. She was on the grass, racing for the woods and suddenly Bastien knew with absolute certainty that she was going back to the mad vampires no matter what it cost her.

Because in her head, the madness was better than betrayal.

Fuck.

The vampires had taken an affinity to her so if she managed to get to the amphitheater, he'd have lost her to them. He'd be no match for multitudes of mad infected. If she got to them, she would no longer be his wife—she would swear vengeance on him based on a miscommunication.

He ran.

OCTOBER 20, 1867

Within moments the sky opened up and rain sluiced against Sabine's skin. Icy droplets burned against her heated flesh, but couldn't compare to the soul deep numbness that was her heart. Physically she felt, emotionally she was broken.

She'd opened herself up to him. Tentatively given her heart.

Stupid, stupid, stupid.

And then he turned around, took her heart, and

crushed it.

Sabine gritted her teeth as she raced into the night, spinning a sigil in her hand to add for speed. She was desperate and wild, not thinking logically, but she didn't care.

When she'd woken, it was because in slumber she'd been haunted by Nicholas—as he had been wont to do the last several nights—but suddenly, they both evaporated without her trying to. Instead of dreaming, she was in a void of nothingness.

And then she woke.

Groggy.

Stiff.

Pain in her arm.

Pain that was accompanied by a red mark. A needle mark.

She had gotten up in haste, examined her body in the mirror, but the only marks she could determine were old scars, the previous bites from Bastien—including last night's—and a small, thin, line on her neck. She touched it gingerly.

Had someone held a knife to her throat while she was asleep? While she was drugged?

Confused, she had dressed and gone in search of Bastien. Which was when she'd overheard him talking to Salem.

"My lovely little marriage last night?"

"Mmhmm?"

"A ruse. The entire thing a trick. Every word I said bound Sabine to Drusilla because of my blood bond. So now she can't harm her."

It had all been a trick. To use her. To gain her trust and sympathies and then hand her over to Drusilla like a prize boar. She was, again, as she'd thought, a cow to slaughter.

And just like before, she was running. This time, she

knew what the woods held and she knew that Irving, Esther, and Washington, though insane, would side with her. Who had proven they were stalwartly against Drusilla. Something she was not confident about with her husband.

Oh, Hell.

Her *husband.*

Fuck, she was *married* to him.

Regardless of her marriage, she ran, rain dripping down her long tresses, leaking into her eyes. She was running from her heartbreak, her lungs suffused with autumn earth air that couldn't seem to fill them.

"Sabine, you misheard! Please listen to me!"

Bastien was shouting behind her but she didn't spare him a moment. But she also couldn't bring herself to cast at him either, especially since he hadn't thrown a single spell her way yet, either. She didn't want to admit to herself what that meant.

Sabine was fast, but she was faster with her spellwork. Bastien was faster. She cursed out into the night as he gained on her, and once again, like before, like déjà vu, he caught up to her at the wrought iron fence before the forest.

He caught her around the waist, crashing against the iron bars. She didn't have the energy to fight him. She didn't have the energy to cry. She just stared at him through the rain.

"Was that all I was good for? Hmm? A ruse? And then you'd have your fun and cut me loose? What was it all for, Bastien? Huh!?" She was spiraling, utterly fucking spiraling. "I warned you on the way here. I warned you if you killed me—and I don't care how indirectly—I would use that rage and turn into a demon so vicious it would make Nicholas look pathetic."

"It wasn't a ruse!"

"Lies! I heard you talking to Salem. I found the needle

mark in my arm. You had me incapacitated so you could—what? Collect your loyalists and commit to Drusilla once again? Offer me up as an appetizer?"

"I didn't know how the vows work! I had only just found out and I was ranting to Salem about it."

"A convenient tale."

"The truth, Sabine."

Sabine rolled her eyes but couldn't do much else as he had her wrists locked in the manacles of his hands. Even so, she didn't know what she'd do. Not knee him in the groin—not if she could avoid it.

A tear slid down her cheek. "I can't trust you." She inhaled sharply. "Maybe I'm too broken. Used too many times over. Did I ever tell you about me and Benedict?"

Bastien's brows knitted. "Your professor friend's husband?"

Sabine let out a mirthless laugh. "Yes, that is the one. He was my lover first. It was brief, casual, purely physical on the romantic scale. He was virtually a hermit-scholar who'd never been with a woman—understood enough from anatomy texts, but that was all. I'd been through a rash of failed suitors and was ready to swear off males at all until we decided to come to this agreement so he could learn and I could be find pleasure and be respected. Which could be ended whenever, by whomever."

"Who ended it?" he asked softly.

"He did. The moment he met Lucia. It was like magic. I saw it happen. I knew in that moment our education was done. And I was fine with it. He wasn't my beau. I didn't love him like that." Sabine rolled her lips in pain and frustration. "But then Nicholas did worse. Used me to get to her. Attempted so much malevolence and destruction in the name of his twisted love for Lucia. But it wasn't love, it was obsession. Control.

"And again, I was pushed to the wayside. Second-best. Second choice. Just like now, I am second to your Drusilla."

"That's not true—I am trying to end her. She is *not* my Drusilla. That's what I was telling Salem."

"It matters not. I am too far beyond repair. Or maybe it's just that you're not trustworthy."

"You can trust me," Bastien pleaded. His eyes were so open and earnest it was almost enough to trip her up.

"Can I?" she queried. "You admitted you initially brought me as a ticket here—perhaps you lied when you said you changed your mind." She bared her teeth. "Maybe you did all this because you're secretly in love with Drusilla."

Rage entered his silver eyes.

"Does this feel like I'm in love with Drusilla?" he asked.

And striking out like a snake, he kissed her.

Deep.

Hard.

He tilted her mouth to meet his, plunging his desire into her as his tongue slid between her lips. She couldn't help the moan of pleasure that slipped out of her.

Sabine met his kiss with the same hungry passion, but just as quickly, tore her mouth away.

"You're proficient in artifice."

"That is not what this is."

"Yet you do not deny it."

"I don't. You know I am. How do you think I survived those early years with the Malady, Sabine?" Pain screwed up his face. "I was mad each and every night, driven to basic instincts and hallucinations, bloodthirsty cravings, and nothing in my mind made sense. I was worse than what Irving and Esther are now. It is why I know you're still not safe there no matter how you may be angry at me. They try, but it is not always enough. I dedicated myself to the restraint, but before that, I learned how to charm by day, to do what I needed. It was self-preservation, love," he said. "Much like you shutting me out is."

"Do not psychoanalyze me, Bastien Emmons."

"I can't not. For I know you, Sabine Emmons, soul deep and heart full. I made my promises to you—not her—and whatever games she played were of her own independence. I am yours. You are the only one I've ever been true with. Yes, it began with deception, but every moment here with you has been verity."

Sabine's mouth parted and something within her split down the middle. She didn't know how to close the fissure that was swallowing her whole so she did the only thing that could tether her to reality.

Her mouth slammed into his, vicious and hungry. Her hands were still bound by his so she rolled her hips, seeking him, begging with her body what words she could not summon.

Bastien's body answered hers. His kiss was heady, intoxicating, utterly lifesaving. He released her hands only to shuck up her dress. He groaned when he found the garter on her thigh he'd insisted she keep on last night, and nothing else.

Now freed, her hands tangled in his hair, wrapping around his neck. Bastien hitched her thighs around his hips, pressing her soaked core against him. Her back was suddenly against the fence, wet and slick with rain. One-handed, Bastien went for his buckle and pulled out his cock.

Before either of them could think, he was inside her, fucking her ruthlessly against the iron. Her ankles locked around the small of his back as he rammed into her over and over in a feral claiming.

She was kissing him, pulling his lips between her teeth while her pussy quivered around his thick length. He was driving deep within her, every thrust came with an upward roll of his hips, so divine as it ground against her clit. Her climax was close, careening off a cliff. As it hit, it consumed her, her whole vision sparkling with bliss. Sabine screamed as her core clenched around him and with a few more thrusts he came too, each pulse of his orgasm spilling into her—possessing her.

Sabine panted as her climax dissipated, her forehead knocked against Bastien, both of them out of breath.

After a few moments, he slipped from her and they disentangled. She righted her dress and he tucked himself away, and as she did, she realized she'd become grounded through the process.

But with it came clarity.

With his body he'd settled her.

With his mind he'd hurt her.

She loved him, but it was too dangerous to trust him. And she couldn't trust him. He'd tricked and lied and schemed all his vampiric life. She couldn't believe he'd changed just for her.

She knew what had to be said.

"We are married only on paper, and whatever transpires between us is purely physical."

Bastien stilled. Frozen in the rain. "What are you saying? Are you saying—?"

"I am saying," she interrupted. "That our marriage is a proxy, but we may use each other's bodies. That is all."

"But…I love you."

Sabine looked at him sadly, her own heart breaking.

"I wish that were enough."

And then she walked away in the pouring rain, each step taking her closer to the Hell-forsaken manor.

OCTOBER 20, 1867

Still drenched from the deluge, Bastien rejoined Salem after Sabine requested time alone. He was desolate, walking on thin ice, and desperate to repair the damage that he'd done— that his previous character had solidified.

Sabine was so scarred from the past and he kept hurting her with doubts. She was so on edge that the slightest confirmation of her terrors had her believing her self-worth was minimal. But she was wrong. She was so much more.

But he hated himself for making her feel that way.

That he'd added to this damage.

Boots squelching across the black and white floor, Bastien found Salem where he'd left him, smoking a new cigarillo. Salem looked him up and down impassively, only raising a single midnight brow and releasing a cloud of smoke as a reaction.

"Well, I presume that did not go over smoothly."

Bastien glared at him.

Salem appeared chagrined.

"Sorry, mate. Want to tell me about it?"

"No," Bastien responded, flopping onto a seat and snagging a decanter of brandy from the bar cart. He took a generous swig. He spoke roughly as it burned. "In fact, I want nothing more than to never talk about it and destroy Drusilla once and for all."

"You do realize if she dies, the blood bond is gone and we go back to nightly insanity?"

"We don't know that for sure."

"That's the plausible reaction and risking any other consequence is selfish."

"I *am* selfish."

Salem assessed him. "But not stupid." Dawning realization hit him. "Who are you planning to bond us all to?"

Bastien drank again.

"Me."

"But the corruption…"

"I will not be the tyrant she is. I will not demand tithes or control. I will not have a fucking sacrificial island. I will seek new treatments and pursue a cure. Already Ember Fever and the Wasting have been cured, Midnight Malady is next."

"Until demons create a new disease and efforts go to that instead."

"That is a possibility, but again—the cures were just found recently—surely our cure is imminent."

"You have a lot of trust in this," Salem said slowly, as if staving off his own emotions.

"Hope is a finite thing, but so are our lives. If hope is what takes me out, so be it. But I will no longer be at the Mistress's mercy. It ends now."

"What do you want me to do?"

"Who have you gathered against Drusilla's loyalists?"

"Kaldette, the twins, Alice, Quinton, Claude, and everyone else you know about."

"We can add Irving, Esther, and Washington to that list. They're partial to Sabine and want Drusilla dead."

"And when are we going to act?"

Bastien thought for a moment, organizing the plans he'd secretly concocted over the years of visiting Hollow Place, the maps and schematics he'd acquired. The weaknesses and follies he'd discovered. The new issues regarding the hallowed ground. All calculated into a few mental lists.

"In four days."

Salem's brows rose. "That soon?"

"The stay at Hollow Place is only partway through November and Sabine is nearly free of her curse. Acting quickly will give us the greatest chance of avoiding betrayal."

"And you're certain you want to do this? Take on the corruption of your soul?"

"I have immaculate willpower."

Salem didn't say anything, but with his distinctly dark eyes, he watched and put together what Bastien didn't say. He clapped him on the shoulder, thanks and sorrows in his eyes.

"There's no one better I'd trust to have my lifeforce bound to."

Bastien swallowed the emotion and nodded.

"Meet me here at midnight and we'll discuss further."

And then, with another clap on the shoulder, he left, off to find the others and start putting plans into action.

In the absence of Sabine's welcomeness, Bastien made himself busy by putting together his coup. Kaldette and Quinton, fond of pyromania were part of a contingency plan, but ensured they knew if their steps needed to take effect.

For the original plan, he encountered Hoult and Renfield, both haughty fools, but fiercely independent—having been chafing under the Mistress's restraint for years. The allure of a blood bond without the dedication was enough to draw them into the fray. They were to barricade exits when the loyalists attempted to flee. All the others committed to their cause were directed to apprehend and fight whomever thwarted them.

All of them understood the risks.

All of them accepted them.

Meanwhile, Sabine remained cold and curt to Bastien.

Midnight came too soon and then Bastien gathered all the vampires and went over the plan in full detail, committing them all to secrecy and treason for a new future.

OCTOBER 23, 1867

Drusilla was hosting a heinous event in the woods. A gladiator-style battle royale, mad vampires fighting till first blood or death—depending on which the crowd dictated. The winner received fresh blood and a scrap of sanity.

It was inhumane.

Agatha had arrived in her suite with a black velvet box tied with a matching satin ribbon. Nothing said but a nod and when she left, Sabine discovered a gown and a mask.

It was of a rabbit's face. The ears rose up like horns,

the cheeks curving over her lips. It was dark brown and macabre, holding a sinister air. She'd heard of cursed objects, and even though this one fit the bill, it wasn't one.

Probably.

Nervously, she stripped out of her leather leggings and creamy blouse. For someone who loathed dresses, she had been wearing many as of late.

Dressing in the quiet suite, Sabine had more than enough time for self-reflection. And with that, self-loathing. She had let herself be duped again, and this time deeper. For that, it hurt greater.

Sighing, she pulled on the gray-violet gown, the cap sleeves draping over her upper arms, the sweetheart neckline accentuating her generous chest. Her hair was left deep red and unbound, while the mask was fastened over her face. The material was oddly sculpted to perfectly mold over her cheekbones and nose—as if it had been specifically made for her.

That fact unsettled her.

Bastien had left her alone, as per her request, and even though she'd asked, she still felt the loneliness soul deep. Not to mention pure exhaustion. Nicholas was still haunting her dreams, tormenting her. The most recent one featured illusions of their previous dalliances that turned her murderous with rage.

A knock at the door disturbed her just as she was applying a lip cream. When opened it, sigil ready, she lowered it when she saw Bastien standing there.

"A rabbit?" he asked simply.

"Not my first choice."

"Neither was mine," he replied, lifting the mask that dangled from his finger.

It was that of a wolf, silver so bright it was painful. Its

lips were peeled back in a snarl; eyes narrowed over a heavy brow. The ears, like hers, peaked up in sharp little horns, but unlike hers, appeared truly sharp.

The symbolism was not lost on her.

Fuck, Drusilla had a sick sense of humor.

Gingerly, Bastien offered his elbow. "Ready to go?"

Attendance was mandatory.

"I am."

Not speaking, they left the room and made their way through the forest. In anticipation for the event, warlocks had carved a path glowing with numerous sigils, cocooning around them like a tunnel of prisms. Light shone in variegated colors in a direct path to the amphitheater, flittering with everything from protection, to deflection, to wards. When they arrived at the stone stage the wards continued in a bubble above and around the arena, anyone not pre-screened to enter would have no success in infiltrating it.

Reynard, masked as a red fox, honey-brown curls falling foppishly over the edge, greeted them with a slimy smile. The irony was not lost on her, what with the legends of Reynard the Fox—trickster and hero. Clearly delusional. A non-reality-based sense of self.

Sabine bit her lip and tried her damnedest to not roll her eyes. She was not certain she succeeded.

"Welcome to tonight's exclusive event," Reynard leered. "You two have special guest seats in the box with the Mistress."

Because of course they did.

"Such an honor," Sabine said dryly.

"Yes," Reynard bit out, sickly sweet. "It is."

Fear skittered down Sabine's spine but didn't let it show.

With a nod from Bastien, the two of them found their

seats beneath the midnight. The special guest box was a temporary construction, gauzy black curtains festooned over a pergola with five cushioned chairs under armed guard.

It was mere yards from her cell.

Drusilla was sitting in the centermost one, garbed in a white shift, like that of the Romans, a black and white tiger's mask over her tiger's eyes. Half of her dark hair was wound up in small knots, like that of a jungle cat's ears, the rest falling loose and braided, rings coiled into the plaits.

Beside her on the right was an empty spot—presumably for Reynard, and beside that was Veronica, her mask that of a golden eagle, her gown similarly shaded with diamonds applied carefully over her bodice. To the left of Drusilla was two empty spots.

Theirs.

Carefully, they made their way to their predetermined spots, sitting delicately upon the plush cushions. Immediately, servers in plain domino masks swooped in with trays of drink. Sabine tentatively selected a clear flute. Bastien took a red one.

"Thank you for the honor of sitting in your presence," Sabine said through tight teeth. "It is unprecedented."

"But no doubt appreciated, hm?" Drusilla returned.

"I just said that," Sabine bit out.

Drusilla's head snapped toward her both in shock and anger. Sabine just met her eyes emotionlessly. Cocking a brow, the mistress slowly turned to the stadium below where an announcer—whose voice she did not recognize—was calling attention for the first fight.

Torches formed a ring around the stands, the fire dancing with sigils. It was the only form of brightness against the opaque night, no moonlight to be found. It was ominous, oppressive, and gloomy. So much stilled beneath the wards, sounds of birds and bats blocked so that the absence of sound made the entire scene eerie and wrong.

Sabine held her breath as the first names were called—like an appetizer—as Reynard took his seat next to Drusilla, chatting with her companionably.

"Tonight, we begin with our first champion, Lestat!"

A tall, sandy haired mad vampire strode onto the stone, dressed in tan leathers and a white piratic blouse. His eyes chased every small movement, taking in everything like a predator. He circled the announcer whom was encased in a ward of russet light, impenetrable against attack.

"And our second champion, Irving!"

Sabine's stomach dropped from under her.

While not her favorite and most trusted vampire, she'd known him and he had taken her side, fought to free her from her cell and the woods.

Sickness roiled in her gut, fear mixing with anxiety. Her fingers curled over the arms of her chair, trying to dig into the wood, to peel splinters between her nails. The world narrowed beneath the mask, her breaths tight.

"I'm here," Bastien whispered, taking her hand. He squeezed it. "I'm here."

Sabine nodded, at a loss for words and desperate for comfort in that moment. It didn't matter that she had horrifically mixed feelings about him right now, she needed him.

Taking comfort in Bastien's touch, she waited for the fight to commence.

And commence it did.

Irving lunged at Lestat, feral black claws out, fangs bared. Lestat took Irving by the waist, slamming him to the stone. Irving's skull cracked against the ground with a reverberation that shook the arena. Sabine's heart stuttered, but Irving got up and threw a punch.

The fight continued with tackles, claws, and punches, but when blades were thrown into the ring, it all escalated. They both took up two, wielding them like extensions of their bodies, swiping faster than her eyes could track.

A chill breeze crested over the stands, fluttering the curtains. Gooseflesh erupted over her exposed skin and she shivered from cold and fear.

Roars of fury echoed below, the sounds animalistic—raw. Clashes and the singing of metal on metal lit up the sky. It was all high tension, adrenaline-fueled, insanity.

It was a performance, and it was sick.

After a few more grueling moments, Irving was crowned the victor with Lestat groaning on the ground, holding a half-severed arm.

The crowd had begged for mercy and relief seemed to glow in his eyes. It seemed despite the madness he really didn't want to take a life.

The next fight sent fear down her spine just as bad as the first, for it was Esther and an unknown vampire with terrifying eyes. They were the sort of pure evil only reserved for the worst demons in existence. There was nothing more vile.

Sabine squeezed Bastien's hand harder.

Esther was vicious.

She didn't hold back, tearing the vampire limb from limb, fangs covered in blood by the end, her maddeningly sharp ears spattered just as much as her black-tipped fingers.

Esther was crowned winner when her evil opponent was declared dead.

The body was dragged out and Esther was escorted through a doorway. Shock flooded through Sabine. If Esther was capable of that…

She was suddenly very grateful Esther had decided to side with her.

Fights increased in ferocity, and then a true battle royale began. Ten vampires tossed in together; one left to survive.

Washington was amongst these.

Nerves were shattered as crows of delight went up around her. Sabine felt nauseous. A sheen of sweat beaded on her brow, the mask claustrophobic and hot. Despite the chill of the autumn air, she was overheating. Suffocating. Her breaths came quickly.

Bastien was there, though. "I'm here. I'm here."

He said nothing more than that, and she wasn't sure if anything more than that would be helpful. Because what could he do? He was as much a prisoner here as she was. Perhaps she was more so, but by how much more?

She realized with that thought process she was opening up sympathies that she couldn't afford. Shaking her head free of it all, she paid attention to the battle again.

And wished she hadn't.

She tuned in just in time to see a vampire tear Washington's heart from his chest, the mad vampire faltering while blood poured from his mouth. A pang of grief struck her, horrified as Washington's body hit the ground with a lifeless thud. His eyes were wide and unstaring.

Blank.

Gone.

Sabine swallowed her gorge and pressed her lips together to keep from letting out a small sob.

He hadn't been a dear friend, but he'd saved her life. And she hadn't been able to repay that debt. For all he was, there was a kindness to him, and it had been ruthlessly snuffed out.

"I can't watch this anymore," she whispered, thankful she'd gotten the edge seat, at least one spot removed from the mistress.

"You must," Bastien returned softly. "I'm so sorry."

She knew he was right, but it still stung.

For the rest of the event, she slipped into her mind, constructing a safe haven there. One that was filled with oil paints and blank canvases. Fuck, she'd missed her art. She imagined the strokes of the abandoned church Winnie lived in, the spires that soared into the sky. She pictured the palette in shades of warm gray and orange, hit with a sunset as bright as a flame.

It was peace.

It was not this war.

Eventually, the monstrous spectacle ended and they were allowed to leave. Sabine stood as quickly as she could, eager to escape. With Bastien in tow, they made for the exit, just in time to see bodies being carted out.

Including a decomposing corpse that was undoubtedly Idris.

Sabine let out a sob of despair, the sound harsh in the night. She put a hand to her mouth, trying to muffle the cries that begged to be released.

How? When?

It was her fault. All her fault.

His face was bloated and gray, limbs stiff. Bugs fawned over him, digging at his unseeing gray-aqua eyes. His mouth was filled with maggots like too many teeth.

This time, Sabine couldn't contain it and all the contents of her stomach came spewing up to the forest floor. She heaved and heaved until there was nothing left, her throat burning from acid, her eyes swimming with tears.

There was no doubt in her mind that this wasn't an

accident. Drusilla had predetermined this. Organized this sight.

Rage turned incandescent within her and she vowed to do whatever possible to kill her.

OCTOBER 25, 1867

Bastien woke, thrashing as hands grabbed him. They had his arms and legs, another set around his throat, a third—fourth?—hauling him bodily by his torso.

He was carried from the room, gagged by cloth and magic, watching in terror as he was torn from Sabine's sleeping form. Her back was to him, protecting herself, curled inward from the pain. Guilt struck him as he tried to fight free of the hold, all to no avail.

Dragged from the room, his last vision of his slumbering wife was Veronica leaning over her.

He screamed, but there was no sound.

His heart broke as the door slammed, the resounding bang an accompaniment to his split organ. He was wailing into nothingness; nothing could get past his muffled state. So, fueled by rage, he fought harder. He freed a leg and managed to kick the face of one of his kidnappers and a masculine curse lit the dark hallway.

Someone cracked the butt of a knife against his temple and temporarily his vision blacked as pain streaked across his brain. Every throb of his pulse was an anvil's hammer to his skull, the new headache a thief to his resistance.

When the night air struck his face, he knew instantly where they were taking him. Knew that it was among the mad. Just like the fights the other night, he was doomed to his fate.

Suddenly, it all felt futile.

Suddenly, it all felt meaningless.

But then, a spark.

Sabine.

His wife.

She needed him. He needed her back. He needed her to trust him. She needed to know that she was wanted. That she was his first choice—his only choice. He needed her more than he needed air.

Invigored, he remained placid and bided his time, waiting for the face he prayed he could trust in the forest.

The canopy of leaves crossed over them, obscuring the moon and stars, adding a glom that unsettled. That made everything feel damper and more compressed. Like a hand of a giant, slowly closing in. Every sound echoed, every step thundered. Night creatures were hellish beasts. Simple whispers were murmurs of the dead. It was all too eerie and those who carried Bastien reacted to it.

Before long, they arrived at the crumbling mausoleum surrounded by wine red roses and ichor black brambles, the thorns thick and sharp. They were stark against the bleached white stone, made even more striking by the recent rainfall.

There, on the mausoleum's steps was Drusilla.

She looked vindicated.

Bastien hated her.

Her fascinator was a gothic medley of feathers and roses and lace over her brow, made more morbid by the raven skull and ribs sewn into it. She tipped her head back, a move in power, and stepped closer, Reynard at her heels.

"There are words on the wind, Mister Emmons."

His kidnappers dumped him on the ground and removed his vocal bindings. He stood, brushed himself off, and tried to maintain as much composure as he could.

"Well, we are in the Mad Woods, it would be odd if we didn't hear whispers on the wind."

"You are far too witty to be serious. And unfortunately, enough, do not have the cleverness to match." Drusilla sneered. "You have been staging a coup against me."

"Have I?" he asked innocently, stalling for time.

"Your little rebellions must come to an end. Why do you fight me so? Why not submit? Be mine in all ways. You will be welcome to all I can offer."

Bastien's lip curled back from his teeth. "I will never spend a moment in your embrace. You are repulsive to my very bones. I despise you. I dream of sowing your bones on the shores of this damned island, watching the void of the sea take you once and for all."

Drusilla scoffed and clapped. "Macabre and theatrical. My, what love has done for your spine."

Bastien just seethed silently.

"It's a shame," she sighed, descending further from the

steps. "We could have had glory, but instead you squandered my gifts for a little whore."

"Do *not*," he hissed. "Call my wife that."

Drusilla was mock affronted, offering an affected air. "But is that not what she is? Is she not the harlot that dabbled in casual dalliances? Who has a spurned former lover? That spread her legs for whomever would have her and it wasn't enough?"

"Shut up."

Fury was incandescent in his veins.

"Seems I struck a nerve. Is that because that floosy was getting beneath young Idris before he met his untimely end?"

"I said shut up! Shut up!"

Drusilla grinned maniacally. Her teeth were too white, fingertips too black, ears too pointed. The madness was creeping in. She had to form another blood bond to stave it off. Otherwise, she'd succumb to Midnight Malady and take them all with her.

"I wonder how she'll feel when I tell her you'd taken someone to bed. In your grief and loneliness, just needing some contact to feel…" She smiled brighter. "Well, I'm sure she wouldn't act accordingly, especially when I threw charming and adoring suitors after her. She prefers only the male form, yes?"

Bastien suddenly realized what she was going to do.

She'd created a wedge between him and Sabine. Hoping such pain and resentment would drive her to push him away. To pursue another. So that he could fall to jealousy and heartbreak. So that Drusilla could be there to comfort him. To take him in her arms. To bed.

And then she'd turn Sabine into a vampire as her next blood bond and force her into the eternal struggle he was desperate to be rid of.

And he'd made her job ten times easier by breaking Sabine first.

"Don't you dare touch her!"

Drusilla cackled. "Oh, it's far too late for that." She approached him carelessly, heedless of the sigil he'd unconsciously summoned. "I'm sure she'll take to her new life just fine."

Then, to add insult to injury, she patted him on the cheek.

"In the meantime…let the bloodletting begin."

And then his veins were opened and his blood spilled to the forest floor.

OCTOBER 25, 1867

The grogginess Sabine had woken with was alarmingly—and unwillingly—familiar. She woke slowly, clearing the cobwebs from her psyche as she became aware of the rapid knocking on her door. She came to a bit further, putting a hand to her head peering blearily out from behind the canopy of her bed.

Wakefulness grew and with it the realization that the knocking was rather pounding.

Stumbling out of bed, Sabine got her bearings and

made her way to the door. It was when she opened it and came face to face with the sight of Salem's panicked face that Sabine realized she'd woken and Bastien was not there.

"Where is he?" she demanded, suddenly lucid.

"Drusilla took him," he said lowly, stepping into the room.

She shut the door behind him, adrenaline battling against whatever sedative she'd been given. When she checked her arm, sure enough, there it was again—the red mark. A needle's evidence.

Fuck.

"Do you know what she's going to do to him?"

She didn't ask what she'd already done, because frankly, she was too scared to know.

"My best guess is her favorite torture," Salem told her solemnly. "Draining him of blood and depriving him of more. It's almost a certainty to trigger complete and permanent insanity. It's what she's done to most of those locked in the woods."

Sabine's stomach dropped.

Not to Bastien.

Not to her Bastien.

"There's a ship booked for passage, but it'll only linger an hour after dawn before departing."

Springing into action Sabine tugged on a crimson coat over the blouse and leggings she'd gone to sleep in, donned a belt with blades and holy water, laced up thigh-high boots, and tied her hair up in an uncharacteristic knot.

"What are you doing?" Salem queried.

"Going after my husband, what does it look like I'm doing?" Sabine slid a long blade into her boot for good measure and strode out the door. "Are you coming?"

Salem didn't hesitate. He immediately jumped into

action, leading Sabine out the door. What she hadn't realized upon her drugged waking was that Salem was already similarly outfitted. Around his waist were vials of holy water, and a spellbook hanging from a chain and about his torso was a bandolier full of knives.

She realized if she'd have said no, Salem was going to get him anyway.

A rush or gratefulness went through her. Despite it all, she was glad Bastien had a friend who dared to go after him. It reminded her all too much of how she and Lucia had once set off to rescue her husband and how Nicholas had pursued them.

With that reminder, she readied a cutting sigil, prepped for battle like she had once—thankful it wasn't through a blizzard this time.

"Why do you have holy water?" Sabine asked as they travelled through the manor. "I meant to ask—since this island is supposed to be hallowed."

"I knew the blessings on the land were failing and my theory was demon attacks would start becoming an issue. Just in case, I brought a trunk full of bottled holy water." He paused, seeing her vials. "Why did you?"

"I've learned demon attacks come at the most inopportune times and never leave anywhere without them."

"Fair enough."

Descending the outside steps, Sabine had an eerie feeling. They hadn't seen anyone in the manor upon their exit. There were dozens staying at Hollow Place, yet they hadn't encountered a single one.

Dread crawled up her spine.

"Where is—?"

A sudden scream rent the night with an accompanying roar.

Sabine and Salem shared a look before tearing off to the shore.

There, demons were crawling from the edge of the ocean, Hellfire gates demarking the shore. All the warlocks were on the beach already battling it out with demons coming from a separate gate, nearer to the woods.

Sparks jumped from the gates as demons poured from them, summoning infernal runes and hellhounds. Claws ripped through the sand and wings beat deafeningly against the wind. A bonfire lay trampled from battle, warlocks on fire fought against demons of fire. In the night, clashes of blades were blinding against the firelight, slashes of silver and embers of orange fought through the gloom.

Guilt warred in Sabine as her thoughts told her this was the perfect distraction to slip into the woods unnoticed. But at the same time, she was leaving everyone to fend for themselves when she knew she could do something. She hesitated, but fortunately, the decision was made for her because the hallowed land had disintegrated right at the steps surrounding the hill of Hollow Place and followed the line to the woods.

They couldn't make it to the forest without being sighted and chased. Especially if a hellhound caught the scent.

Sabine and Salem joined the fray, cutting the fringes of the group, herding them back to the beach. Sabine's crimson magic sliced while Salem's emerald sigils exploded through the air. They made fireworks out of demon blood, ichor spraying in tenebrous arcs. A splatter fell across Sabine's face, bisecting her nose.

And then Nicholas arrived on his hellish steed.

"Motherfucker," she swore against the night.

Salem glanced over. "A friend of yours?"

"Quite the opposite, actually, dear."

"Figured as much. Shall we take to the forest?"

"We shall."

And then they cut through the demons with renewed vigor. Meanwhile, Nicholas, emerging from the Hell-Portal, dismounted from his hellhorse and sauntered over without haste.

"Sabine, honey, you can't hide from me…" Nicholas taunted.

Either Nicholas didn't realize how far the hallowed grounds went, or Sabine was wrong about much still remained.

Sabine prayed it was the former.

She'd learned that nothing pissed him off more than not getting a rise out of her. So, by not responding, adding an air of nonchalance, Nicholas internally combusted. No matter what he said, she resolved to stay silent.

Salem and Sabine attacked a demon together while Nicholas pursued unhurriedly, taunting all the while. Pet names, memories, curses.

"What happened to lover boy before? You moved onto this chump already?" he asked, pivoting.

Salem spared her a glance with a brow raised. "A real gem you got there."

"Don't remind me. Quite possibly the deepest regret of my life."

"Could have fooled me," he said flatly as a destruction sigil tore through a demon.

Sabine cast him a scathing look and tackled her own demon. Holy water spattered a demon as she smashed a vial against its indigo blue chest, and a two-toned scream ripped apart the sky.

"Fucking hell," Salem snapped, covering his ears. "I see where mortals came up with the myth of banshees."

"So sure they're a myth?" she queried back. "Vampires were once myths too."

Salem glared, his black hair falling over his brow to deepen the dark of his eyes in a more menacing fashion. It had little to no effect on Sabine as she simpered and darted to the Mad Woods.

They just crossed the boundary, the path which had been woven with sigils just nights before when Salem let out a cry of pain. Sabine turned just in time to see Salem fall, Nicholas mere steps from her. She gasped and stumbled further into the woods.

Nicholas's eyes flickered from gray to red in an unsettling flip. As if a mirage were shimmering over them only to dissipate. They settled on red as he approached, grinning too bright, morbid against the angry red stripe of his face. Sabine could even see the faint line where her sigil had broken one of his teeth when she'd killed him last year.

"You have been a trying little cunt," Nicholas bit out.

Sabine's eyes flickered to Salem in concern; a red matting of his hair marred the back of his head. Not a good sign. She hoped Nicholas hadn't killed him.

"You haven't been the most pleasant company either," she snapped back.

Nicholas rolled his eyes. "Spare me your theatrics." Nicholas nonchalantly toed Salem's arm. "Is this the new boytoy?"

Sabine held back a snarl. His familiar Vonorian accent ground on her nerves. It wasn't a pleasant reminder of home like Bastien's was. It was a painful thorn of her darkest nights.

"He is of no concern to you."

"Oh, on the contrary, Sabine Van Arsdel, you are my only concern."

"Emmons," she spat.

Nicholas halted. Surprise dancing across his face. "What?"

"It's Emmons," she said, unable to help herself. To claim something he couldn't touch. "It's Sabine Emmons."

His face screwed up in rage. "You're *married*?"

"I would apologize for not sending an invite—we decided we already had too many enemies present—but I truly feel no sorrow."

"You're a cold-hearted bitch, you know that?"

"Cry me a river, you primordial git."

Nicholas stepped forward menacingly—then stopped.

They both looked down and saw the nearly incandescent line that prevented him from reaching her. The wall was invisible, but impenetrable. They both looked up at the same time, slowly, as their eyes met. Rage entered Nicholas's, delight, Sabine's.

Sabine cackled and then quickly formed a sigil, blasting him back with pure force. He flew back thirty feet, carried by her vindicated fury and unexpected glee. Nicholas landed on his ass, sliding backwards through the debris of the forest floor, his fingers claws to the yielding carpet.

With Nicholas temporarily down and disarmed, Sabine quickly crossed the line of safety, knelt down to Salem, hooked her arms beneath his, and dragged.

"Always fucking rescuing men," she muttered.

Her distraction wasn't enough because Nicholas was up again and already racing for her, forming a violent purple sigil, before she'd crossed over.

Five more feet.

She heaved, but he was dead weight. Panic loosed through her, but she couldn't abandon Salem. Not when he could be the only person truly on her side on this Hell-forsaken island.

Nicholas was ten feet away.

Two feet to the line.

She hauled ungently, using every molecule of her strength and pulled Salem to safety just as Nicholas slammed into the hallowed wall.

Breaths sawing out of her, she grinned to her trapped ex-lover. Flipping him the middle finger, she hooked her arms under Salem once again, pulling him further into the forest. Now, their biggest concern was the mad vampires—she just hoped Irving and Esther sensed her before someone else did.

Nicholas yelled after her. Nothing clear, all unintelligible raging nonsense, so Sabine ignored him. She pulled Salem deeper into the canopy of trees, the violet sky disappearing against the falling ceiling of leaves. Leaves which were strewn across the path in a rustling labyrinth.

Nighttime critters scurried and chirped around her, birds flittering and tweeting between each other, the waning croak of frogs joined the song of crickets, all of it Sabine had taken as reassurance. Every time the mad vampires were near the forest had been quiet, with it being so alive, she felt less paralyzing terror. She hadn't let down her guard, but she knew for the moment that she could breathe.

But then came the dawning realization that they needed to find shelter. Especially if Salem would remain unconscious for much longer. She hadn't seen any structures in the woods during her few ventures in, but that didn't mean they didn't exist. However, there had been no mountains to provide a cave, and there'd been no shacks constructed by the prisoners here.

Nothing.

"Fuck," she whispered to herself.

Undeterred, Sabine continued pulling Salem, fashioning a red sigil in front of him for protection, another of warding, and a third of silence. Fuck, if only Bastien were here with his proficiency in wards—this would be so much easier. But the whole point was rescuing him, so the idea was moot. More than moot, it was stupid and cyclical.

She didn't know how long she pulled him along before the night creatures silenced, but when they did, she was instantly alert.

Gaze flickering, Sabine searched the skeletal trees, peering around the trunks for any movement. It took a moment for her eyes to adjust, and when they did, she breathed a sigh of relief.

"Irving."

"Hello, One." He crunched through the undergrowth. "What brings you to my corner of the woods? Were you in the neighborhood? Should I have known of your visit, I'd have put on the tea."

"I need help, Irving." She looked down at Salem, worry knitting her brow. "Salem is hurt and Bastien has been taken."

Irving grew solemn. "I have seen your devoted husband, One. He is under duress, refusing to submit, tortured, just to be under duress, to refuse to submit, to torture again and again. He refuses to forsake you for the mistress, One. He will not renounce your bond and spouts treachery at her."

Sabine's heart ached. "Is he still alive?"

"He is. Though, only because the mistress needs him. He is needed and wanted, but he does not want nor need her, he needs and wants you, One. He is left alone only for one hour, one hour is all he gets, one hour is all we need."

Guilt and determination gnawed at her. "Can you help me?"

Irving drew closer, excitement gleaming in his eyes.

"Is it time, now, One?"

"It is time," she confirmed.

Irving clapped in joy. "Let's finish this then, One. He is alone only the hour of dawn—no more, no less."

Irving helped her with Salem and she glanced over at him. A question on the tip of her tongue. She resisted asking as Irving helped, but curiosity ate at her too deeply.

"Irving, why don't you act like you have bloodlust?"

"Oh, One. That is simple. I do not have it."

"What do you mean?"

"The bond takes it away. That is what the Mistress takes from us and pulls into herself. It is our madness that stays. The madness that needs her. It is a balance, One, see? And more and more she needs them more to push the corruption, to push the bloodlust deeper within her, where it can be submerged down, down, down."

"But you are no longer bonded?"

"No longer bonded, but she took the lust and left me mad. It is not so bad as it could be worse, and worse is not better than what I am now."

Sympathy flittered through her as she followed his lead with Salem. Irving seemed to know where he was going, so she didn't ask questions.

"I am sorry, Irving."

"Much appreciated, One. But it is not so bad, as bad could be worse, and worse is much worse than I am now."

Sabine sighed and nodded, tasting blood in her mouth. It was the coppery tang of exertion in her lungs, not the pooling of a wound. Thirst made her throat dry and she wished she'd brought water before making her hasty decision.

A short time later, the three of them arrived at some ruins not far from the amphitheater. It was three pillars, felled in a triangle, broken stone forming a fence around them.

Irving waved his hand and copper magic misted in the air, pulling back like a curtain. He ushered them through the intangible sheet, and waved his hand behind them. The magic sealed itself and Sabine found herself in a warded clearing.

It was warmer within the wards, quieted by a sound dampening sigil. Moss carpeted the space, leaving it spongy and soft. Sabine tugged Salem over to a patch and situated him carefully, still worried about his living status.

She placed two fingers to his neck.

A strong pulse.

She breathed a sigh of relief and rocked back on her heels, sitting back and flopping to the ground.

"One is safe here," Irving said. "We all have claimed our territory and this is mine. Protected by magics and respected by claims, this is mine and no one shall pry. My spells also make it look as if no one is home, we are invisible, not to be seen, no one shall bother, One."

Sabine leaned on an elbow. "No one can see us in here?"

"Not even if the stand right there," Irving said, pointing to a tree just outside the perimeters of the pillars.

Relief deflated her chest and threatened to spill tears. "Thank you, Irving."

"Thank you, One. For caring." He offered a nervous smile. "Sleep now. I shall watch the forest and watch the friend. You need to sleep to save your heart. I shall wake you before the sun rises, then we will find Mister Bastien."

Sabine nodded.

Forming a sigil for warmth, Sabine curled on her side and fell to slumber, deciding to trust a mad vampire for once in her life.

OCTOBER 26, 1867

Pain. Bood. Thirst. Madness.

It was the same. Over and over. Under and under.

Tiger's eyes, Reynard's eyes, memoryless eyes.

Swimming through a labyrinth of thoughts that didn't make sense. A sea of disconnect. A wave of confusion. Trod and stumbled, the path wound and wound, like a snake of sinister intent.

Blood and blood and blood and blood.

Laughs.

Taunts.

How much more?

Lancing pain, blinding light. Knife and sun and blood.

Wife and son and blood.

Wife and son?

Had he a wife and son?

Red hair and dark eyes shimmered to mind.

Yes, a wife.

No, a son.

Raw grief. Raw longing. Raw desolation.

Coalescing in the darkness.

Opened eyes, white ruins, black trees, starlit sky.

Goodnight, hello, where was his mind, he did not know. Where was his one? His one hello. The one he said good to know.

Bastien blinked.

The madness receded.

He lay in a pool of blood, his black shirt soaked, his silver necklaces caked and dried with it. His mouth opened, desperate to slake the thirst. He blinked again and looked around.

He was in the Mad Woods by the mausoleum, and there, on the steps was Drusilla, wiping her black tipped fingers on an embroidered handkerchief. Reynard was wiping off a blade—one, he realized, was used to cut him a thousand times. Beside Drusilla and Reynard was Veronica, smoking a cigarillo between gloved fingers.

Hatred wound through him.

Murmured conversation reached his ears but nothing clear enough to hear. He focused, but he was so tired, his sanity slipping with the dawn.

"—come back—" Reynard.

"—dawn and then—" Drusilla.

"—sleep before insanity, and he—" Reynard.

"—she'll be here soon—" Veronica.

"—she loves him, so yes—" Drusilla.

Bastien wasn't sure what the conversation meant, but he understood it entailed him and his wife.

Sabine.

He fought to the surfaces of consciousness and sanity, but the press was too heavy and it rushed over his face, closing over his head.

Under, under, under he went. Blackness settled and spread, poison in his mind, venom in his veins.

Pain. Blood. Thirst. Madness.

OCTOBER 26, 1867

Soft gray-violet greeted her when Irving jostled her awake. The sky was lightening, dawn on the horizon, their one chance rising.

Sabine got to her feet and brushed herself off, glancing at Salem. He, too, was stirring, and relief rushed through her.

"Salem woke while you slept," Irving told her. "I tended and tended and tended to him. He is now well, as you can see. I told him slumber shall heal, and heal he did."

"Thank you, Irving," she said softly.

He nodded in appreciation.

Readjusting her vials and blades, Sabine made her way to Salem and tapped him on the shoulder. His dark eyes flashed open, alertness arriving before recognition.

"Your old friend hit me in the head," he grumbled.

"Definitely not a friend."

"Definitely not."

The three of them waited for the sky to change, ears tuned for sounds of approach. It was unlikely that Drusilla and her loyalists would pass directly by them, but if they were keen enough, they may detect an absence or hiccup in the sounds of dawn creatures.

Biding their time, they hovered in nervous stillness awaiting the near imperceptible change. But it did come—subtle, but there. They paused a few minutes longer, listening intently for a crunch or snap underfoot. None came. But when the dawn creatures started up again, they set off their pursuit of her husband.

Intrinsically, Sabine knew where he'd be. Something within her tugged her, as if by the core, to a separate area of the Mad Woods. With both Irving's leading and Salem's confident stride, she was reassured of this feeling.

And then Veronica stepped from behind a tree with two mad vampires in tow.

Sabine acted without thinking, her speed aiding her in a cutting sigil as she battled with a defensive sigil in retaliation. Both smashed into Veronica, slamming her into the ground. Irving and Salem took on the vampires, flanking her and quickly battling it out.

Not letting up, Sabine clutched one of her daggers and pounced on Veronica, pressing it into her jugular.

"Pretty witless, Sabine," Veronica cooed venomously. "Where oh where are you supposed to go?"

"Where is he?" she hissed.

"You'll never find him," she taunted.

"*Where. Is. My. Husband*?" she hissed, emphasizing each word with more pressure on the blade. A bead of blood slipped down the metal.

"You are truly melodramatic."

"Are you sure you want those to be your last words?"

"They—"

Sabine sank the knife to the hilt.

Veronica's dark eyes widened in disbelief as she gurgled, blood spilling down from her neck and through her fingers that uselessly tried to staunch the bleeding. Sabine pulled the dagger out and blood spurted, arcing across Sabine's coat.

Sabine climbed off the other warlock, cleansing herself with a sigil as Veronica lay dying in the Mad Woods. She couldn't find anything in herself besides vindication—despite taking a life.

Both Salem and Irving successfully dispatched their own vampires, a little worse for wear, the former sporting a new slice across his cheekbone.

"Everyone hale and healthy?" Sabine asked.

"Fucker got me good," Salem griped. "Almost took out my eye."

"But at least you'll have a dashing scar to make up for it."

Salem glared.

Sabine acted innocent.

Suddenly, Salem put a hand to his head and wobbled.

"Oh," he managed breathlessly.

"What?" Sabine queried.

"Memories," he whispered. "Memories that were taken by Veronica. I…fuck, she took so many."

Sabine glanced over at Veronica's deceased form.

"Anything particular?"

"Just anything involving her."

"Surely nothing sexual."

With an eyeroll from Salem, they began trekking again.

Just as shards of sunlight broke through the canopy of trees, bringing the chill of autumn mornings, she spotted him.

Sabine broke into a run, heedless of threats. Panic rushed through her, powering every step as the scent of blood suffused her. She slid through the debris of the forest, leaves rushing up around her as she came to Bastien's side.

Blood was saturated in the ground, thousands of cuts lining his bare chest and arms. His skin—what she could see of it—was stark white except his fingertips which were coal black. His ears, which she could see poking from the dark of his hair were pointed.

"Bastien, no, no, no, no, no."

The Midnight Malady was taking hold, seeping insanity into his mind. The physical manifestations were alarming, but worse so was his complete lack of consciousness or response.

She fought tears as she searched for a pulse, waiting, her own heart racing. After a moment, she felt it, thready, but there.

Relief powered through her and without a second thought she took one of her blades and sliced open her arm.

She hissed in pain as blood poured from the cut. It was stinging and throbbing, but she ignored it in favor of saving her husband. Sabine lifted him into her lap, pressing her bleeding arm to Bastien's lips. She prayed over and over that it would work, that it would be enough.

"Please, please, please," she whispered.

Moments passed.

A full minute.

Her blood continued flowing into his mouth, dripping down his throat. No response. Her heart hammered with terror. She didn't want to lose him.

Suddenly, he twitched and then fangs sank into her arm. She gasped and his silver eyes flashed open. His pupils were the size of pinheads. She'd never seen so much of his mercury eyes before.

A thrill of fear went through her as he drank; but instead of pulling away, she cradled his head while he watched her unblinkingly.

She didn't know how much he'd taken, but she knew she'd need to stop him soon before he drained her or light-headedness rendered her useless to their plight and escape.

"Enough, brother," Salem said carefully, placing a firm hand on Bastien's shoulder.

Bastien tore from Sabine's wrist with a hiss, long fangs on display. The fangs paired with his pinpoint pupils was horrifyingly animalistic, but Sabine didn't startle. She simply drew a healing sigil over her wound and covered it for good measure.

"*Enough*," Salem repeated firmly. "You don't want to go killing your wife, now, do you?"

Bastien blinked, his pupils growing in size.

"Wife?" He looked at her—truly looked. "My wife," he said softly.

Sabine nodded.

"You came for me."

She nodded again.

A tension thrummed between them, a heated exchange, breaths held. His silver eyes flicked to her lips— they parted. She watched his mouth, still covered in her blood, but that did nothing to quell the racing desire that tore through her.

Salem cleared his throat and the tension broke.

Bastien shook himself from the reverie. Softness entered his eyes, replacing the yearning. "Thank you."

"Don't thank me yet, we still have much to do before we're in the clear."

Bastien glanced around, confusion marring his features. "What are we doing?"

Sabine grinned. "It's time for your coup, darling."

OCTOBER 26, 1867

A day late, but better late than never. And it was all thanks to his wife, who'd taken up the mantle in his stead.

Bastien's love for her grew greater, especially as she wrangled all the other vampires into submission. Madness still lingered on the fringes of his mind, but with her at his center—like she was his sun, not his son—he could remain tethered to something.

He didn't know if she still held love for him, or if instead hatred had been sown in its place, but it mattered not, for his heart was hers and there was nothing that could be done to change that.

Salem explained succinctly that he'd organized the rest of the rebellion in his absence and the group would meet them on the escape ship after torching the island, leaving Drusilla's loyalists trapped. Though, that effort was eased by a demon attack last night, where there had been multiple fatalities. But time was finite and they were losing precious moments.

He was also informed that Sabine had just killed Veronica and memories regarding her would return.

Bastien turned inward and discovered, yes, indeed, there were memories. A whole friendship diminished away into fragments. Dalliances, dances, games. There was laughter and there was hatred. But all of it had been taken from him. Veronica had chosen in this twisted, one-sided friendship.

He felt violated.

They set off and Esther joined the group a few short minutes later, having woken from her territory and curiously sought out the commotion. He'd sworn he'd seen her during his bloodletting, peering out from branches of tress like a wildcat. But he couldn't be certain.

Despite his blood loss, he was following the group as they set off, slightly airy and nebulous in his gait, but determined. He was leaning on Salem, there, but not there.

They broke from the edges of the forest and Irving and Esther halted. They stopped, staring out at the clearing, the ocean just out of reach, a small cargo ship bobbing placidly at the dock. A smoldering bonfire sat on the beach, dead warlocks and demons scattered across the shore and grass. At the manor coils of smoke rose from the windows.

The coup had begun.

"This is where we leave you for now," Esther said, a

tinge of unease in her voice. "We will do our part when it comes time."

"Once Drusilla is dead, you will be free of the woods," Salem told them. "When that time comes, run for the ship."

Esther and Irving nodded sagely.

Bastien was surprised when Sabine wrapped her arms around Irving and Esther—disregarding her own safety.

"Thank you for everything," she murmured, just loud enough for Bastien to hear. "Farewell for now."

Irving stiffened, but returned the hug. Esther did similarly, nuzzling the side of Sabine's head.

"Thank you, One. For making us feel worth something more than the worthlessness Drusilla has deemed us. For you have deemed us more and more, forever more, but nevermore than before."

Sabine patted them and slowly untangled. She held their hands.

"See you soon, darlings."

And then she pulled away and crossed the clearing, sigil held aloft.

Screams rent the morning, billowing smoke engulfing the manor as flames streaked from balconies. The cloying scent filled the air, paired with the comforting scent of wet earth and crisp fall air, a morbid juxtaposition against the warring scenery. Red and orange leaves mimicked the red and orange flames, the crash of the waves like that of the pounding on doors that took up the cacophony as vampires fled the arson.

Bastien could see his rebels, but in pursuit were loyalists that had managed to escape. Judging from the speed in which they were traversing the ground, the loyalists would reach the ship before them.

Despite being less talented with offensive magics than

others, Bastien formed a destruction spell and cast it towards Elvira. She went down with a shriek, the lower half of her right leg obliterated by the cast. Her own chartreuse magic sputtering with their shock and pain.

Just then, Bastien felt something strike him in the spine. He stiffened before searing pain exploded through him, and sent him sprawling. Pain temporarily blacked out his vision, but when he turned himself over, muddied by the trampled ground, he found Drusilla standing over him like a grim reaper in white.

OCTOBER 26, 1867

"You wretched little welp," Drusilla seethed. "Worthless cretins, worth less than grit and grime."

Sabine spun in surprise and was met with a vicious backhand from Reynard. She let out a yelp of surprise as she hit the ground, her cheek hot and smarting from the blow. A power sigil formed quickly in her hand and she blasted Reynard with it, his turn to fall.

Drusilla held Bastien, trapped within her burgundy magic, sigils dancing around his throat. Sabine knew if she tried anything she would seize, and the magic would take Bastien's head. And regardless of how she felt, she did not want her husband decapitated.

Sabine froze as she took in the scene.

Salem had taken it upon himself to restrain Reynard, the former holding the latter by magic and blade, Reynard struggling futilely as the knife's edge dug into him. The rebels were battling it out with the loyalists on the lawn, and while Drusilla drew breath, Irving and Esther could not help.

"Surrender to me and give up this nonsense, senselessness," Drusilla growled. "Join the ranks. Become one of us. One of us. Forever and ever."

Sabine blinked. "What?"

Drusilla wanted her to become one of the vampires? To be blood bonded to her? She didn't want her dead?

Sabine stared at the mistress, black taloned fingers, knife sharp ears, maddened eyes. The insanity had taken her further—and not just by inches, by miles. She could see the fraying of her psyche, the labored breathing, the skittering gaze.

Her blood bonds were weak. Too many deaths. Too many broken. And that's when it hit her with a startling clarity, like that of a shooting star.

Bastien's blood bond was gone.

Irving's words came back to her.

"The bond takes it away. That is what the Mistress takes from us and pulls into herself. It is our madness that stays. The madness that needs her. It is a balance, One, see? And more and more she needs them more to push the corruption, to push the bloodlust deeper within her, where it can be submerged down, down, down."

"But you are no longer bonded?"

"No longer bonded, but she took the lust and left me

mad. It is not so bad as it could be worse, and worse is not better than what I am now."

What Drusilla hadn't realized during her favorite torment sessions was that by draining him of blood, she'd effectively severed the blood bond within him. There was nothing linking them together anymore. It is what she hadn't figured out over the years, but Sabine had in mere moments.

Drusilla was destroying her very own sanity and corrupting herself further with every destruction and death.

And now there was nothing forbidding Bastien from killing her.

Sabine didn't know how, but she needed to convey to him the knowledge she'd just discovered. She stared at her husband, praying he would understand her signals.

Hands up, Sabine pressed forward.

Drusilla stiffened.

"You can't kill him, you can't afford his loss," Sabine said slowly. "You can't kill me, you need me. You needed me enough to bond us to you another time with a façade of matrimony." Her eyes flickered to Bastien. "But you broke your own vows. Your own blood bonds. Bleeding them broken."

Drusilla snarled. "I bled them so they'd learn not to cross me. Never me. Never crossed, only bled, left with a needle in their head."

Sabine flinched at the insanity-induced babble. She needed to tread carefully.

"But you bled them so broken they were no longer yours."

"They are always mine. Mine, mine, mine."

"Care to test that theory?" Sabine said kicking a rock. Drusilla's attention flicked, and quickly, she formed an illusion sigil—too fast for Drusilla's distracted eyes to track—

and under its guise, mimed stabbing to Bastien and mouthed four words.

The bond is broken.

Despite his unwell state, understanding dawned in his eyes.

The sigil dissolved and Sabine maintained her hands raised in mercy. Pretending as if nothing had happened.

"I think it best you allow us to go our separate ways, Mistress," Sabine offered.

"Never," Drusilla hissed.

Just as Bastien drove a blade through her heart.

Drusilla gasped and her magic fell away. She stumbled backward, her perfectly white gown blooming red, like a rose in snow, as blood dripped down her body.

Bastien tumbled to the wayside and Sabine dashed for him as Salem and Reynard ended up in a tussle. Drusilla stared uncomprehendingly at her hand, at the blood that marred it from her severed heart.

"How?" she managed, blood flooding over her chin.

Sabine leveled her with a heavy look, fingers twisting toward the ground. "Every time you drained one of your bonded, you were breaking the bonds. You kept their bloodlust but nothing else. And that continued to destroy you, slowly. And it only got worse as other bonded died. You were the villain in your own story, Drusilla. You sowed your own destruction, now you reap your end."

Drusilla's eyes flared with disbelief, her mouth opening and closing, spilling only blood and never words.

Sabine stared at the mistress as a spell came fully formed in her hand, one of complexity that heralded an inferno. And then, sigil held, Sabine sent the spell into the ground and watched the fire race toward the manor where it swallowed it up in a violent conflagration; tearing apart

Drusilla's legacy once and for all as her life faded into the soil.

OCTOBER 26, 1867

With Drusilla's death, Bastien expected an explosion or a snap as the bond broke, but he felt nothing. He rubbed his chest, as if trying to stimulate some sort of feeling, remove some numbness. Something. But there was nothing.

Perhaps it was because as his wife had revealed, the bond was already broken.

And that's when it hit him.

The bond was broken.

He was free.

They were all free.

Bastien stared down at the mistress. Her icy skin was

cooling with the mask of death, her eyes lifeless and staring—once fierce and hard like a tiger's eye gemstone. It was odd to see this villain so lifeless, despite making efforts to ensure she became one with the worms. Even her chestnut hair seemed lank and dull.

Once a force to be reckoned with. Now nothing.

Bastien heaved a sigh of relief, shuddering out of him. It wavered through him like the flames devouring the white monstrous manor. It ate everything, leaving decimation in its path.

And then he sobbed.

Loss and relief twined through him, part of himself damaged beyond repair, the rest of him rescued. He'd sacrificed so much of himself for her whims. His very soul was blackened and damaged but he was *free*.

Sabine's hand found his and hauled him to his feet. He got to them shaking, taking in Sabine like she was his salvation. Like she was a rescuing angel.

Reynard was choking on his loss, grieving Drusilla in a loud and wrenching way. He was half held, half groveling, Salem keeping him down, despite the fact Reynard didn't seem to want to fight anymore.

Bastien met Salem's eyes and he nodded once.

Salem took Reynard's life.

No longer were the sounds of grief, only the crackling of the fire and the crash of the waves.

They'd made it.

Dark eyes met his silver ones, sharing a moment. Bastien wanted nothing more than to kiss Sabine. To thank her in every word and every action. To pour his devotion and appreciation into her with everything he had.

But he knew he couldn't.

Because she wasn't there with him.

Restraining himself, he cupped her cheeks and pressed his forehead to hers. He closed his eyes and she did the same in response.

"Thank you," he whispered.

Sabine's hand went to his chest—a comfort and a boundary.

He backed off.

"We're going to miss our boat if we linger much longer," he told her.

"Yes, you're quite right."

Without communicating further, the three of them boarded the ship, safe from one danger, still fleeing another. Due to the lack of Drusilla's influence, the holy blessing of the land would disintegrate further and demonic reach would grow. They couldn't afford to stay—especially if any of the loyalists survived the fire. They just needed to stay on the water for a few more days. A few more days and the curse would expire and Nicholas would no longer be a threat.

After that, it would be Sabine's decision where they ended up and if their marriage would continue in any capacity. The prospect of it ending gave him a physical pang and he had to rub his chest to assuage it.

"Is your chest okay?" Sabine asked as they crossed the dock. Her eyes were full of concern. "I've seen you touch it a few times. Are you wounded?"

"Not physically, love."

Sabine flinched but nodded.

They boarded the ship without ceremony, meeting the rest of the rebels, thanking them for their efforts. They were informed that Drusilla and her closest confidantes—Veronica and Reynard—were eliminated, and the responses they received were mixed, but overwhelmingly was the feeling of relief. Of freedom.

And then something else struck him.

No one was descending into chaos.

No one was falling to madness.

No one was victim to the bloodlust.

Bastien slowly looked at Salem, who at least had the decency to look chagrined.

"You're the new bond sire," he breathed in astonishment.

"I had to," Salem said flatly. "You were gone and the plan was in action. It was a sacrifice I had to make." He bowed his head. "But I will endeavor to be the sire you would've been. I will not hold these bonds as leverage. I will not coerce. All will be free. I will carry this burden alone."

"I would have done it," Bastien whispered.

"I know. And that's why I had to."

Emotion choked Bastien's throat.

Salem, selflessly, had taken the burden of the choice he had made. It was *his* plan. It was *his* decision. Yet Salem had to take the fall for it.

Two figures dashed from the woods and the familiar blonde banner of Esther's hair paired with Irving's slim frame sent a gust of liberation through him. They boarded, sequestering themselves to a corner away from everyone.

On the ship, Bastien's adrenaline high waned, and with it, his insanity wavered. He could feel the fringes of madness trying to hold on by its fingertips and that prospect terrified him. Was he permanently like this now? Teetering on the precipice of reality?

He shook himself from the concerns and vowed he'd fight for his mind to be the best thing for Sabine. Because she deserved to know someone would fight for her, even if it was themselves they were fighting.

THE
SEA

OCTOBER 27, 1867

They were sailing and his thirst was savage. Due to Drusilla's torture sessions, his bloodletting made it so that his hunger for blood was elevated. He tried to fight it, but when a warlock who was supposed to be a tithe got a papercut, he had to admit to himself his self-restraint wasn't at its strongest.

His fingertips were still blackened; his ears still knife sharp. It was clear he wasn't handling himself as he should. Even though he'd bonded with Salem, it did not take away what Drusilla had done.

Through the night, he fought himself. As the midnight waves lapped at the ship, he laid next to his wife, a valley of distance between them. He tried to start conversation several times, but no words emerged from his open mouth. It was when Sabine sensed his tension that she broke the silence.

"Are you well, Bastien?"

He cleared his throat. "I'm thirsty."

She got up on an elbow and looked down at him with stern dark eyes. "Are you asking me something?"

"Yes. No. I don't know."

She watched him a beat longer before she spoke.

"You can feed off me. And if anything sexual happens between us, know that I am giving consent now, but it is purely physical. Is that understood?"

Bastien nodded.

"It will remain that way until I decide if want to stay married to you."

"I accept that." He inhaled sharply. "Whatever you choose. Just know that I love you, no matter what."

It was Sabine's turn to inhale sharply this time.

"Understood."

Slowly, Bastien moved over to her, so slow and careful. Situating himself beneath her, his wife still propped on her elbow, he gently nosed her throat. Sabine let out a small sound, one he couldn't quite distinguish. Opening his mouth gently, he let her have plenty of time to pull away, and when she didn't, he sank his teeth into her throat.

Sabine moaned as the euphoria-inducing saliva hit her system. Her hands flew to his shoulders, digging into his chest, clenching and unclenching his shirt. He drank for a few more moments before she started grinding her hips against his thigh.

Bastien froze, his cock hardening. He knew she'd given her consent, but he knew it meant more to him than it did her. Then again, he'd told her he'd loved her and she still agreed.

Struggling with himself, he felt the give. He'd praised his self-restraint, but when he was on the brink of madness, recently drained, with the woman he loved begging with her body for him to fill that tight little—well, he was only a man, and she a beautiful and vivacious woman.

As Sabine's hand drifted down to his length, desire shot through him like a meteor. His eyes rolled back as he moaned into her throat.

"That's right, husband," she murmured. "Only I can make you feel like this. Right?"

He nodded aggressively.

Sabine's other hand undid the buttons on her blouse and her shirt fell away, exposing her perfect breasts and taut pink nipples. He wanted those in his mouth more than the blood currently filling it.

Bastien licked a path down her throat to her breasts, and then suddenly paused. Should he stop? She was under the effects of the vampiric bite. Not in her right mind. He should—

Sabine, seeming to have sensed his hesitation grasped his cock roughly through his pants. "If you don't fuck me right now, I am going to be very upset."

"But your—"

"I wanted to fuck you before you bit me. I may not know where our marriage is, but I know where our bodies are, and I know you're the best I've ever had. So, with that said; please fuck me."

Bastien, needing no more prodding, divested them of the rest of their clothing. With Sabine still above him, he let the tip of his cock press against her slick entrance. He was letting her make the final move. And she did.

Sabine sank down onto him, her tight pussy clenching

him so spectacularly he thought he saw divinity. She began riding him, slick and warm, grinding her clit against him. He gave her what he could, turning them to their sides so that he could fuck her properly.

Hips undulating, they moved together, Bastien grabbing her ass to create better leverage, ensuring he created that upward roll of his pelvis that she loved. Her hands were clawing at him and he loved it, and he could tell she felt the same way because her delicate inner muscles were fluttering around him.

"Are you going to come on this cock, pretty wife?"

"Shut up," she moaned, biting her lip as she bucked against him.

"So sensitive. So close," he teased.

He pinned her down and gave her exactly what he knew she needed and soon she gasped and arched off the bed, pretty mouth forming a perfect O as her orgasm crested through her. She squeezed around him and he could hold on no longer, that tension at the base of his spine uncoiling as he spilled into her with a groan.

The final waves of their shared climax waned as he slowly pumped in and out. He realized immediately that he wanted to go again, but not only that, he wanted to hold her, play with her hair, tell her sweet nothings, and just talk.

The pain that came was unprecedented and sharp.

Bastien tore himself from her and tumbled from the bed, anxiously grabbing his discarded clothes. He was shaking as he dressed, not meeting her eyes.

"I can't do this again," he whispered.

"What do you mean?" Sabine asked, a hard edge to her voice.

"I can't just be physical with you. I'm sorry, I thought I could do this but—I'm sorry, I need more. I can't do this unless its more."

There was a breath held. Silence so acute it was screaming. He didn't dare look at her.

"Okay," she said, simply.

"Okay?" he echoed.

"Okay. I can accept that. But I don't want you drinking from anyone else. Only me."

Slowly, he nodded. "Okay."

"Okay," she said again.

He didn't look at her as he left the room, darting for the stairs and crossing the deck to the stern. He leaned over the rail, staring at the ebony waves, the glitter of moonlight over the ripples, and tried not to be sick. Bastien's breath sawed out of him, fringes of anxiety eager for a fingerhold. He pressed his brow to the rail, praying for the moment to pass.

He would have his answer about her soon.

He just didn't know if he'd like the answer.

OCTOBER 30, 1867

The last several days had been excruciating. Not in the physical sense, but in the sense she desperately wanted Bastien, but couldn't convince herself to open up to him. She'd been hurt, and she was so scared it would happen again.

She could think of so little with the stress surrounding her, but she was reassured by the fact that there was only one more night left of the curse and then she'd be free. That Nicholas could never touch her or haunt her again. That she could get a decent night's sleep. And that she could truly decide what she wanted to do with her husband free of duress.

It still haunted her though. The way he couldn't look at her after they'd been intimate. The way he'd forced himself from her, struggled into clothes and couldn't meet her eyes. She'd hurt him, she knew she had, but she had no idea how to fix it without compromising her own boundaries.

So, she'd accepted them and let him leave.

It had been days since and they'd barely spoken. Even now, with him beside her, one of her signature red coats fluttering in the wind as they leaned against the ship's rail near midnight, they didn't talk. He was in black and red, just as she was, a silver gothic cross hanging around his neck, similar jewelry adorning his vest and fingers. Like her, he had blades and vials of holy water on his person, still not at ease, still not settled.

Vale Wood was not far in the distance, but they'd made an agreement with the captain to remain aboard until the first of November—no questions asked.

The ship bustled with activity behind them, the hired crew working in tandem with the rebels and former tithes. A system had been worked where blood was given consensually, all information regarding Midnight Malady no longer withheld. Salem rose up as natural leader, ensuring everyone's safety and cooperation. Sabine had been beyond grateful for what he'd done, especially in light of Bastien's torture. Had he gone through with his plan, she wasn't sure if his mental capabilities would've been able to handle it. It was Salem who had ultimately saved them.

Sabine was looking out over the churning waters as the clouds swirled with malevolence when the first crack of thunder struck. It rumbled out across the waters, lightning scattering on the horizon.

Illuminating the oncoming ship.

A bell of warning went up from the crow's nest, hurried feet sounding behind her. Sabine turned to watch the frantic movements of everyone around, an argument going up between a crewman and the captain about the logistics of keeping the sails up in a storm versus outrunning the likely foe.

The decision was made for them as a cannonball shot into the water just shy of their hull.

Sabine met Bastien's eyes with terror and conjured a speed spell aiming it at the sails, and a second sigil forming a protective bubble. Bastien created his signature wards and others followed suit, but they were not fast enough.

A cannonball struck true and screams went up.

Destruction and incendiary spells lashed the wards, smashing across Bastien's silver magic with shatters of blue and purple. The attacking ship was gaining on them and it became painfully clear that they had more warlocks aboard, and more adept ones at that.

"We need to outrun them!" Sabine yelled to the captain.

Bastien caught her around her bicep. "We can't hit land. We still have another night to go," he said lowly, fear in his silver eyes.

"I know," she said lowly, her own eyes hard as she met his. "But we cannot risk everyone here for me. Not when everyone's safety is in peril."

"Fuck everyone else, I just care about you."

"Including Salem?"

That silenced him.

"We need to get away from them. We do not have the power to fight, and if this ship is damaged on water, we may all go down. Land will give everyone a fighting chance."

Fire crackled along the hull as warlocks frantically tried to douse it. And despite the ocean water to aid them, something was accelerating the rate of the flames and more and more smoke was rising to the deck, getting trapped within the wards.

Esther and Irving were coughing up the smoke, distracted by it as their yellow and copper magic wobbled with the effort. Irving bowed over, almost tossing his spell directly into the water below.

"Bastien, you need to drop the wards. We'll die of smoke poisoning if not."

"Then nothing will stop the assault."

"Then open one side."

Bastien did as bid and it helped some, but as their back became exposed, the attacking warlocks grew clever. They directed their spells to strike behind, and when they did, they hit not only the ship, but warlocks aboard.

Screams went up, fear and pain tinged, everyone scattering, trying in vain to organize. The argument between sail or no sail had been dropped, some warlocks forcing the sails with speed and force spells, others defending their travel and attacking when they could.

Everything fell into chaos as her mind struggled to process. It could have been hours, it could have been minutes, but whatever time it had been, it was not enough.

One fateful blow struck the ship true and the entire thing was a sinking inferno.

Sabine looked to Bastien.

"We need to jump."

"Are you mad?" he asked in astonishment.

"This ship is a lost cause and the lifeboats are gone," she hissed as thunder rumbled. "We need to jump. We're not far from Vale Wood."

"Nicholas will get you," he despaired.

"It's a risk we have to take."

And then, quicker than a blink, Sabine formed a destruction sigil. With all the power she could summon, she lobbed it at the opposing ship just before she climbed onto the flaming rail, and jumped.

OCTOBER 31, 1867

The water was fucking cold. It closed over her head like a fist, sucking the breath from her lungs. She launched for the surface, casting beneath the water, assembling warmth, stability, and cognition in record time.

As she broke the surface, gasping, she saw the residual bubbles and ripples indicating Bastien had likely jumped in after her. Her hair was plastered to her forehead and she hastily pushed it back, spitting sea water. Through her tangles she saw the two ruined ships, her final cast enough to send it to the brink—other spells finishing it off.

Bastien came to the surface, gasping, eyes wide.

"Holy fuck, it's fucking cold," he rasped, teeth already chattering.

"Make a warming spell," she commanded, her own hovering around her in a halo of red.

Bastien's own silver spell formed over him, his chattering fading.

The ship was slipping beneath the maw of the ocean, other warlocks having had the same idea as them, descending into the drink with gasps and splutters.

A familiar face swam up to them.

"Find some debris and paddle to shore, we're going to be at it a while," Salem said, lips blue.

Sabine and Bastien found something to buoy them and began swimming towards Vale Wood. Salem was shouting over the conflagration, waves, and thunder, screaming for everyone to do as he'd bid them. Some heard, some did not, but he didn't stop yelling.

The ocean bit at them, eager to drink them up, but they fought and paddled. With the current strong and the sky angry, their fatigued minds and muscles were in a dangerous state.

"Find—"

Suddenly, a spell struck Salem in the arm and he screamed in agony. Blood bloomed on the surface of the ocean, and Sabine saw that his arm was almost completely severed.

"Oh, fuck!" she cursed, swimming over to him.

Trying to stay afloat, she tried a healing sigil, but it barely had an impact. She tried for something more practical, and holding onto his debris, she tore the lower hem of her blouse and made a sling.

"We need to keep it in place!" she shouted. "I don't know the first thing about medical care—I am no nurse—but I know you shouldn't move it."

Bastien was beside her, helping where he could. Salem was moaning in pain, hardly lucid.

"We need to get him to shore," Bastien said, concern flickering between his friend and her—his ally and his wife.

She nodded. "Let's go."

They dragged him, heedless of everyone else, Salem fading in and out of consciousness as they swam. It was freezing, but thanks to their magic, they were warm—albeit wet.

The pursing ship was ruined, but the loyalists were marveling at the damage to their vessel. Invaders were monitoring the deck, which was nearly underwater, and pillaging and assessing. Sabine prayed the three of them were too insignificant for them to care about.

Despite the three of them being the catalyst for Drusilla's downfall.

Sabine's stomach dropped and she ensured she kept alert of the threat still behind them. Anxiety threaded through her as she realized nowhere was safe. Not behind, not below, and not ahead. Everything was wrong, everything was out to get her. If only she'd survived on that Hell-forsaken ship for one more day.

It didn't do to dwell on that though, so Sabine shook her head free of her paranoia, and towed Salem to shore.

Dawn was breaking as they neared the docks. The sky was lit

up in streaks of gray-yellow and gray-violet, the water dark as a void. They could see merchants on the docks, sailors and fisherman strolling in the early morning. Sabine and Bastien were exhausted, muscles screaming for relief, Salem unconscious due to pain or blood loss.

The waves continued to lap at them, threatening to drag them down to the depths below. Rocky shores came into view, individual stones becoming clearer. Barnacles climbed up the stilts of the dock, water damage dyeing the wood dark.

So close.

"Just a bit further," Sabine rasped, her throat raw from inadvertently swallowing salt water. She was so unbelievably thirsty. "Just a bit more."

Through a haze of delirium, they made it to the rocks, dragging themselves as sunlight struck them. For a moment, the three of them lay there, gaining their breaths, rocks and sand sticking to their skin while water still fell against their legs. Sabine's hair was like seaweed, soaked and stuck to her face; her flesh chilled and chafed.

Bastien, across from her, was fading. His eyes fluttered, skin pinkened, black hair like ink across his brow. He was fighting the fatigue, but he was also still recovering from Drusilla's machinations in addition to the arduous swim.

Salem was still unconscious, his arm mangled. Sabine could see the bone against the minced muscle, all the gore on full display. It made Sabine's stomach twist and her gorge rise.

"He needs a healer," Sabine told Bastien.

"I know," he rasped. "Just…just give me a moment."

Sabine nodded lethargically.

On the docks Sabine could hear sailors gossiping, something about a sudden spree of deaths—a plague? A serial killer? She tuned into the voices, grousing about heads being lopped or bodies split.

Panicked alertness flooded through Sabine.

Nicholas had not been idle.

A moment passed and Bastien hauled himself to his feet. Sabine joined him and together they got Salem up the beach and to the city. It didn't escape her notice that she could see her apartments just over the ridge.

"We can get him to a healer and head back out on the water by nightfall. If we wait out the night on another ship we can beat the curse."

"We?" she asked.

"We," he confirmed. "I'm not leaving you."

"Okay," she said, swallowing hard. "Healer, and then back to the water."

Bastien nodded and the continued down the street.

She was right back where it began.

Wind from All Hallow's Eve nipped at them, biting and cold. The veil between Vale Wood and Hell would be thin tonight and Nicholas's powers would be even greater. Samhain was the most sacred night to warlocks and the most opportune to demons. Demon attacks were far more common this night than any other, and Sabine had the abysmal luck to be cursed exactly, too.

Feeling self-pity, Sabine allowed her thoughts to spiral as they got Salem up to the street. If he died, it had worse consequences than just their emotional turmoil. If he died, all the vampires could go mad tonight. None of that needed to be paired with All Hallow's Eve; it was imperative they found Salem a healer.

On the street, patrols found them, and fortunately they did not question their story of late-night drinking and a friend who'd fallen off the docks and sliced his arm. Sabine and Bastien's soaked states were explained by jumping in after him. The patrols scoffed at them for their drunken stupidity, but guided them to the nearest infirmary.

Salem was immediately seen and swept away upon entrance to the sterile white room. The healers ushered them away while another healer checked them over for injuries despite their denials. After reluctant assessments, Bastien and Sabine were taken to a room where they were given blankets and water.

Together, they sat huddled on the bed, seeking comfort and warmth. Sabine tucked her head against Bastien's shoulder as he tipped his against her, the two of them nodding off.

"Thank you for staying," she whispered.

"Always," he mumbled.

Sabine startled awake as a healer tapped her shoulder. Her eyes flew wide as the surprised young woman stumbled back. Bastien awoke, similarly alarmed, a wobbly sigil in his hand.

"I'm so sorry!" the healer apologized. "I didn't want to wake you, but we really need to assess you."

"Oh," Sabine said, heartrate slowing.

The healer softly checked them over and after a diagnosis of exhaustion with a prescription for sleep, she dismissed them with promises to send a courier should urgent news be needed, but reassurances that they had him in hand.

Relieved, they promised to visit the next day.

Back out on the street, the sun had risen, but had brought little warmth. Sabine sighed, heaving out a pained breath. Her throat felt like it had been raked over with hot coals. She toed the cobbles, staring at her soaked boots. Her clothes were relatively dry, courtesy of some spellwork, but her boots were stubborn.

"Have you any contacts at the docks?" Sabine asked.

"A few," Bastien returned. "Any requests?"

"Something dry with a bed."

"Luxury tastes. A woman after my heart."

Sabine couldn't stop the giggle that burbled out of her. "I know, quite the high demands, I'm not sure you'll be able to meet them."

"It'll be a feat, for sure, but one I will indulge."

"How kind," she continued, falling into the comfortable flirting they'd developed.

"Anything for my wife."

Sabine's heart did a funny flip. Something warm spreading through her, a settling and comfort. Was she…? No, she couldn't think of that right now.

Just then, screams took up the street and a whistle blew.

"*DEMONS*!"

"Oh, for fuck's sake!" Sabine groaned. "Never a fucking break!"

A roar sounded from the direction of the docks and it didn't take a genius to figure out who had sent demons on the day of the year where the veil was thinnest to block the way to the water.

Another whistle screeched through the air from behind them, closer to the city center, another warning of demons erupting.

They were being herded.

"Motherfucker," she cursed as she readied a sigil and took off for the dock.

"Sabine!" Bastien yelled. "No, this is what he wants!"

She knew, but there were more demons behind them, and they needed to get to the water. So, if she had to go through demons to get to her salvation, then so be it.

Bastien followed and when they came upon the street the demons had spawned on, they skittered to a stop.

Bodies littered the road, demon and warlock alike, magic flew in a rainbow motley, clashing against infernal runes of deepest black. Hellfire raced around, wingbeats thundering overhead, claws scraping stone.

There were at least two dozen.

"Oh, seven Hells," Bastien cursed.

The fight was brought to them and quickly they were separated. Everything was a blur of blades and color, sparks and crackles lighting the air, the scent of blood of offal thick in the streets. Sabine's boots slid in the aftermath, her hands aching with the rapid movements.

Suddenly, a familiar head of strawberry-blonde hair caught her attention and Sabine froze.

"Winnie?"

Winifred spun, hazel eyes wide, cheeks flushed. Her mouth opened in an O and she rushed over to Sabine. Her hands went to her upper arms, patting her down in shock.

"Sabine! What are you doing here, dear?" Winnie asked, her very faint Vonorian accent slipping out.

"I could ask you the same thing!" Sabine said disbelieving. "I told you to flee, that Nicholas would use you to get to me."

"Yes," Win said, brows drawing together as she ushered Sabine to an alley. "But that time has passed, has it not? I mean...you have returned, surely, it's safe now?"

"No. No, Win, it's not. It is very much not."

Winnie sighed, watching the demons disperse on the street beyond them. "Well, that is most unfortunate."

And suddenly Sabine felt the now horribly familiar prick of a needle and something ice cold inject into her blood.

Sabine slapped a hand to her neck, her perception tilting on its axis as she stared at Winnie in shock. Nausea tipped through her as her vision swam.

"Win…what…?"

"He told me the truth, Sabine." Winifred's voice was warped. "How you'd hurt him. Now, I just want to help him."

Betrayal tore through Sabine as she lost the battle with darkness.

VALE
WOOD

OCTOBER 31, 1867

Bastien was clawing his way through the waves of demons when he saw Winifred sedate Sabine and drag her away.

Fierce, protective rage ripped through him as he battled the demons in his path with vigor. He used power and magic he didn't know he possessed, risking his sanity in the process. He watched in perceptible steps as his fingers blackened, felt his ears prickle with a new arch.

He was drawing from a well of power that Midnight Malady festered in. Not only was he dangerously low on reserves of energy, he was low on his grip of reality.

When he broke free of the demonic masses, he'd lost sight of Sabine and Winifred. He whipped his gaze around, panic turning his blood to syrup, slowing him down, making him erratic.

Where had Winifred taken her?

He darted down the alley, following the most likely path, but after several minutes of running it was clear there was no trail to follow and no bystanders to witness them.

Bastien realized with a sick clarity that this had been planned. The demon attack was a ruse. It was all organized to get Sabine. All those deaths were for Nicholas's plight and he'd recruited Sabine's friend to do it.

Another betrayal to add to Sabine's list.

Another time she was chosen second.

Wrath poured through him at the repeated slights to his wife and he vowed that he would endeavor every day for her to know she was his first choice. His only choice. Always.

Bastien paused in the street, mind working in overdrive and he tried to figure out what the fuck he was supposed to do. He had no leads. He had no idea what connection Winifred or Nicholas had to anything. He knew Sabine, but Nicholas would not lead her to something she preferred, and his existence limited all water options. But that did not narrow it down by much.

An idea lighted through him.

"The library," he whispered to himself.

And then ran.

He wasn't sure how he'd made it to the library steps, but he had. When he'd crashed through the doors, he'd startled the receptionist whose spectacles fell off her thin nose, saved by the gold chain about their neck.

"I never—!"

"Please," Bastien wheezed. "I need help. I need information."

The receptionist huffed. "Well, you could have been a bit less rushed about it, but what can I help you with?"

"My wife's life is in danger. She has been taken. I can spare no time. I need information on tracking spells."

The receptionist straightened. "Explain."

So, Bastien did.

Within the hour he was coached on how to create a tracking spell. He'd never been entirely proficient with all the magics, but luckily these were similar to wards. The receptionist—Odelia—was careful to only teach him the tracking spell for locating based on concern and welfare, not one of stalking—making sure he was no villain in a domestic dispute.

He appreciated her care.

"Do you have anything of hers you can use as an anchor?" Odelia asked, green eyes narrowed behind her gold spectacles.

Bastien slumped. "I have nothing. She has recently lost everything due to this curse."

Odelia gave him a look of sympathy. "Do you have any token of your marriage? Something you share? It will make it a bit more difficult as it is bonded to you as well, but as long as some of her essence is attached to it, then it should work."

"Nothing," he said. They had no rings. They didn't have the handfasting ribbon anymore. All he had was the—

"What about a bond? Like magic? Or bodily fluids?"

Odelia's long, oval face twisted in confusion.

"What sort?" She noticed his hesitation. "You do not need to give me specifics; I just need to know the nature of it."

He didn't want to divulge that he'd been regularly drinking his wife's blood and engaging in blood bonds.

"Blood."

"Of all the bonds that would be the strongest. And certainly, since you have nothing else that is your best bet."

Odelia walked him through the machinations of the spell—the attachments, the tuning, the movements—she did so all with a scholarly air, her light brown hair tied in a no-nonsense bun that added to the visage, but what betrayed her were her kind eyes.

When Bastien produced a wobbly spell, Odelia cheered him on. A rush of disbelief and pride went through him.

He did it.

"Oh, by the way—you should take this. You can never be too careful. Shouldn't be too hard to use."

Odelia reached beneath the desk and handed him something large, long, and—oh.

"Magic can only do so much," she told him, no nonsense, even though what she'd given him was…well, ridiculous.

With a hasty thanks, Bastien took to the street, following the delicate throb of the tracking spell that led him to where this curse began.

The woods.

OCTOBER 31, 1867

Consciousness slowly dripped through her, awareness stumbling behind it.

Sabine's head was hanging against her chest, which was bound by chain. Her back was pressed against something rough and uneven. After an experimental touch she deduced it was bark. She was chained to a tree.

She could smell leaf rot, wet soil, crisp air.

Nodding in and out, Sabine peered through bleary

eyes, seeing decaying leaves, trees all around, skeletal branches, and a fading sky.

A fading sky.

Fear spiked through her as she stared at the horizon.

"No, no, no, no, no," she repeated like a lament, thrashing against the bindings.

But it was to no avail, she was bound physically as well as magically.

"He'll be here soon," a soft voice said.

Sabine's head whipped to the sound and found Winifred standing at the edges of her periphery, slowly coming into focus. The familiar strawberry-blonde hair and hazel eyes hurt to see. They were features she'd trusted, opened her heart to after being hurt so deeply last year. They belonged to someone she'd begun to care for, to trust.

Her only friend in Vale Wood.

Who'd betrayed her.

Who, like everyone else, chose someone else over her.

Who'd decided she was second-best.

Always second-fucking-best.

A hysterical near pained bark of laughter slipped out of her. Tears of either fear or anger or sadness brimming in her eyes as she laughed, and laughed, and laughed.

Oh, what folly.

Oh, what a joke the universe was having at her expense. It was too good. This couldn't be written.

"What's so funny?" Winifred hissed.

"You," Sabine managed through peals of laughter. "You, you stupid bitch." Her voice was breathy, ragged. "He's just using you. He's manipulated you like he manipulated me."

"No," Winifred growled. "You were the mastermind behind everything. You were the one who'd sought fortune rather than heal him of his Wasting, and when he tried to stop you, you killed him."

Sabine laughed.

Oh, what a clever lie. A clever construction, indeed. Built from crumbs of the truth, but the whole loaf misshapen.

Nicholas had indeed been afflicted with the Wasting, a sickness Benedict had cured, but when he wanted the cure made public, Nicholas had decided only certain people should deserve it—to even know of its existence. Nicholas was the one who'd sought fortune. She'd been the one to stop him.

And yes, she'd been the one to kill him.

And she didn't regret it. Not for one fucking second.

"Truths mixed with lies, Winifred," Sabine managed. "I killed him, yes, but not for money—because of his greed and duplicity."

"No, he told me how he'd been wronged, how you've run from your actions, how your friends have forsaken you."

"Did I mention his specialty is illusions?" Sabine said, not even deigning to acknowledge the lies Nicholas had filled Winifred's head with.

She was stuck.

There was nothing that could be done.

Her magic was muted, her hands tied, and she was so fucking tired. She couldn't do it anymore. Her heart hurt, it ached, it cracked. The fight had gone from her.

This was how it ended.

On the last night of a curse.

On the last fucking night—so close to outrunning it.

The last rays of the sun were sinking below the tree line and Sabine was still laughing hysterically.

"Good luck, Winifred," Sabine managed through peals of manic laughter. "You're going to need it."

A new figure appeared and Sabine closed her eyes.

"Unchain her," a familiar voice commanded.

Sabine's eyes flew open.

It was not Nicholas, the hellish rider, as she had thought. It was Bastien, her husband, who'd come after her.

"*Bastien*," she breathed, longing mixed with relief in her voice.

"Hello, love," he purred, striding toward them with a spell bobbing before him and a shotgun slung over his shoulder. "I've missed you."

Sabine let out a breathless sound. "I missed you, too."

Bastien beamed, and then, in one smooth motion, unslung the shotgun from his shoulder and had it braced in his two hands—pointing at Winifred.

"Are you going to release her, or shall I?" he asked.

"She's a killer," Winifred opposed.

"As am I. This information changes nothing."

"She must pay."

"For what?"

The rounded vowels of his words sent shivers through her body. They were the sounds of home. His voice was the sound of home.

"For what she did to Nicholas."

"Her wretched imp of an ex-lover?" he asked dubiously. "The one who's been decapitating people on Vale Wood streets?" Ah, so he'd deduced what she had. "The vile toad who's been haunting Sabine's dreams for weeks?"

"He would never," Winifred gasped.

Bastien sighed and glanced at Sabine. "He got his hooks into her, didn't he?"

"Indeed."

"Ah, most unpleasant. Well, if this unfortunate conversation doesn't steer in the direction I wish, then I should be forced to use this—" he brandished the gun, "it's loaded too, you see. So, perhaps keep that in mind when you make your choice."

"You are siding with a murderess," Winifred hissed, nearing Sabine's chains.

"Yes, yes, the murderess is mine, you can have the murderer if you wish. I must forewarn you though, I've heard tell that he is a selfish wretch and will use you to further his own gain. But if that is your thing, then who am I to judge? We all have our kinks, hmm?"

Sabine's heart cracked. Half was overjoyed at Bastien's presence. At the easy wit and humor he extended. The other half was feeble, devastated by the loss of Winifred's friendship—at her delusion. She hardly even sounded of herself.

"Chop, chop, Miss Todd," Bastien said. "I'm running a strict schedule."

Winifred glared venom as her fingers touched Sabine's chains. Sparks of pear green magic danced between her fingertips and then the chains fell away.

The physical freedom gave her an immediate rush, her lungs finally expanding like they'd been dying to do, but the magical freedom was like a high. Her crimson magic burbled to the surface of her skin, shimmering through her blood like starlight and warmth. It incited a wakefulness in her that dissolved all the remaining drugs from her system.

She felt alive.

With the gun still trained on Winifred, Bastien urged Sabine over to his side. She stumbled over as Winifred stayed by the tree, eyes hard, lip curled.

"She may be unbound, but she cannot run," Winifred snarled.

A crack sounded from down the path, hellish red blooming into existence, shadowy black magic forming the gothic spires of the gates. Fully formed, with the scent of brimstone pungent in the air, they swung open.

They were too late.

Sabine gripped Bastien desperately as horse and rider leapt from the Hell portal, autumn leaves chaotically kicked up in their arrival. Nicholas was as he always was—pale, haunting, white haired, red-eyed. He was wearing the white suit and capelet he'd donned the day of his death, the silver chains and medallion over his breast, the ivory details adding to his ghostly visage.

Nicholas galloped up to them, stopping as his horse reared up. Bastien tucked Sabine behind him while Nicholas jumped off in a dramatic swirl of pale fabric. He walked toward them slowly, theatrically slow, malevolent eyes burning brighter than any ember of Hell.

He was exuding triumph. Like he'd believed he'd already won. Like all hope was lost.

Sabine would not give in. Not until her last breath.

"It is time," Nicholas announced in a booming voice.

Sabine didn't respond.

Nicholas stared at them, eyes hard, before turning gray and flickering over to Winifred. She beamed the moment their eyes met. She twisted the cream skirts that flared beneath her snug tan corset, shrugging her blue and green plaid cloak behind her shoulders to better reveal the low neckline of her dress to Nicholas.

"Thank you so much, sweet Winifred," Nicholas said, sauntering up to Sabine's former friend. "You have truly shown your dedication to me."

Nicholas gently cupped Winifred's cheek while she leaned into it, her own hand gingerly going to his. Tenderly and romantically, he leaned down and placed a chaste kiss to her mouth. Nothing like what Sabine knew Nicholas was capable of, and nothing like what she knew Winifred preferred from her enthusiastic exploits—though, she did shy from public displays. The whole thing seemed like a farce.

Winifred hummed in bliss before Nicholas took a step back.

"You have no idea what this means to me," he told her softly.

And then with a thin stiletto, he slashed her throat.

Winifred's hazel eyes widened to orbs, blood was a fountain from her throat, scarlet bathing her pretty outfit she'd probably put on just for him. The scent of copper filled the air, the metallic scent on the wind more potent than the woods around them. Her pale fingers went to her throat, betrayal burning from every inch of her being.

Sabine couldn't help but feel a surge of pity. Winifred had once been her friend. Misguided, yes, but not evil. And Sabine had once been tricked by him just like Winifred had been, the only difference was that she'd figured it out soon enough and was able to escape.

Winifred's eyes went flat and her hand fell slack as she tumbled to the ground with an ungraceful thump, staring at nothing.

Callously, Nicholas formed a violet sigil and Sabine recognized the incendiary shape for what it was. He cast it at Winifred and it took up her body, burning it to a crisp.

And she was gone.

Emotionlessly.

"Right," Nicholas said, wiping his mouth with a handkerchief before using it to remove the blood from his blade. "Now that, that is done and over with, let's get on with why we're really here."

"You killed her despite the fact she was helping you?" Sabine asked dubiously.

"Astute observation, Professor Obvious."

The barb was dual ended. He knew as well as she that she was no professor. Lucia was. And it was just another reminder of her short-comings. Of her being second-fucking-best.

Sabine gritted her teeth. Nicholas was truly deplorable. More than she'd ever thought. It was heartbreaking to realize the man she'd pined over for years was actually a monster.

"Why are you even bothering with this curse?" Bastien asked. At some pointed he'd levelled the shotgun at Nicholas. "Why not leave her be? You are dead, you have done wrong, why must you keep doing this?"

Nicholas bared his teeth at Bastien. "If I do not do this, then Hell takes my soul for good. Hell can obliterate it and I will be nothing. I will not take that risk."

Bastien sighed. "Fair enough."

And then Bastien cocked the shotgun and fired.

OCTOBER 31, 1867

The kickback of the shotgun was a reverberation through his whole body. His shoulder smarted from the blow, an ache that was reminiscent of the one time he'd dislocated it. Gunpowder filled his nostrils, the blast still echoing in the air.

Where Nicholas's head once was, was gone.

Nothing but a stump of a neck that didn't bleed, the charred ends like burnt chalk. He was hardly a person anymore—a husk—and the gunshot was evidence of that.

His head had been obliterated into something like

dust. Like a marble sculpture crashing upon stone.

Now, a headless horseman, Nicholas stood there, statue still. He was unmoving and un-falling. Bastien wasn't sure what state the haunted specter was.

Decapitation was typically a surefire way to kill something—even undead—but the texts about the Hallow Curse hadn't described this being an option.

"Is...is he dead?" Sabine asked, hope on her bated breath.

That would be too perfect, wouldn't it, darling?

"Oh, for *fuck's* sake!" Sabine groaned. "You cannot be serious."

For Nicholas no longer had a head, so he no longer had a mouth. But apparently now, he could speak directly to their minds.

And he took a step.

"Do you remember where the bridge is?" Bastien asked Sabine urgently.

"Yes."

"Then go," he ushered her. "I love you."

Raw emotion entered her eyes and then she did the unimaginable.

She kissed him.

Grasping him by the collar of his shirt, she tugged him in and slammed her mouth to his. Her lips were divinity and bliss. He moaned into her mouth as he deepened it, sweeping his tongue against hers. She quickly returned it, then pulled away.

"Come back to me," she whispered.

Then she ran.

Nicholas was still striding towards him as Sabine dashed away. Bastien steeled himself and summoned sigils as he met Nicholas step for step.

She will be mine in eternity.

"That begs to be seen."

A sight joke? Nicholas sneered. *You think I have no vision? I can see all in an elevated sense, little prick. I know exactly where you are, which is why I know exactly where she is.* He paused. *And so do my demons.*

Sabine's surprised and infuriated yell took up the forest as Nicholas raised his hands as deformed demons pulled themselves from individual-sized Hell portals in the ground. They clawed through the soil, lipless and lidless. Eyes like eggs, maws of razor shark's teeth. Their flesh was mottled and black, like decay warmed over, threads of purulent red running over them. Their talons tore rivers in the earth as they emerged, lanky and skeletal.

Seven in all, and likely seven more wherever Sabine was.

Bastien knew Sabine could hold her own, but he still couldn't avoid the flash of fear that sparked through him.

Warding was his specialty so that's what he began with. He secured wards around himself and then he doused the end of the shotgun in holy water—as he'd done on the trek to the woods—and readied destruction and cutting sigils. His silver magic gleamed like mercury as it shot through the night, bright as the starlight that hung in the canopy about the naked boughs. The moon was shy of full, but brighter than lamplight.

All the silvery night light illuminated the woods in stark relief this Hallow's Eve. Nicholas's monstrous form was lithe as he climbed atop his hellhorse, and due to perspective, the moon was suspended right where his head should be.

Farewell, Emmons. If I have time after I kill her, I shall come back for you.

Then Nicholas kicked his steed into action and Bastien

was left fighting the demon minions. They galloped after Sabine and his rage sent him into a flurry of movement, his wards keeping the creatures at bay.

Three demons were dead, crumbling into black dust, their Hell portals swallowing them up. The other four were scrabbling over his wards, shearing through them, shredding each sigil. Luckily, Bastien was ready. As soon as there was a window, Bastien blasted a shotgun shell through it and sent a demon careening into the night with half a head.

Hi shoulder was aching, but he didn't stop.

The remaining three were dispatched similarly in quick succession, and once their portals closed behind them, Bastien dropped his wards and gave chase.

Finding them didn't take long. Sabine was stranded on the bridge, demons on either side of it, having been summoned separately. Nicholas was on Bastien's side, taunting from the bank, his hellhorse trotting anxiously.

She was fierce and fiery on the stone arch, the water rushing beneath in a vicious rage, swollen by the recent storms. Her deep red hair was a punishing flag in the wind, her throat marred from his bites, yet she looked like a warrior goddess—if one existed. Her red jacket was torn, silver buttons hanging on by threads, while her shirt resembled something that once was white, but now imbedded with dirt and grime, was closer to a muddy gray. Her leather pants had tears in them and her thigh high boots were a little worse for wear, but none of that mattered—she was still ethereal.

Sabine's crimson magic sliced through the night, faster

and more severe than his had been. She sliced with precision, cut without hesitation; all of her spells were blades sent to kill.

I can do this all night, Nicholas taunted.

"Actually, you can't," Sabine fired back as she sent a power sigil into Nicholas's chest. It nearly unseated him, but he held onto the reins. She cackled.

Nicholas's own violet magic flew through the air, forcing Sabine to duck as they traded blows. She dodged them easily enough, but they slowed, while his arriving demons did not. Soon, the bank was overrun with them, clamoring over each other, chittering and chortling with hunger and glee. So hungry were they that a skirmish broke out between them and some even dispatched others.

Bastien, blasted his shotgun through the masses, sending demons into the depth of the river where they screamed upon contact. Evil and the soulless could not cross running water, and so as soon as they touched the brackish waters, Hell pulled them under.

Nicholas spun with Bastien's assault, but Bastien did not stop. In fact, his next shot was at Nicholas, taking him in the leg. He staggered, a chunk gone from his thigh, more of that burnt chalk consistency around the wound.

You insolent welp.

"That's such a mild insult, come on, now. Speak truly dirty to me."

Nicholas no longer had a face, but if he did, Bastien knew he'd be sneering.

You truly are a match made in Hell.

Bastien put a hand over his heart in mock affection. "Why thank you." And as he pulled his hand away, he whipped a cutting sigil towards Nicholas.

It struck his arm and he roared.

Nicholas's attention was now on Bastien. Injured, but not incapacitated, Nicholas assaulted him with violet. Sigils he couldn't name slammed against his wards that he'd hurriedly constructed, one cutting through and striking him in the chest. He crashed the ground, wheezing as a scream reached his ears.

It sounded eerily like his name.

Nicholas hovered over him, headless, heartless, and hopeless, and then, with one of his little stilettos, he punctured Bastien's lung right beside his heart.

He gasped in agony. Nicholas yanked it out, just as something struck him, sending him to the dirt beside Bastien. Blood flowed freely from the wound, pressing against his lung. Beneath his ribs, too much blood and not enough air. He gasped again, trying to hold pressure to the wound.

There she was beside him. Nicholas flat on his back while Sabine delivered merciless blows to the horseman, both of blade and spell. Her voice was like a banshee's screaming insults and deplorability that Bastien could no longer decipher.

He felt his ears sharpen with the signature tickle, his breaths grow shallow, his vision fade. Already his grip on sanity was turning to salt between his fingers, each granule falling down, down, down.

Surely, his fingertips were just as blackened as Drusilla's had been. Blackened and bruised like his heart. Blackened and bruised like Sabine was turning Nicholas into. Blackened and bruised like—

He lost his train of thought.

Bastien's eyes were trained on Sabine and he thought it was nice that the last thing he'd ever see was his wife in a murderous rage, destroying a spirit of Hell.

OCTOBER 31, 1867

Bastien was dying.

She knew it in her heart, she knew it as her soul was rending, reaching for him with fading fingers. Their bond was more tangible in this moment as it was disappearing than she'd ever felt it.

Sabine was decimating Nicholas. Part of him were so far gone they were dust, chunks missing from his chest, parts of his arms, legs. She'd opened up the wound from his center again, revealing nothing but a blackened hull of chalky white powder. As the curse was nearing its end, he was fading into ash.

Nicholas's fingers were crushed, so unless his hands were lent the same spectral ability of his voice, he was unable to cast. He was utterly at her mercy as she pummeled him with everything she had. Everything she lost. Everything he fucking deserved.

Her fists were bloody by the time he stopped moving. By the time his voice stopped taunting and cursing her in her mind. By the time he was more dust than man.

Sabine's throat was raw and she didn't realize why until she noticed she was sobbing. Her cries were interspersed with screams, all of it shredding her vocal cords. Fingers shaking, she looked at the mess of blood and grime and gore. Watched them tremble as she left the shreds of Nicholas's abandoned form, rags of his once pristine white clothing all that remained.

She dragged herself over to Bastien who was unmoving. Her hands went to his face, filthy, but there. She tipped his face towards hers but received no response. Her heart clenched as she found his limp hand on his bleeding chest, the flow stilled to a dribble. Pressing her ear to his heart, she listened for a beat. It was there, feeble, but true. She shuddered a breath of relief.

All over him she poured healing spells, desperate, wobbly, sharp, all forms in every attempt. She pleaded with whatever powers that be that he'd pull through. That something would take.

Sabine noticed his fingertips. Black, fading to his normal tone at the knuckles. She pushed his hair from his ear and saw the point. Sharper and deeper than she'd ever seen them. She realized even if she succeeded in healing, the madness would consume him.

She did the only thing she could do.

Opening her wrist, she pressed it to his mouth, praying that her blood would be enough. She ignored the pain as her blood spilled down his throat, time ticking by painfully slow. She wasn't sure how much time had passed, but she watched as the blackness receded from his fingertips, his ears rounding out. She was bringing him back from the edge of madness, yet it wasn't enough and she was fading.

Her eyes crossed, her energy waned. She blinked slowly. She just needed a rest. She closed her eyes, wrist still to her husband's mouth, and settled her head on his chest.

OCTOBER 31, 1867

Moonlight shone into his eyes, warm weight was on his chest, and the taste of blood was in his mouth. He blinked slowly, staring up at the canopy of the woods over him. The earth was cold and wet around him and when he looked up, he noticed a sprawl of auburn hair and a pale hand on his neck.

Pale.

Too pale.

Alert, he looked more clearly.

Sabine was not meant to be that pale. Her skin had a

golden tone. He jolted up, cradling her in his arms. Her head lolled and terror struck through him.

"Sabine?" He brushed the hair back from her face. "Sabine?"

She didn't answer.

He felt for a pulse and for a moment—a heart-stopping moment—there was nothing. But eventually he discovered she was alive. He looked her over, trying to figure out what had happened.

Last he remembered, Sabine was beating Nicholas to a pulp and his sanity was slipping.

Bastien looked at his hands and saw the barest tips of black on each finger. His ears, when he reached up to feel, were rounded with the slightest point.

Panicked, he picked up the wrist that had been at his throat. There, a slash was across her forearm, dribbling blood, raw and angry.

She'd drained herself to save him.

Hurriedly, he formed healing spells over her, closing the arm wound, scanning the rest of her body for any other wounds.

"Please, please, please," he whispered, pressing his lips to her brow. "Come back to me."

It was an echo of what she'd said to him.

They were so far from healers. He'd lose her by the time he got her to an infirmary. He was desperate.

Tears slid down his cheeks as a horrible idea came to him.

"Please forgive me," he whispered, voice cracking.

And then he cut his arm and pressed it to her mouth.

She had lost so much blood, the only thing that could fix it was more blood. The problem was that only those with Midnight Malady could replenish their blood supply via oral intake. And one needed to first drink the blood of someone with Midnight Malady to become afflicted with it.

He was damning her to a life of blood drinking, the risk of madness right on the fringes of her restraint, yet if he didn't do this, she'd be lost entirely. It was a risk he selfishly had to take.

And he was that, *selfish*.

If Sabine hated him afterward, fine, he'd live with that. As long as she was *alive*. As soon as she was aware, he'd offer the blood bond so she wouldn't suffer the nightly bloodlust and share the weight of the disease, extending each other's life.

The blood bond would secure their immortality, but it would also damn them in the process. Should one die, the other was at the mercy of unreality. They needed each other henceforth, whether that was together or not, he wouldn't force her. He wanted her to choose.

Regardless, he was doing such a villainous thing for the most irreproachable reason. It was love, the most unimpeachable offense, and he was so in love with her it hurt. The idea of her dead was unfathomable. So, he was doing the only thing that could keep the object of his heart alive.

It was sometime later, the blood dripping down her throat, that her eyes fluttered open.

A sob spilled out of him and he wrenched his hand away.

"I'm sorry, I'm so, so sorry," he babbled incoherently. "Please forgive me."

"Bastien?" she asked, her voice foggy.

"I'm here, love."

"Am I…am I dead?"

"No, no, you're not. I…I did the only thing I could do."

Sabine's clever, dark, midnight eyes flickered from his eyes to his wrist. A pale hand went to touch her lip, finding the blood there.

"Oh," she said softly. "Am I—do I have Midnight Malady now?"

"I think so."

"Oh," she said again, brows screwing up in concentration. "Well. Do you want to give me the blood bond so I don't go mad, then, please?"

Surprise jolted through him.

"You're not…you're not angry?"

She cracked a thin smile, her teeth pink. Her *fangs* pink. "I am no idiot. I know you would not have done this, had you had any other choice."

"But I am selfish and—"

"And you put me first." Her eyes softened. "You kept choosing me first. Over everyone else. Despite everyone else doing differently. You chose me. Over and over again." Tears spilled over he lashes. "I think I was afraid to accept that I really wasn't your second-best. And I think it was easier to reject you before you could cut me."

"I would never," he said softly, kissing her hand.

"I know that now." A breath shuddered out of her. "I love you, Bastien."

His heart cracked from joy. "I love you, too."

She smiled again, brighter.

"So, about this blood bond?"

Bastien explained the logistics of it, carefully and gently, mindful of her weakness still. The exchange would be equal and necessary, a few words, and it was formed.

Sabine nodded and took out a blade.

"Does it matter where I cut?" Sabine asked.

"Wherever you want me to drink from."

Sabine nodded and lightly slid the blade against her collarbone. She winced from the sharp sting, but soon a thin trail of blood wound down her breast.

Bastien inhaled, feeling his cock stir in excitement. Beneath the blood and dirt, she still smelled like her, like Sabine—cinnamon and vanilla. Slowly, reverently, he spoke the words.

"With this blood we are bound, in protection and harmony." He licked up the spilled crimson. "You are my sire as I am your thrall, you are my thrall as I am your sire. This bond is forged in equal measure." He tasted more blood. "I vow that I am yours. To serve and protect, to honor and guard." Another taste. "Bound be our blood."

He took a final mouthful and then pulled away.

"Now it is your turn."

Bastien took the blade from Sabine's trembling fingers and he sliced the same place, opening his collar for better access.

Sabine repeated the first line.

With this blood we are bound, in protection and harmony.

She licked his blood and he shuddered in desire, feeling sparks crackle across his skin.

You are my sire as I am your thrall, you are my thrall and I am your sire. This bond is forged in equal measure.

Blood. Shudder. Lightning.

I vow that I am yours. To serve and protect, to honor and guard.

Taste. Eyes close. Incandescent light.

Bound be our blood.

The final mouthful and Bastien wanted to explode.

"Were those always the words of the bond?" she questioned.

"No, I altered them. I did not want any power dynamics between us. The original words did not include the mirrored phrases of sire and thrall. It also claimed the bond was forged in obedience. I didn't want that."

Sabine cupped his cheek. "I do quite appreciate that, darling. It was the least you could do after turning me into a vampire."

Bastien flinched and she softened.

"Too soon?"

"Perhaps."

"Ah, well then, my apologies, darling. Maybe in a few days."

Bastien cracked a smile. "Maybe."

As the bond slotted into place, a Hell portal opened.

Beside them, the form of Nicholas that Sabine had destroyed had slowly, ever so slowly been regenerating itself. Pulling the pieces she'd minced back into itself, trying to form what was lost.

But then, a wind swept from the brimstone portal, a dragging zephyr and Nicholas's form began to move. Hell sucked Nicholas back from whence he came. Every morsel of his damned soul and every crumb of his desecrated body. A swirl of black and white dust followed when his fine clothes got sucked into the flames, the red light swallowing them whole.

The hellhorse rode into Hell willingly, letting out a strained whinny as it leaped through on ember hooves, its flaming mane disappearing into whatever abyss of Hell

Nicholas belonged to.

When the last speck of dust was vacuumed into the portal, it snapped shut with a metallic clang and the portal dissolved, taking with it the bite of sulfur.

It was midnight.

Hell had taken its rider.

And the curse was gone.

SABINE EMMONS

NOVEMBER 1, 1867

"Bastien," she began nervously, twisting her fingers. "I want to make it clear now."

"Okay," he said softly, betraying no emotion.

"I choose you. Today and all of my days. You are my first choice. I wish to continue our marriage in full."

Bastien's silver eyes positively glowed. "I choose you, too. You are my only choice. The only choice I'll ever have."

"So, we continue?" she asked hesitantly.

"We continue," he confirmed.

Emotion struck her and she wrapped her arms around his neck, heedless of the filth, and kissed him. She wrenched his head back by his hair and devoured him. Her tongue battled against his and suddenly he was lying flat on the ground in the woods.

Her hands were all over him, his over her. She roamed over his face, neck, chest. He clutched and grasped her hips, waist, whatever he could get his fingers on. She was atop him, grinding on him, riding him through their clothes before he ripped her blouse down the center.

Bastien sat up, his mouth exploring her chest, mouthing against her breasts before he found a nipple and pulled it in his mouth. She threw her head back and moaned. They were so hard against his touch, peaked and begging. Mixed with the potent desire and the chill of late autumn, she was alive in the most feral sense.

Her hands clawed at his clothing, rending buttons from their holes, stitching from stitching until his pale torso was on display.

Bastien tumbled them into the forest floor, reaching down to drag off her pants. They quickly made do with his, and without any preamble he was sliding his thick cock into her wet cunt.

Their fucking was animalistic. Claiming. He drove into her relentlessly as she clawed at his back, her hips undulating with his punishing thrusts.

Sabine used what strength she had to turn them over again, plunging his length deeper within her. She rode him hard and fast, fucking him among the leaves and dirt, streaking him with all the evidence of the woods. His black hair was a mess of twigs and leaves, and she presumed hers was in similar disarray. Even so, she did not stop. Her rhythm was rough, grinding down and lifting up, Bastien's mouth pulling her nipples, his teeth grazing them to heighten the sensation.

Her orgasm was climbing rapidly and she fucked faster, chasing it.

"Come wife," he begged. "I need it. I need you."

"You have me," she rasped as she came, his name tipping from her lips. "Forever."

Her mouth opened in a soundless O, her climax tearing through her with all the force of the sea, streaming incoherent euphoria through her blood.

As her pussy squeezed him, as she rode out the waves, Bastien came too. He moaned her name, spilling is climax into her, his orgasm hot and desperate.

When the pleasure faded, they lay together a while, wrapped in each other's arms, warding and warming sigils hovering around them in scarlet and silver. Bastien's fingers threaded through her hair, hers playing nonsensical patterns on his chest. For a while, they reveled in survival as the moon bathed them in its cosmic glow, starlight winking their pride at them.

It was the afternoon when they rose from Bastien's bed after a very late—or very early, depending on your perspective—session of lovemaking. It was slow and languid, deep and rolling. Sabine came slowly, the orgasm tumbling through her like a wave on the shore.

Bastien made them coffee with cinnamon, and she perched on his dining chair, staring out over the city. She was dressed in one of his white button-ups, like so long ago, yet so much had changed. She sipped her hot coffee as Bastien came up behind her, kissing her temple.

"What are you thinking about, love?"

"I am thinking I am done with Vale Wood." She turned to face him. "I would like to return to Vonor, if you wish to."

He smiled. "I'd love nothing more."

She grinned. "When shall we go?"

"After we visit Salem."

"A sound plan."

Salem was recovering remarkably well and would be deemed the picture of health tomorrow. They had filled him in on the results of the curse, in addition to Sabine's new status. Salem paled momentarily, but nodded solemnly, understanding the severity of the situation.

They welcomed him to join them back to Vonor, but he refused, saying there was something else he wished to do, but would be in touch. He wanted to watch over all the vampires that had bound themselves to him, to discover their fates and if they had survived the sea.

Sabine and Bastien bid him farewell and left to book passage. The ship was set sail on the third, so they had until tomorrow to get all their Vale Wood affairs in order.

It was quick. Not much of a life was left here for either of them, but they had each other.

NOVEMBER 3, 1867

Magic enhanced passage had its perks, most notably the quick journey from Vale Wood to Vonor. The trip was set to be halved by Mortal standards, and based on her previous sailing she deemed that accurate.

Sabine and Bastien leaned against the stern of the ship, watching the deep blue waves part against their massive ship. Vale Wood was long in the distance now, and she had no intentions of returning. There was nothing left for her there but bad memories.

She sighed and Bastien squeezed her tighter, her back quite warm against his front.

"Are you well?"

"Just bad thoughts I am eager to leave behind."

He kissed her cheek. "As am I."

"I've missed Lucia and Benedict. I believe they've had their baby by now."

"Will I get to meet them?"

"Of course, you're my husband. You're part of the family now."

"I love hearing you say that."

"Well, husband, start getting used to it."

They stayed like that, wrapped in each other's arms, Sabine's black gloved hands resting on his forearms. She stared out at the horizon, watching the sun slip, no longer fearing nightfall and a headless horseman's curse.

She was free.

She had survived.

Yes, she now harbored a deadly secret—one that made her crave blood—but she was alive and it was controlled.

And love had conquered all.

VONOR

NOVEMBER 15, 1867

They docked in Vonor and Sabine was hit with such a surge of nostalgia that she nearly cried. The gothic spires were so familiar, the architecture, ancient stone, stained glass and leaded windows, horses and carriage, it was all that of home.

       Sabine and Bastien walked hand in hand off the ship. They had little to no belongings after the entire ordeal of Hollow Place and the curse. Autumn was giving way to the first breaths of winter, the chill biting their cheeks. Bundled up in layers and spells, Sabine and Bastien maneuvered the streets, a fine dusting of snow taking up residence. Sabine knew where she was going like the back of her hand. Within the year, so much within her had changed, but so little of this world.

When they ascended the steps of the townhouse, Sabine shook out her long auburn waves and brushed snow from her black cloak. She turned to Bastien.

"Are you ready?"

"Always."

Sabine knocked succinctly and after a few moments she heard footsteps on the opposite side. When the door opened, she was met with a tall figure with a messy head of brown hair and familiar green eyes.

Benedict broke out into a riotous smile.

"Sabine!"

Benedict gathered her up in a chest-crushing hug. She squeezed him back, emotion raw in her heart.

Fuck, she had missed them. More than she'd let herself admit.

They separated and then Sabine glanced over at Bastien. She smiled and took his hand. "Benedict, I'd like you to meet Bastien. My husband."

Benedict's brows flew to his hairline.

"Well, this seems like a conversation we should not have on the front step. Come in, Lucia will be ecstatic you're here."

"How is she?"

"Come see for yourself."

He ushered them in where the scent of citrus and cloves mixed with bergamot suffused the house. He guided them to the living room, the red one that she'd spent so many evenings in, drinking and playing games with her friends. A fire crackled in the hearth and there were already boxes of Christmas decorations half opened.

The familiarity made her ache.

"Lucia, my love, you'll never guess who has just arrived."

"Who?"

Sabine heard a soft voice ask, one of her favorite voices in the world. Tears sprung to her eyes as she rounded the entryway.

When she entered, she found Lucia on the sofa, pillows propped around her, a blanket over her lap, and a tiny bundle in her arms. Sabine instantly broke, tears running down her face.

Lucia took perhaps two seconds to process before she was sobbing uncontrollably, her crystalline blue eyes shining with tears.

"*Sabine*," Lucia practically wailed.

Sabine went to her and collapsed at her side. Her knees pressed under the sofa as her head rested against Lucia's thigh.

"I've missed you so," Sabine whispered.

"I've missed you, too."

Above her, something shifted and then Lucia's arms were around her, pulling her up. She hugged her best friend tight, never daring to let her go. They remained entwined, soft murmurs from their husbands behind them. Lucia smelled as she always did—citrus and cloves—and it was home.

Finally, when they pulled away, Lucia smiled, a heartbreakingly pure smile.

"You're here? You're here to stay?"

"I am," Sabine confirmed, tucking a strand of Lucia's jet hair behind her ear. "And I have much to tell you."

"As do I." Her gaze flickered above them.

Sabine turned, realizing Benedict had scooped up the baby during their moment. He returned the tiny bundle to his wife's arms.

Lucia smiled, fatigue lining her tear-rimmed eyes. "Meet your goddaughter. Estella."

Sabine's throat was thick as she stared down at the tiny creature, absolute perfection with dark, downy curls, and the grayish blue eyes every newborn had.

"She's beautiful," Sabine breathed, awed.

"I know. Would you like to hold her?"

"I would, but first—I'd like to fill you in on many things before you allow me the privilege. Starting with my husband."

EPILOGUE

OCTOBER 31, 1877

Her husband was atop her, kissing a trail down her throat before sinking his fangs into her. She hummed in pleasure as her hands roamed his perfectly toned back, the muscles carved in familiar lines beneath her fingertips. He drank from her slowly and decadently, a thrill going straight down her body to her clit. Sabine ground up against him, seeking friction.

When he'd had his fill, it was her turn to tumble him

over in their downy white sheets, straddle him in her flimsy nightgown and sink her own fangs into his throat. Bastien hummed in pleasure, lifting his hips like she had done, his hard cock a wondrous ridge between her thighs.

She hummed in delight as his blood slipped down her throat, the scent of crushed leaves, smoke, and apple filling her nostrils as she drank.

It was always like this, drinking from each other, having discovered how to keep Midnight Malady completely at bay, staving off the insanity by treating the disease with equal measure, no power imbalances, no hunting anyone. Sustaining each other. It was information they'd quickly passed onto others afflicted, and to Benedict and Lucia who had moved on to studying other immortal diseases—including Midnight Malady—after the Wasting and Ember Fever were completely cured.

Only, after ten years still, Midnight Malady did not have a cure or a vaccine; only a treatment plan.

But that was all right. It hadn't impeded their life by much.

The arousal from the bite was as familiar as it was potent, but she knew this day, of all days, they wouldn't have time to fulfil it. All Hallow's Eve was too exciting.

"Mama!"

A sweet and lilting voice called from the doorway before a three-year-old-sized warlock leaped onto their bed. A head of black hair nestled itself comfortably below Sabine's throat, tiny arms wrapping around her, his little back against his father who placed a soft hand and kiss upon his head.

"Good morning, sweet Dorian." Sabine kissed her son's sleep tousled hair, "Should we get your little brother up?"

"Yes! Apples!" His big, dark eyes were wide, filled

with the kind of joy only children could have.

"Ahh, indeed, we shall go to the festival for caramel apples."

They'd worried about the ethics of having children while afflicted with Midnight Malady, but after tests and other vampire couples having children, it was deduced that it didn't pass onto offspring that way.

Sabine deposited Dorian in Bastien's arms before slipping from the bed. Donning a long robe and fluffing her long auburn locks behind her shoulders, she went down the hall to her youngest's room. Carefully opening the door, she entered, but the moment the knob turned, her nearly one-year-old was up, babbling excitedly.

"Mama, mama, mama," Leander cooed, reaching up with his sweet, pudgy arms.

He'd inherited her dark auburn waves, already they were thick and falling over his brow.

She plucked him up and kissed him good morning as Bastien brought in Dorian, chatting about auntie *"Loo-Sah"* as he'd yet to pronounce Lucia.

She beamed.

This was her life, her family, her love.

She'd chosen them as they'd chosen her.

"My love," she whispered to Bastien.

"My only love," he returned softly.

Ten years ago, he'd chosen her, and ten years later, he was still choosing her.

Murderess, coquette, curse, and all.

AUTHOR'S NOTE

Regarding Sabine's name. I had accidentally copied a name by a fellow indie author, Kayla Edwards. Her character featured in *City of Gods and Monsters* is Sabrine Van Arsdell. Mine is Sabine Van Arsdel (now Emmons). We have had a discussion about it regarding my mistake—I had written *The Nightmare Curse: A Christmas Carol Retelling* very early post-partum with my second daughter and I was very sleep deprived. That was a mistake I made and I apologized for. Kayla is completely okay with it.

Regarding the publishing delay. 2024 was not my year. The first quarter of this book was written during the worst time of my life and during that time I stopped writing. It was months I went without writing. Before returning to this story, I wrote a contemporary romance Christmas one-shot and a whole other contemporary romance book before I felt ready to return to this book. It was a trial of love and I can easily say the hardest book I've ever written, but I love it so dearly.

ACKNOWLEGMENTS

Once upon a time I never thought I'd write this. But it is here, and it was a labor of love with a huge host of support behind me.

First and foremost, my husband, Michael. Thank you for all your love and support. Thank you for choosing me. I love you. I could not be where I am without you.

To Tess, thank you for always being excited whenever I share whatever annoying detail I have about my books. Thank you for being there for me. Thank you for being a dear friend. Thank you for it all.

Anna, thank you for your unfaltering friendship. Thank you for being there, even if it's just sitting beside me at the kitchen island while I write and you read.

My Safe Space. I never have enough words for you all, but thank you eternally for all you do. Thank you for letting me rejoice in my wins, languish in my losses, share my art, and vent about whatever has taken my mood. I love you all.

Thank you, as always, to Vivienne and Rosalie. Thank you for being you, I love you. Oh, and Rosalie, thanks for falling asleep on me as I wrote "the end", it is a memory I cherish.

To Leah, I will never forget your kindness that gave me the energy and confidence to continue. Thank you so much, you have no idea the difference you made.

Thank you to all the writing and bookish friends I've met along the way. Thank you for encouraging me and loving the idea of this story. Thank you to everyone who shared my posts, thirsted after Bastien art, and engaged with all my socials.

And finally, as always, thank you, Dear Reader, for picking up a little indie author's book.

ABOUT THE AUTHOR

Kayla McGrath has been writing since the age of thirteen out of spite, having read a book with a love triangle that didn't go her way. After that, it became a passion. If she's not writing, then she's reading, or drinking endless cups of chai. Kayla lives on Vancouver Island with her husband, two daughters, and two dogs.

She is the author of the Cold as Iron trilogy, the Infernal Curses series, the Love and Other Tropes series, and A Deathless Empire. The Hallow Curse is her eighth book.

You can find her on TikTok (@kaylamcgrath_), and on Instagram/Threads (@kaylamcgrathbooks).

MORE BOOKS BY KAYLA MCGRATH

THE COLD AS IRON TRILOGY
This Broken Memory
These Ruined Dreams
Our Shattered Fates

INFERNAL CURSES
The Nightmare Curse
The Hallow Curse

A DEATHLESS EMPIRE
A Deathless Empire

LOVE AND OTHER TROPES
Love & Other Tropes (Emmett & Illiana)
Romance Thy Enemy (Mina & Graham

www.ingramcontent.com/pod-product-compliance
Lightning Source LLC
Chambersburg PA
CBHW031740180726
48283CB00005B/1601